We were hun

We stalked our prey. They were everywhere below, huddled together in their villages, sleeping, thinking they were safe. But they dreamed. Their dreams rose from their minds like smoke from a fire.

We hovered over a particular village, plucking dream filaments at random, following them back, letting their images unravel: hunting bison on horseback, stalking deer, pounding gold into sheets and making jewelry, making love with your friend's wife.

Dawn was near. Dream-hunters hunted best at night. We retreated before the advancing day, floating back the way we had come, dropping back to the garrison, going back to our bodies . . .

DREAM GAMES

KARL HANSEN

ACE SCIENCE FICTION BOOKS
NEW YORK

"Dreams Unwind" appeared in the May 1985 issue of *Omni* magazine.

DREAM GAMES

An Ace Science Fiction Book / published by arrangement with
the author

PRINTING HISTORY
Ace Original / May 1985

ISBN: 0-441-16691-1

Ace Science Fiction Books are published by
The Berkley Publishing Group,
200 Madison Avenue, New York, New York 10016.
PRINTED IN THE UNITED STATES OF AMERICA

BOOK ONE

DREAM-LOVER

1

Grychn Ronmartha-Williams was already bored with the party.

She stood by herself on the patio, amid scattered garments, watching some of the other guests frolicking naked in the swimming pool. She was average height for a standard Terran, one hundred seventy cm, and slender, with a mass of seventy kilos. Her hair was white and cut as short as ermine fur; her eyes were ocher. She had lithe arms and legs, a narrow waist, and breasts unrestrained by gravity. She wore a single strand of singing pearls around her neck and matching earrings. Her skin was brown and smooth and taut in the right places—from appearances she could have been twenty years of age. In fact, she was almost a hundred, and at that, was one of the youngest people at the party.

The naked bathers splashing in the pool all looked uniformly young. Some of them were nearing their millennium. Most were over five hundred years old. All still had the vibrant vitality of apparent youth.

Grychn ignored them when they shouted for her to join the fun. She was dressed appropriately enough for water sports in a sheer chemise and ruby slippers, with nothing else underneath. It certainly would have been easy for her to slip out of both and jump into the pool. Her jewelry was waterproof. But for some reason, she just was not in the mood. She was bored and a little depressed.

Not that there was anything wrong with the party itself. The other guests certainly seemed to be enjoying themselves, partaking of the usual diversions: peptide, mnemone, dream-games, sex. Grychn knew that the problem was within her own psyche; she had been bored since coming back to Earth. Her ennui had started even earlier, when Detrs became a legitimate business-man—crime was more exciting than commerce. But now she was also having more and more frequent at-tacks of melancholia. Her twin boys, age eight, were her only real interest, and she would not have them much longer. Lady Blue would be coming to take the boys away from her any day now. She had not figured out how to save them from Lady Blue. With them gone, she would have no reason to live.

She had thought she had been hurt as much as possi-ble when she ran away from Ceres and Marc Detrs, tak-ing the two baby boys with her. Now she knew she could be hurt even more.

A servbot approached with a tray of drinks. Grychn selected a glass of white wine and went into the house and wandered about. She seemed vaguely out of sorts with the party, as though she had arrived in the middle and had never become integrated into its chemistry. Part of it was that the parties seemed more and more like the parties her father used to have, the ones he made her attend as a child for the amusement of his guests. She had run away from home to escape such humilia-tions. But she had been feeling the same way in other situations lately. She knew she should go to a psycho-mat and take a little hypnotherapy to iron out the wrinkles that had developed in her psyche, but even that took more effort than she could muster.

A sudden anxiety sent her downstairs to the play-room. Three boys were hunched over a holographic game board, each wearing a psihelmet. The tiny figures of combrid Ghost Cavalry fought with Marindians on the board. They looked up as she entered. After a quick, "Hi, Grychn," they went back to their game. A nandroid stood by dutifully. The boys were safe.

The twins, Craig and Christopher, were Grychn's sons. The other boy, Alix, was the Saraltr's son. He was half a year older than the twins. They were second cousins, but could have been brothers by their appearance. All were towheads with hair as white as Grychn's, blue eyes, and brown skin. They were becoming gangly with the awkward angularity of a preadolescent growth spurt. They were inseparable and usually took turns spending the night at one or the other's houses. Grychn loved all three of them more than she had once thought would be possible, as much as she had once loved Detrs. Losing them would be harder than running away from Detrs had been. She tried not to think about how short a time was left.

Although the twins looked identical enough that even Grychn had trouble telling them apart, their personalities were really quite different. Craig was more assertive, the leader, while Chris was content to follow his lead. Craig was manipulative and devious, Chris open and sincere. Craig was always worried about something, while Chris never worried. It was almost as though when the zygote cleaved, the halves were different parts of the whole. Grychn sometimes thought Chris should have been a girl—his mannerisms seemed feminine, his personality more female. She would have loved it if he had been her daughter instead of her son. Alix was different from both Craig and Chris—he was more a loner and could entertain himself. He did not open up easily, keeping his feelings hidden. Lately all of them had been acting peculiar. Grychn could not figure out what was wrong with them. The twins were waking up with nightmares. They seemed to be taking an unhealthy interest in sex—once she had caught them masturbating each other. She had said nothing then, deciding it was normal curiosity. They seemed to know more about sex than they should, even though she had not told them of it yet.

There were some things you still needed a father to pro-
vide.

Satisfied that nothing was amiss with the boys,
Grychn went back upstairs.

She walked through the sitting room. It had become
the official "peptide parlor" of the party, where the
pepheads congregated. By now most of them were
sprawled naked on the floor, lost to the euphoria of
neuropeptide. Saraltr, Grychn's cousin and hostess of
the party, was being a good hostess indeed, holding a
liter bowl of peptide between her hands. She too was
completely naked. She had long amber hair that cas-
caded past her waist and eyes as blue as frozen topaz. A
singing sapphire pendant hung between her breasts. She
dipped her tongue in the bowl, lowered it over the open
eye of a pephead, and let the peptide-laden saliva drip
into his eye. She repeated the ritual with each pephead.
They began stirring back to life: penises stiffened, nipples hardened, glands exuded. Blue fire burned from
their eyes. The pepheads began a frantic sexual coupling
with one another.

Grychn knew that Saraltr had switched from endor-
phin to endocaine and endosterone—speed and sex
steroids. That was one of her favorite tricks at parties.

Grychn left the room as Saraltr accepted the sexual
ravages of her frenzied guests.

Other diversions were taking place in other rooms.
Immortality lent perversion a certain legitimacy.

Petraltr, Saraltr's legal husband, had hired the best
pedimorphs their Guild had to offer. Grychn had seen
them arrive, strutting in with cocky arrogance, proud of
their androgynous build, shiny yellow curls, up-turned
button of a nose, big blue eyes, and pouting lips. She
did not even glance into that room. She did not have the
stomach for pederasty, even if it was with legal hybrid
surrogates. But she knew most of the guests would visit
a pedi before the evening was through.

A seance was taking place in one room. A psiber
crystal stood on a pedestal in the center of the room.
Ghosts hovered above it, trapped in the warp the crystal

created in the psiberfield. The ghosts appeared as shimmering vortices of multicolored light and represented the persona of one of the living brains of cybermind. These personas could travel out in the psiberfield at night, to prowl about the psychic ether. (Sunlight disrupted their energies too much for them to become manifest during the day.) It was considered great sport to catch these wandering ghosts and tease and taunt them until they begged to be released. That the captive ectoplasm might have been a friend or relative made the sport that much better.

Another room was devoted to the disciples of pain. Grychn watched them writhing in their shackles, as a whipsman flailed them with an alphalash. More subtle humiliations would soon come. A splendid dominatrix with raven-black hair, dressed in chains and leather, gestured for Grychn to join the fun. She laughed and shook her head and walked away. She knew eventually she might come back to that room, but not just yet.

Grychn was still bored. One could find the same amusements at any of the parties going on elsewhere that night and every night. It had been the same for the past seven years she had been back on Earth. She was tempted to leave Earth again. Though she hated to admit it to herself, she would have liked to have seen Detrs again. Sex with him was the best she had ever had. Maybe it was because he was the first.

She wandered upstairs. A dream-game was in progress in the upstairs parlor. Grychn stopped to watch, although there was not much to see. A dozen guests lay on the floor wearing psihelmets, connected to a central macroprocessor by criss-crossing red lasewires. The same lax expression could be seen on each face: eyes staring open, mouths agape, tongues protruding. Each player's mind was inside the macroprocessor, engaged in a role-playing fantasy game. Each player's score, based on his success at manipulating his role within the game, was automatically tabulated by the DPU. Huge wagers had no doubt been placed on the outcome.

Dream-games could last indefinitely. Usually a timer

was set within the dream-processor to terminate the game after a predetermined interval. Otherwise, players had been known to starve to death before the conclusion of a game.

Dream-gaming had attracted quite a cult-following among Earth's immortals. Grychn had not yet tried it here.

She had spent six months as a tiderider playing the dream-games of the mind-casinos of Chronus. Although that had been seventy-five years ago, she had not forgotten the experience. She was afraid if she got started again, she would not want to return to reality.

She was not that bored yet.

Grychn was the daughter of Lord General Williams, a founding member of Earth's War Lords, who directed the successful suppression of the most recent Hybrid Rebellion. Her mother was the Lady Ronmartha, the famous cyberneticist. "Father" and "mother" were legal terms and only meant she had been gestated from the same lot of gametes as they had—her genome was a different blend of their genes. Neither the Lord nor the Lady had ever had actual sex with the other, as far as Grychn knew. A hundred years ago carnal procreation was considered imprecise, as well as a little vulgar. Fertilization was achieved in vitro. Her prenatal life had been spent in an artificial womb succored by a synthetic placenta. Her birth had been an expulsion from the sterility of the fake womb into an even less friendly world. Her infancy was spent in the care of mechanical nursemaids, and her childhood shuttling back and forth between "father" and "mother," to both of whom she was only of brief and occasional interest.

She had run away at an early age and had become involved with off-world revolutionaries. A fourteen-year-old girl could easily be seduced by the intense camaraderie of a guerilla cadre, especially one who had been deprived of real love. At the age of sixteen, she was one of the most famous terrorists in the system. The high-energy sex and violence of a terrorist group was like a narcotic—one's perceptions were dulled to the point it was difficult to return to a rational life-style. Grychn still had fantasies of those years, especially when she was having sex. Sometimes she had to resurrect images of rape and rampage in order to have an orgasm. She felt guilty about her fascination with violence, but had not sought therapy. She did not want to lose the thrill it brought.

She had first met Marc Detrs when they were children. The Lord General's estate bordered that of the Detrs'. Her father was too busy plotting the war to spend much time with her, but she found a second home at the Detrs' estate. Grychn spent more time there than at home, preferring a live playmate to the company of household androids. She had been drawn into the dark insanity of Marc's parents' drug-fueled sexual abuse, and had helped him kill them and disguise their murder to look like an accident. She could have run away with him, but was afraid to then. A few years later, she ran away herself and learned to enjoy killing.

She met Marc Detrs again on Titan. He was a combat hybrid at a garrison there, and she was a terrorist revolutionary fighting with the Elves. Detrs was the trooper who captured her for the spooks of Corps Intelligence.

They met again as tideriders in the mind-casinos of Chronus. Grychn had been put there by the spooks as bait, to help them follow Detrs in his quest for a chronotropic crystal. He and Grychn found the crystal on Iapetus, and Detrs made the mistake of looking into it, which gave him a certain capacity for precognition. They left the crystal and Kramr, the spook who followed them, buried in an ice cave beneath a glacial avalanche.

The next seventy-five years had been mostly happy for Grychn, especially the first few decades. She had stayed with Detrs while he used his precognitive ability to amass a considerable fortune, first as a pirate, then as a gambler and financier, and finally as a legitimate businessman. She loved their years as pirates and criminals—the thrills were almost as good as being a guerilla. Being legitimate was not as much fun. She missed the excitement of violence. They traveled throughout the solar system, visiting the nicest resorts and staying at the finest hotels. They had built homes on most of the planets and moons.

Starting about ten years ago, Detrs had become moody and withdrawn. He began to have nightmares and would awake in the night screaming. During the day he mumbled to himself. He lost interest in his businesses and established trusts to manage them. He decided he was a Prophet and his precognition was a divine gift, which should be shared. He seemed to lose interest in Grychn as well. She had hoped the birth of the twins would help their relationship, but it had deteriorated even more, until she could no longer stand it. The final fission had come when Detrs founded the monastery on Ceres. Being the consort of a wild-eyed religious oracle was more than Grychn could tolerate. If not for her babies, and if she had known where to start looking, she would have tried to find a guerilla group to join. Instead, she had taken the twins and returned to Earth. Now she was not sure that had been the right decision. Maybe she should have stayed with him and tried to work things out. Maybe he would have come to his senses if she had stayed.

Coming back to Earth had been a mistake though. She missed the life-style of the Outer Moons.

Life on Earth had changed a lot in the past century. The only humans left on the planet were the immortal aristocracy, numbering a few million. The common classes, once numbering in the trillions, were now completely gone, depleted by a combination of a millennium of emigration to the colonies and conscription into the Foreign Legions. Earth's legions were themselves becoming depleted from lack of new recruits, and the ranks were increasingly being filled with units of hybrid personnel. Terra's glory was dimming, her power fading. Without replacements for her troops, the next hybrid rebellion might well succeed.

Earth's Lords and Ladies had bravely tried to replenish the population, even to the point of attempting "natural" procreation in the old vulgar manner, but without success. They had waited too long. Their DNA was fatigued, defective—beyond the repair of the cleverest genosurgeons. Their children did not live past adolescence. Grychn's own twins boys were nearing the critical age.

Grychn knew the human race was dying. But because those who were left were immortal, their death chant would last for a long time.

And the death throes were pleasant enough. Earth's bioengineering factories produced androids to perform mundane tasks, controlled by a massive electronic/neurologic computer called cybermind. Crystalyst-mediated matter annihilation meant unlimited power was available for Earth's now scant population. Automated factories produced abundant supplies of consumer goods, food, and other comestibles. Tribute of all kinds still flowed to Earth from her colonies.

Earth was a paradise. Sprawling cities had been razed, the rubble groomed into parkland. Her air and water were clean and pure. Her industry was all underground, carefully out of sight. Her immortals were healthy and wealthy, with the vitality of perpetual youth. What difference did it make if they could no longer breed? They had an eternity of leisure to enjoy.

So Grychn had thought when she had come back to Earth.

But now she was bored.

Almost bored enough to be tempted to play the dream-game again.

"Did you arrive too late to play the game?" someone asked.

Grychn turned to see who had asked the question. A sailor stood behind her—a real Asteroidian sailor, with coal-black skin, silver nictitating membranes over his eyes, suction-cups on his fingers and toes. "You look as though you wished you were playing."

"I'm not a devotee."

"But you were once, a long time ago."

"How did you know?"

He smiled sadly. "I lost six months in the mind-casinos once. I saw a familiar look in your eyes."

"You too," Grychn said in a low voice. "But you also escaped. Not many of us have."

"I was lucky. A friend rescued me."

Because sailors looked so much alike, Grychn looked at him closely. But she did not think she recognized him. "I haven't seen you at any of the parties. I'm Grychn Ronmartha-Williams." She held out her hand.

The sailor shook it. His suction-cups tugged at her skin. "Damiel Bwaman. You haven't seen me before because I've been out of circulation for the past few years. I just got back to Earth today."

"What have you been doing for the past few years?"

His answer was a second too late in coming. "Racing in the twelve-meter trials for the Ceres' Cup."

"Do you own your own boat?"

"The *Kalispel Condor*."

The name meant something. "Oh!" Grychn said, remembering. "You're Lord Bwaman."

"Of course."

"The expatriate Terran War Lord who had himself hybridized into a sailor."

"At your service."

"You knew my father, Lord General Williams."

"Of course. How is he?"

"I wouldn't know. I haven't seen him lately. Our relationship is somewhat distant. He hasn't forgiven me my youthful excesses."

Damiel laughed. "Interplanetary terrorism is a little more than youthful enthusiasm." He smiled at the look that came to her face. "Don't be surprised I remember who you were. You were quite infamous for a short while. A lot of us still remember your exploits. I'm surprised you were allowed back on Earth."

Grychn laughed. "I'm supposed to be harmless now. Besides, 'interplanetary terrorism' is dead. Almost all of us were captured and hypnoed back to normal with operant lobotomies. I wouldn't even know where to find a guerilla cadre anymore. The War Lords felt so secure in their victory that they granted a general amnesty after the last rebellion collapsed. Earth's prodigal sons and daughters were forgiven. Would you mind if we left here? I'm becoming a little uncomfortable."

"Of course not." He took her arm and they walked away. "Still tempted sometimes?"

"To dream or blow up buildings?"

He laughed. "Either one."

"Of course I'm tempted by the dream-game. Aren't you?"

"Sometimes. How about blowing up buildings?"

"That too."

They walked down a hall and out to a balcony overhanging the patio and pool. The pool party was still in full swing below. The sounds of laughter and splashing could be heard plainly. Grychn and Damiel sat at a small table on the balcony. They could see naked bodies coupling below—some in the water, some on cushions along the pool's apron.

A servbot found them and left a glass of wine and a mnemone stick.

"You don't drink?" Grychn asked as Damiel sucked acrid fumes into his lungs."

"Not on Earth. Out there," he waved his hand upward, "I drink Earth wine, because it helps me remember home. Here, alcohol just makes me sleepy. Mnemone has less of an effect on sailors. We stay functional under its influence."

"Why did you become a hybrid—a sailor?"

"I wanted to win the Ceres' Cup. No Terran craft had won it for five hundred years."

"Is that the only reason?"

"I was bored with life on Earth. The Hybrid Rebellion was crushed, peace and stability had returned to the system. There was not much excitement for a War Lord, just the endless parties and sex and peptide. Besides, cybermind had taken over most of the real planning. We just rubber-stamped its decisions. I was ready for a change."

"I'm bored myself," Grychn said.

"Become a sailor. Or a sphinx. You would look good as a cat-woman."

"Do you think so?" Grychn bared her teeth and growled. She leaned over and bit Damiel's hand.

He did not pull it away. Human teeth could not hurt a sailor's skin. He laughed. "See, I told you you'd make a good sphinx. You already have cat mannerisms."

Grychn turned him loose and smiled. "I'm afraid of hybridization. When I was a rebel, the Elves and the Marindians and the sphinges all wanted me to become one of them. But I wanted to be myself. I still do. I'm standard Terran. True human. That should be enough."

Damiel snorted. "Look at them," he said, pointing to the pool. "Those are what remain of your true humans —jaded hedonists who can no longer enjoy the pleasure they seek. You are a dying breed, you true humans. You will either have to change into something else or die."

"Nobody dies anymore except by accident. Have you forgotten the anti-agathic genes?"

"No, I haven't. It's been a thousand years since the first 'immortal' was produced. A thousand years is about as long as one can cheat entropy."

"You mean the anti-agathic process is limited to a thousand years?"

"Generally speaking. There are other ways to cheat entropy its due."

"What other ways?"

"Hybrid vigor. Mix a little xeno-DNA into the genome."

A knowing look appeared on Grychn's face. "So that's why you became a sailor."

Damiel smiled. "One of the reasons, anyway. I thought it would be better than psychic integration into cybermind." He laughed. "Now I find I think like a sailor. I have the desires of a sailor. I am tempted too much by the *up and out*."

"What else tempts you?" Grychn asked, rubbing her foot on his leg beneath the table.

"What do you mean?" Damiel knew what she meant.

"What other games do you play? What diversions do you prefer? Pedis? Pain? Peptides?"

Damiel laughed. "I'm just a simple sailor now. Completely unsophisticated. I prefer the simple pleasures."

"Like sex?"

"That would do nicely."

"Right now?"

"Why not?"

"A man after my own heart." Grychn pulled him up from the table, along the hall, and through a darkened doorway into a bedroom. She kissed him and pulled him down on a bed of wombskin.

"You seem to know your way around," Damiel remarked.

"I've been here before."

As she received his thrusts, Grychn once more had to fill her mind full of images of fire and blood, before the parasympathetic release would come.

Later, after making love, they lay together in bed. A servbot had found them again and offered them refreshments. It would not leave until they had taken something. Servbots were persistent in their duties, if nothing else.

Grychn sipped another glass of wine. Damiel sucked mnemone.

"What are things like out there now?" Grychn asked. She was thinking of Detrs.

"On the surface, peaceful and stable. Underneath, I think trouble is brewing. The legions are spread too thin and are understaffed. I don't think we could suppress another rebellion."

"Will there be another rebellion?"

"Who knows? Maybe. If the right leader comes along who can unite all the hybrid races."

"Which side will you be on?"

Again, his answer was a second too late. "Earth's, of course. I'll always be a Terran at heart, even though I know it's a lost cause. And you?"

"Neutral, I suppose. I don't think I could fight again." Grychn knew she was lying. Nothing would give her more pleasure than spraying an autopulser into a troop of combrids, seeing blood splatter the crystal trees of Titan, watching flesh give up its oxygen in fire to methane air. She told another lie: "I lost too much innocence in the last rebellion."

"You were on the wrong side then. Maybe your side will win this time?"

"I suppose. But I'm going to sit out this one anyway."

"If war comes, you might not have a choice."

"What do you mean?"

"The War Lords might draft you into their service."

"Me? A Lady? They can't."

"Don't be too sure of that. There aren't any more commoners and they won't trust hybrids. Lords and Ladies are all they have left to conscript."

She rolled over and kissed him, stroking his penis hard, then straddled him, rocking up and down with her pelvis.

"Don't say anything for a while," she said.

"OK," he agreed.

This time the images came unbidden.

2

Grychn awoke with sweat cooling on her skin.

At first she thought she must have awakened from a nightmare. She often had dreams of the Rebellion, frequently seeing comrades die again as their images cycled out of hippocampal gray. But there were no war images lingering in her mind. Something else had awakened her.

Damiel lay beside her, still asleep. He had not awakened her. She looked at her ring watch—it was 0400. Something else had disturbed her sleep.

She listened carefully, thinking the boys might be having another nightmare and had cried out in terror. She heard the sound again—a faint, high-pitched hum.

She got out of bed and went to the window, just in time to see an iridescent blue sphere drifting away. Lady Blue!

For a moment, it seemed as though her heart had stopped. Then blood began pounding in her ears with her heart's palpitations. Sweat poured from her skin.

She ran out of the bedroom naked, bolted down the hall, and jumped into the stairwell. P-grav slowed her descent through the air. All she could think about were her sons. The boys' room was in the basement. When her feet hit the basement floor, she was off and running. She flung open the door to their room and rushed inside.

A faint odor still lingered in the air—noscamine. She remembered the smell—Ghost Cavalry used it in gas grenades to put villages to sleep before search and destroy missions.

As her eyes adjusted to the light, she could see Craig and Chris asleep in their beds. She sighed with relief, but her sigh turned into a gasp when she saw that Alix's bed was empty.

Lady Blue had visited.

She had taken Alix away.

Grychn collapsed on the floor. Her mind was numb with shock. She felt relief that Craig and Chris were safe, but the loss of Alix was just as hard to bear. How would she be able to tell her sons that they would never see their cousin again?

She had to find Saraltr and tell her.

Grychn climbed back upstairs. She looked in the peptide parlor first. Naked bodies were sprawled in a heap on the floor, gleaming with peptide and their own mingled secretions. She untangled them until she was sure Saraltr was not there.

She began looking through the house. The dream-gamers still dreamed, and would do so until dawn—the dream-game was as restful as REM sleep. Saraltr was not among them. Ghosts were still trapped in the seance room, but the people there had found more interesting amusements. A few people were still collared and shackled, skins still glowing with protons, but the dominatrices had left. Guests could be found in almost every room, engaged in various activities. Those who were still conscious were not surprised when a frantic, wild-eyed naked woman burst in on them—after a thousand years, surprises did not come easily. Most invited her to join them.

Grychn had looked through almost the entire house without finding Saraltr. Only one room remained. She had saved it for last, afraid it would be the one.

She opened the door. Saraltr was there, with Petraltr. They lay together naked, with a pedimorph between them. Saraltr's fingers still held the pedi's tiny penis. Secretions matted its yellow curls flat to its skull. Its eyes were open and faded blue from waning peptide. Its chubby fingers clutched Saraltr's breast.

Grychn could have killed just then. She had killed for less in her youth. Images of death rose in her mind: poisoned babies, bellies bloated; children with arms and legs torn off; frantic husbands cutting out their unborn sons from their dead wives' bellies. That was the legacy of the Lords of Earth.

While Lady Blue was taking away her son, Saraltr was in the pederastic embrace of a pedimorph. She knew Detrs had been right to kill his parents; she had been right to become a terrorist. The old anger returned. The old rage burned bright again.

But she did not kill. She would never get away with it on Earth. She would end up at cyborg labor or be sentenced to serve in the legions. Someone had to take care of the boys.

She went back to the boys' room and picked up her sleeping sons, carrying each of them over her shoulder with a strength she thought she had forgotten. They did not awaken—noscamine still gripped their brains. She strapped them into the back seat of her skimmer, climbed in herself, and shot away at Mach two.

She had decided to leave Earth. She would find a guerilla group to join. The rebellion would flare up again. The boys would fight by her side.

But first she had to figure out how to save her sons' lives.

Damiel Bwaman stood in the window, watching Grychn carry the twins to her skimmer. As it streaked away, he smiled to himself. The Prophet had been right, as always. Lady Blue had come to take the boys' cousin, just as she would come for them. Grychn would try to prevent that from happening. Damiel must be sure that it did. Future events depended on the twins joining their cousin in Lady Blue's embrace.

Damiel shook his head. He wished he understood why what was to happen had to be. It seemed cruel and unnecessary. But he had faith in the Prophet; he would obey his orders.

Damiel went to his own skimmer and told the autopilot to take him home. As he flew over a countryside lightening with dawn, he dozed. His thoughts were not as troubled as they had been when he was human. Sailors' xeno-DNA brought enough racial memories to push away human nightmares. His dreams were those of flight: soaring in the air on outstretched wings, wheeling in thermal updrafts, singing into the wind.

Damiel had been among the first of the immortals. He was nearly a thousand years old. If he had not undergone hybridization, he would already have suffered entropic dementia. No one knew for sure how long his hybrid vigor would persist. No one but the Prophet, and he had not said. But those thoughts did not concern a sailor's mind. Entropy must be served eventually.

Damiel had nothing more to prove to himself. He had had more lovers than he could remember. He had killed more men than he cared to remember. He had been one of the most powerful War Lords. His treatises were still studied by students in the colonies and had not yet been forgotten on Earth. He had won the Ceres' Cup.

His xenogenes had also brought him wisdom. He knew now the cybermind had to be destroyed, that men were better ruled by other men, no matter how prone to error human minds were. If he died in the struggle, so be it, so better to serve Entropy.

For a thousand years, he had feared death.

Now, in his own twilight, he knew there was more to fear. But he was not afraid.

There was Entropy to serve.

In the breakfast room of her own house, with sunlight streaming in through open windows, accompanied by a gentle breeze carrying the scent of blooming flowers, the events of the past night seemed like scenes from a bad dream. But Grychn knew the nightmare had been all too real.

She was eating breakfast with Craig and Chris—she could easily have done without eating, but eight-year-olds were always hungry. She drank a cup of coffee and picked at a pastry, while a servbot tried to keep up with the boys' appetites.

Grychn had not yet told them what had happened to their cousin.

As she watched them eat, Grychn again felt the warm thrill inside that was the physiologic manifestation of love. She could not stand the thought of losing them. There must be some way to keep them out of the clutches of Lady Blue. She would have to figure something out before she could leave Earth.

"I can't wait for Alix to get here so we can go fishing," Craig said, cramming a piece of toast in his mouth.

"Don't talk with your mouth full," Chris scolded.

"I'm afraid Alix won't be coming," Grychn said softly, with a lump in her throat.

"Why not? Is he sick or something?" asked Chris.

"Is he grounded? Did Saraltr find out about . . ." Craig stopped, realizing he might not want Grychn to find out either.

Grychn had trouble continuing. "No, he's not sick or grounded. I'm afraid you won't be seeing him anymore at all." She stopped. The words seemed stuck in her throat.

"You mean Lady Blue came for him," Craig said.

"Neato," Chris said. "Did he get to go with Lady Blue?"

Grychn was incredulous. They knew! "Yes," she replied. "He went with Lady Blue. What do you know about Lady Blue?" She could not remember ever discussing the subject with them. She had always felt too uncomfortable about the concept to talk to them about it.

"Everyone knows about Lady Blue," Chris said.

"Yeah, Alix told us all about her," Craig added.

"What did Alix tell you?"

"He said Lady Blue came for you just before you were about to grow up."

"But only if you had been good."

"Yeah. She takes you to a secret place in the center of the Earth where children never have to grow up."

"All you have to do all day is play."

"They have all the toys and things you could imagine, and if you break something, you just throw it away and get a new one. You can stay up as late as you want. There aren't any nandroids to boss you around."

"Yeah, and nobody makes you do things you don't want to do. Nobody wakes you up at night. You get to sleep in your own bed."

"Who's been waking you up at night?" Grychn asked. She did not know what he had meant.

"Nobody," Craig stammered. "I mean you don't have to hear someone snore."

"I don't snore," Chris said angrily.

"The hell you don't."

"Don't swear boys," Grychn said automatically.

Grychn did not know what to say. She had had no idea an entire myth had evolved to explain Lady Blue. Well, why not? That was the purpose of myths, wasn't it, to explain away unpleasant realities.

"Do you think Lady Blue will come for us someday?" Craig asked.

"That would be neato," Chris said. "We would have a great time playing with Alix. Do you think she'll come for us?"

"Maybe." *I hope not,* she said to herself.

"When?"

"Yeah, when?"

"Not for a while yet." Grychn did not have the heart to tell them the truth. "You're not even close to growing up yet." She hoped that was true.

"Do you think we've been good enough?"

Grychn was about to cry. She turned her face so the boys would not notice. "Yes, you've been good enough.

You've been very good," she said, voice cracking.

"Oh boy, I can't wait," Craig said.

"Me either. Let's go fishing. Can we go fishing?" Chris asked.

Grychn nodded her head.

The twins scrambled away from the table and ran outside, picking up their fishing poles and tackle boxes. A nandroid followed dutifully behind.

After they left, Grychn did cry. When she finished, she did not feel any better. She was a little ashamed of herself. Ex-interplanetary terrorists were supposed to be tougher than that. But it was hard to be tough when you were going to lose two little boys.

Alix was six months older than the twins. Grychn hoped that meant she had six months before Lady Blue came again. Six months did not seem like a very long time.

Later that day Grychn received an invitation to her father's wake. She had not seen him for a long time. He brought back too many uncomfortable memories. Since it would be the last time she and the boys would see him alive, she decided to go.

That night, Grychn was again awakened.

Before the sleep cleared from her brain, she was afraid Lady Blue had come already. She listened for the terrible high-pitched whine. She heard a terrified scream from the boys' room.

She ran to their bedroom naked, not taking time to find a gown.

As she entered the room, Craig sat bolt upright. When he saw her come in, he cowered back in bed and whimpered, closing his eyes tightly, as though he was terrified of her. When she touched him, he jerked away, keeping his eyes closed. She grabbed him and held him to her breast. She felt him take her nipple in his mouth and start to suck on it. His penis stiffened against her belly.

She shook him.

He opened his eyes and looked at her. "Grychn," he said. "It's you. I thought . . ."

"Who did you think I was?"

"Nobody. I was having a bad dream. I don't remember what it was about."

"It's alright now. There's nothing to be afraid of. Go back to sleep." She held him until he fell asleep. As she held him, she remembered how his lips had felt on her nipple and the stiffness of his little penis on her skin. She was ashamed of the wetness that dripped between her legs and afraid of the feeling inside.

Grychn and the twins flew to the Lord General's wake in the skimmer, since it was only five hundred kilometers away. They climbed to twenty thousand meters to cross the mountainous Great Divide, then dropped to eight thousand and streaked over the inland sea at wave-top level. The boys liked flying over water at Mach two, the sonic boom made a nice rooster tail behind them. In less than thirty minutes they could see the flowering trees of New Wichita.

Grychn parked the skimmer on the beach, and the three of them walked the short way to the Cyber Palace.

The palace was a shimmering double duodecagron, a thousand meters in height, impossibly balanced lengthwise on one vertex. It was actually supported within a p-grav field. They stepped into a lift-tube and floated to the top of the palace.

A wake was always a grand party and was invariably well attended. Unlike ancient times, modern wakes were held before the honoree had died, so he could enjoy one last party. Not that death actually occurred, but it was said interfaciation with cybermind was as close to death as one would care to get.

The wake for Lord General Williams was held on the resort island of New Wichita, which was moored in the approximate center of the Kansas Sea. New Wichita was an artificial island and named after the ancient city over whose ruins it floated. Over a thousand years ago there had been dry land where the sea now lay—land that had produced a fair percentage of the Earth's food supply. The water to irrigate those crops had been pumped from a vast underground reservoir, the Oglala aquifer, at a rate faster than replenishment occurred. Wells were drilled continually deeper until the aquifer was drained dry. An earthquake caused the empty aquifer to collapse, which resulted in the overlying land sinking into a great basin, which filled with water, forming an inland sea. Several kilometers beneath the floor of this new sea were deposits of salt, which had been mined when the area had been above water. Water leeched in through the old mine shafts, dissolving the salt and forming vast flooded caverns.

When cybermind was being developed, it was determined that these caverns were now the most geologically stable structures on Earth. Cassions were dropped, and the caverns pumped dry. Cybermind had been built inside those caverns five hundred years ago and had been expanding ever since. Deep inside the earth, beneath five hundred meters of water, it was impregnable to attack.

The Cyber Palace was both a monument to cybermind and the only portal of entry to its physical presence. It was also the traditional place to hold wakes.

At the penthouse level, Grychn and the boys stepped out of the tube and crossed a foyer. Grychn handed her invitation to a receptoid, who scanned it and announced them. They went down the line of dignitaries, shaking hands and kissing lips, until they got to the Lord General.

Grychn dutifully kissed him, holding her lips firmly together, and the boys kissed his cheek. She would have preferred to leave, but since there seemed to be a lull in arriving guests, it would be rude to leave him immediately.

He noticed that and smiled.

"Well, Grychn, it seems we shall have a little time to ourselves. Let me get you something to drink." He signaled a servbot. "Do you still prefer wine?" She nodded. He handed her a glass and then turned and spoke to the twins. "Why don't you two boys go try out the game room? I had it set up especially for you. I think there are some refreshments there."

"Oh, boy!" Craig squealed. "Thanks, General."

"Yeah, thanks, General," Chris echoed.

They ran across the ballroom to another doorway. There was no mistaking where it led—noise and lase-wires spilled out from the game room.

The Lord General watched the boys dash through the door and disappear. He was over a thousand years old, but still looked like he was in his twenties, with unlined skin, firm muscles, sharp eyes. The only outward sign of infirmity was a slight tremor in his hands.

"It's a shame our relationship is not better," the Lord General said. "I'm really quite fond of those two boys. They're the last of my line, you know. It's quite vindictive of you to keep them away from me so much." He smiled at her. "After all, I forgave you. And you hurt me more than you can imagine."

"You never cared about me." Her voice was still bitter.

"I might not have been the father you wanted, but I did care for you."

"Then how could you have done what you did? It was years before I could trust another man."

"Was our transgression that disturbing?"

"It was for me. I was only twelve years old."

"And I was over nine hundred. When you get to be as old as I am, maybe you will finally understand."

"What is there to understand?"

"Lust is the only feeling that withstands the test of time. Greed, power, jealousy, ambition all fade. Lust is the only desire that persists. But passion is hard to maintain. Your senses become jaded, desire harder to arouse. Yet you want to feel the passion again, you want to experience the desire. So you do what you have to do. You do whatever act is necessary. You were a very attractive girl. And you were physically ready."

"But I wasn't emotionally ready. I wanted you to love me. I needed your love, not your lust."

The Lord General shrugged his shoulders. "I had my own needs. You will eventually find you have the same desires. Then you will seek passion in whatever way it takes."

"Not that way."

"We shall see. Eight hundred years is a long time."

"I should have killed you." Fire burned in her eyes. "I should have killed you after the first time. I knew how to do it."

"Who had you killed then?"

"I helped Marc Detrs kill his parents."

"I thought their deaths were suicide?"

"That's what you were meant to think. That's what everybody thought. But we did it and made it look like suicide. I should have done the same to you."

"But you didn't. So we both have to live with that fact, don't we. Someday you'll understand. Someday you will feel the ennui of the immortal."

The arrival of some more guests allowed Grychn to leave. She kissed him on the cheek like a dutiful daughter and left to mingle. She did not know that many of the other guests—her father's and her social circles were not too congruent.

She wandered out to a balcony and watched the wind kick the sea into whitecaps. The wind always blew over the Kansas Sea.

"We've got to stop meeting like this," a voice said from behind.

She turned and smiled when she saw the sailor standing next to her. "Hello, Damiel," she said and kissed him.

He smiled but looked puzzled. "I thought you might have been mad at me."

"What made you think that?"

"When I woke up you were gone, without saying goodbye or even leaving a note."

"Oh! That's right. I had to leave in a hurry. I guess I forgot about you. Sorry."

"What happened—if you don't mind telling me."

"I don't mind. Lady Blue came and took my nephew.

I panicked and took my own boys home. I was afraid she would come back for them.''

"I'm sorry. I don't have any children, but I think I know how you must have felt. I'm glad it wasn't me you ran away from."

"It wasn't you."

"Then maybe we can get together sometime?"

Grychn hesitated before answering. "I don't know," she said finally. "I don't think I would be very good company. I'm worried about the boys. I need to find out if there is some way to avoid Lady Blue's curse."

"Maybe I can help?"

"How?"

"Lord Surgeon Edbryn is my good friend. He's the best genosurgeon on Earth. If anyone can answer your questions, he can."

"Can I trust him?"

"Absolutely. You have my word on it."

She hesitated again.

"What's the matter now?" he asked.

"Can I trust you?"

He kissed her. "Of course," he said. "I'll call Ed and set you and the twins up with an appointment to see him."

"OK." She did not have much choice after all. "Have you paid your respects to the Lord General?" she asked.

Damiel laughed. "Yes. We reminisced about the old days. He was bad enough as a War Lord. I'm not sure I like the idea of him being a ghost."

Grychn smiled. "I think I like that idea just fine."

A gong sounded. The interfaciation was about to begin. Grychn and Damiel walked hand-in-hand out to the ballroom.

A central dais had risen from the floor, upon which sat a crystal sarcophagus. The Lord General stood on the dais. He removed his robe. He was naked. His body was still well muscled; his stomach was flat. Grychn wanted to look away—his nakedness brought back too many memories—but she was caught up in the spectacle and could not.

A medroid placed a psihelmet on the Lord General's bald head, and he climbed into the crystal sarcophagus, lying on white cushions. The top closed and sealed. The sarcophagus filled with liquid DMSO, and there was the faint whine of a compressor. A filigree of frost formed on the outside walls. The temperature inside would be close to absolute zero.

The psihelmet interfaced the Lord General's mind with cybermind, which was just such a collection of networked human and machine minds. Millions of macroprocessors were linked to millions of human minds whose bodies lay frozen in suspended animation, forming a massive gestalt consciousness. A special low-temp neuropeptide was carried into the frozen brains by the psihelmets, which catalyzed thought processes, allowing them to occur at such reduced temperatures. As long as there were no technological failures, the frozen minds would live until the heat death of the universe, some billion years hence. True cognitive immortality had been achieved.

Interfaciation to cybermind was considered quite an honor, a reward for a lifetime of service to Earth.

The dais and sarcophagus began sinking, soon disappearing into the floor. The sarcophagus with its frozen Lord General would be transported to the ancient salt caverns far below, there to rest until the end of time.

The guests resumed partying.

Grychn sent the boys home with their nandroid. She went home with Damiel.

3

They flew to Damiel's place in his skimmer, since Grychn's had gone home on autopilot with the boys.

On the way, they took a detour to the spaceport at Nyssa, so Grychn could see Damiel's twelve-meter yacht, the *Kalispel Condor*. She was a sleek-looking gravship with three p-grav pods placed on struts around a central spherical hull, itself twelve meters in diameter.

The cabins inside were luxurious, with paneling of real teak, gold fittings, silk upholstery, and wool carpeting. There were six staterooms, a galley, a lounge, a control room, and crew quarters. No one was aboard.

Grychn was suitably impressed. She had spent ten years living aboard gravships, when she and Detrs had been pirates, but their ships had been built for speed and firepower rather than comfort.

"This ship won the Ceres' Cup?" she asked.

Damiel nodded.

"Aren't the furnishings kind of opulent for a racer?"

Damiel shrugged. "The interior appointments don't make any difference one way or another. The acceleration comes from your p-grav pods and cannot exceed one hundred G's. Maneuverability is the key to winning races, and that's all in your cybernetics. The *Condor* has quicker cybernetics than any other twelve-meter racer —that's why she won the Ceres' Cup." He smiled.

"Why are you grinning?"

"I thought you knew."

"Knew what?"

"Your mother designed the cybernetics."

"I haven't kept in touch with her either."

"Sounds like you had a lovely childhood."

Grychn shrugged. "I wasn't allowed to choose my parents. So I don't have to like them." She thought of something. "Have you ever slept with my mother?"

"You're not supposed to ask those kinds of questions."

"Have you?" Grychn began to get excited at the thought.

"In a thousand years you can sleep with a lot of people."

"Did you ever sleep with her?" Grychn let her gown slip off and fall to the floor. She stood naked in its crumpled folds. Her singing pearls became warm from the ultrasonics they emitted. Pheromone steamed from her breasts. A normal male could not have resisted. Damiel did not.

He pulled off his pants and tunic and embraced her. She lay on the deck with legs spread. He kneeled and entered her.

"Did you ever have my mother?" she asked.

"Certainly," he answered.

"Am I better?"

"I'll let you know."

"One more question."

"Go ahead."

"Am I better than the Lord General?"

Damiel knew better than to answer that.

Later, Grychn was poking about the *Condor*'s bins and lockers. The ship was fully provisioned with enough supplies to last for months.

"Are you planning on leaving soon?" she asked.

"You never know when you might have to make a quick getaway."

She opened another drawer. "What's this?" But she knew. She stared at the DPU and psihelmets and the vial of peptide. She could imagine the peptide burning in her brain. "Why do you have a dream-processor? I thought you had quit."

Damiel closed the drawer. "For guests," he said. "Sometimes my guests get bored on a long voyage."

Grychn remembered making love within a dream-processor—the sex had been better than any real orgasms she had ever had. Much better. "I want to leave now," she said.

"Right now?"

"Yes, right now."

"Are you afraid of the dream-crystal? Are you tempted?"

"Yes. Let's go. I don't want to come back here."

"OK."

They left.

They took the skimmer to Damiel's estate, a ten-minute flight south to where the Arkansas River emptied into the sea.

Grychn would not talk until they had landed. "Do you have a dream-crystal here?" she asked him then.

"No," he answered, and they went into the house.

Neither one felt like making love again, so they just slept together in each other's arms. It all seemed very tender.

When Grychn awoke, she was alone in bed. Food smells drifted in from the French doors across the bedroom. She got up and padded over. Damiel sat at a table outside on a patio.

He looked up. "Good morning," he said. "Join me for some breakfast?"

Since he was still naked, Grychn did not bother dressing either. She sat across from Damiel, who poured her a cup of coffee. There were several varieties of fruit and cheeses, toast with honey and jams, and several kinds of pastries.

"If you would like something else, I'll have the cook get started."

"No need to bother. This is fine." She picked up a piece of toast and took a bite. A drop of honey dripped on her breast. She reached for a napkin, but Damiel put his hand on hers. His eyes were looking at her breast.

"I'll lick it off later," he said.

"In that case . . ." She let some more drip on her.

Damiel was true to his word. He did lick her clean.

Later that morning, they again sat at the table outdoors. Now they were showered and dressed. Grychn sipped a glass of wine.

"I talked to Edbryn this morning," Damiel said. "He's interested. He can see you this afternoon, if that's convenient."

"That would be fine," Grychn answered. "Will you come with us?"

"Of course."

She kissed him. She knew it was too late to turn back now.

They hopped over the mountains to Telluride and picked up the boys. Grychn and the twins followed Damiel in Grychn's skimmer. Edbryn's laboratory was located in Nyssa, another short hop back over the mountains.

At one o'clock they were sitting in his office.

Lord Surgeon Edbryn did not look particularly distinguished or impressive. He was of average height and slight of build. His eyes were an ordinary blue, his teeth standard white. His one distinguishing feature was his hair, which he wore shoulder length, pulled into a tail by a jeweled band. His voice was surprisingly deep and melodious. As he spoke, Grychn began to feel confidence in him. She believed he would tell her the truth.

After a few minutes of pleasantries, a medroid came in to draw blood and take tissue specimens from the boys.

"Why don't you two boys come with me to another office," Edbryn said. "I've got a few hologames you can play."

"Are you going to talk about grown-up things?" Craig asked.

"That's right."

"We probably already know about it," Chris added.

"Then it would bore you to stay. Come with me."

Edbryn led them out of the office and returned in a few minutes.

"How long will it take to do the tests?" Grychn asked.

"Not long. The actual DNA analysis is automated. Extracting it from the patient's cells is the hardest part. Damiel tells me you want to know if your boys will suffer progeria, and if so, if anything can be done to prevent it."

"That's right."

"How much do you know about genetic physiology?"

"Not much. I don't have a technical background."

"Then let me give you a little background. Hybridization techniques were first perfected fifteen hundred years ago. Using them, bioengineers could modify living tissues extensively, an example of which is sitting beside you." He looked at Damiel. "Next came techniques to hybridize gametes, so true-breeding hybrids could be created. The possible variations of human hybrids is almost unlimited, but less than twenty have seen widescale production: the nine hybrid extra-terrestrial races, the various military models, certain entertainment types.

"Without hybridization, colonization of the Solar System would not have been possible. But the early genosurgeons recognized the danger to the human morphology—hybrid forms might predominate and true humans become extinct. So they created us, the

Terran aristocracy. Ironically, our creation used the same techniques as hybridization, but without using any xeno-DNA. We were to be a shining example of eugenics, and we are. Our bodies are perfect, our features pleasing, our minds are sharp and sometimes brilliant. We do not suffer from disease. And we were given anti-agathic genes, so we do not age. But we are not immortal—death has only been delayed. Deterioration begins sometime after a thousand years. But that is another story.

"Genosurgeons have not had good luck making synthetic DNA. Single genes are not too difficult, but we have trouble creating an entire genome from scratch, especially one that will grow into a higher form. Plants and frogs and rodents can be synthesized, but synmen do not develop cognitive abilities, they have the intelligence of a rat. They can be trained to do simple tasks and by implanting psiwave transceivers they can be remotely controlled by cybermind, but they can never become functional human beings.

"Likewise, cloning techniques have not worked out. Differentiation permanently modifies DNA, and it cannot be brought back to an undifferentiated state.

"So to make human beings, we genosurgeons must modify gametes harvested from living humans. The first generation of the aristocracy was produced from one lot of gametes. The second generation, your generation, was produced from another. By then we had depleted our stock of gametes, which had been obtained from commoners. Unfortunately, we had also depleted our stock of commoners. They had all either emigrated or had been drafted and turned into combat hybrids. The only gene pool still untainted by hybrid DNA was the aristocracy. We harvested some gametes from ourselves and gestated some perfectly delightful little progeny. Unfortunately, they aged rapidly and died as they entered puberty. We thought it might be a problem with in vitro gestation, so we tried in vivo fertilization and gestation—making babies the old-fashioned, natural way—but the same fate happened to those children."

"Why does it happen? Why do they age so rapidly and die?"

"The Hayflick Phenomenon."

"What is that?"

"An observation made a long time ago that cells can divide only a finite number of times and their DNA replicate itself a limited number of times. DNA self-replication is such a complex event that there is a certain chance for errors to occur in the code. Small errors will not be noticed, but as more and more small errors occur, their individual effects become multiplied until faulty DNA is produced."

"That's what's happening to our children?"

"That's what's happening. Our gametes have exceeded the Hayflick limit, even those of the second generation."

"Why can't you repair their DNA?"

"There are too many errors to repair them all."

"Then what can be done?"

"Hybridization before they reach puberty. The insertion of xeno-DNA into their cells will correct the metabolic defects produced by errors in their native DNA. Hybrid vigor, if you will."

"Hybrid vigor. But then they will no longer be human."

"Yes, that's right. But they will live."

"Is that what happens when Lady Blue takes the children away?"

"Of course. Cybermind is practical, if nothing else."

"What kind of creatures do they become?"

"We are experiencing an acute shortage in the Foreign Legions right now."

"Cybermind turns our babies into soldiers?"

"I'm afraid so."

The medroid returned to the office with a printout it handed to Edbryn. He glanced at it quickly and then looked up at Grychn.

"What does it say?" she asked softly.

"There's no doubt they both will suffer the progeria. The error ratio is unacceptably high in their DNA."

Grychn felt stunned, although she had suspected as much. But somehow, not knowing for sure was better. Then at least there was a faint hope. "So my babies will have to be hybridized."

"That or die."

"But why into soldiers?"

"That is the current need."

"There are no exceptions?"

"No. Cybermind has become quite autocratic, I'm afraid."

"Is there any way to have the hybridization performed privately?" Damiel asked. "There must be a small, independent lab around."

Edbryn shook his head sadly. "Not on Earth. Cybermind has become quite pervasive also. There's no way it can be done on Earth."

"Then off-world?" Grychn asked, clutching at a dim hope.

"Maybe. Rumor has it there is a lab on Ceres that could do the work. It's part of some monastery run by a religious crackpot. But I've heard they have topnotch genosurgeons."

"The Entropic Monastery?" Grychn asked. So she would see Detrs again.

"Yes, that's the one. But there is another problem. The children won't be allowed to leave Earth. You're not the first mother who didn't want her children to go into government service. Any child eight years or older is restricted from foreign travel. They won't be allowed past customs."

Now Grychn felt totally defeated. She slumped in her chair.

"Maybe they won't have to go through customs," Damiel said, smiling. "The *Kalispel Condor* could sneak through."

Grychn brightened. "You mean you would take us to Ceres?"

"Why not? It's a quick trip in the *Condor*. She's loaded and ready to go."

"When can we leave?"

"How about tomorrow night? I've got a couple of loose ends that need to be taken care of before I can leave."

"The sooner the better."

Grychn and Damiel shook hands with Edbryn, collected the boys, and left.

On the way out, Grychn leaned over and whispered to Damiel, "Will I see you tonight?"

He whispered back, "No. I've got to run a couple of errands."

The twins giggled.

Damiel spoke in a normal voice. "Bring the boys and what luggage you need and meet me at the *Condor's* berth at 2100 tomorrow night. Would you two boys like to go on a little trip into space?"

"You bet!" they said in unison. "Where are we going?"

"We'll talk about it later," Grychn said, more sternly than she felt, because actually she felt elated. "Now say goodbye to Damiel."

They climbed into separate skimmers and streaked off in different directions.

A hundred G's of acceleration pushed against Damiel, oppressive even though he was immersed in shock gel. Earth dwindled in the rear monitors as the *Kalispel Condor* flashed away. Her departure was not noticed by the Home Guard; camoskin and stealth fields made her invisible to all but the most sophisticated sensors.

Damiel's errands would take him to Ceres. It would be a long time before he would return to Earth.

He felt bad about deceiving Grychn; her devotion to her sons was touching in a pathetic way—he understood her psychopathology. Still it was hardly sport to fool a cripple.

Sometimes Entropy was a cruel mistress.

4

Grychn managed to keep the boys from asking questions until after dinner. By then there was no stopping them. They followed her into the parlor like two excited puppies. She made them sit down before she would answer their questions.

"Are we really going to get to go to space?" Craig asked.

"Yes. Tomorrow night."

"Oh, boy!" Chris squeeled. "Where are we going to go?"

"Ceres."

"In the asteroids?" Chris asked.

"Yes, that's right."

"Where else is there a Ceres, dummy," Craig said.

Chris ignored the taunt. "Why are we going there? What are we going to do?"

"We'll see your father, for one thing."

There was uncharacteristic silence from the boys. Finally Craig asked, "Do you think he'll want to see us?"

"Of course he will."

"Do you think he still loves us?" Chris asked.

"I'm sure he does. I'm sure he's missed you very much."

"Then why hasn't he answered our letters?"

Grychn did not tell them that she had never posted their letters, but had thrown them away. She said instead, "He's a busy man."

"Why hasn't he asked us to come before?"

She also did not tell them that Detrs had pleaded with her to send him the boys. "I'm sure he wants to see you."

"How long are we going to stay?"

"We may not ever come back."

The boys looked shocked. "What do you mean, never come back."

Grychn looked away. "I've decided to move back to the Outer Moons. We have houses on every one. We can live wherever we want."

"But why not come back to Earth?"

"War might break out anytime now. If it does, we might not be able to leave Earth then."

"Is there a Lady Blue in space?" Chris asked.

"No, of course not."

"Then we can't go. Lady Blue will be coming for us any day now. We don't want to miss her. Right, Craig?"

"That's right. We have to be here for Lady Blue. We want to go to the center of the Earth with the other children. We want to see Alix again. We want to get away from grownups. We want to be able to sleep in peace."

"Yeah, we don't want to have to grow up. Who would want to grow up?"

Grychn felt like telling them the truth, that there was no never-never land in the center of the Earth, that the children Lady Blue collected were taken to hybertanks and turned into soldiers to be sent off to foreign garrisons to maintain Earth's domination of the rest of the Solar System. She felt like telling them they would be stripped of their identities and given a standard persona with synthetic memories and artificial passions. They would not even remember their own names. She wanted to tell them that if Lady Blue came for them, they would end up dying in a cold and lonely frontier, without knowing who they really were and that their mother really loved them. Instead she said, "I want you to be able to grow up."

"We don't want to," Craig said with a whine. "We want Lady Blue."

"We want Lady Blue," Chris chimed in.

They began chanting "We want Lady Blue," over and over.

"Stop it!" Grychn shouted.

The boys kept chanting. Their voices blended into a particularly annoying whine. "We want Lady Blue! We want Lady Blue! We want Lady Blue!"

"Shut up!" Grychn screamed.

The twins pranced around, holding hands, continuing their repetitious chant. "We want Lady Blue—We Want Lady Blue—We want Lady Blue."

The sound of their whining voices reverberated in Grychn's mind. Her vision seemed to close in. "Shut up! Shut up!" she screamed.

Grychn chased them and grabbed Craig. She put her hands around his neck, squeezing his throat, shaking him, trying to get him to stop saying "Lady Blue." Chris pummeled her back, trying to distract her. Craig scratched at her eyes, trying to break her grip. But they kept chanting. Grychn closed her eyes and squeezed harder.

Someone pulled Chris off her back. Firm hands removed her fingers from around Craig's neck. "Have the boys been misbehaving, ma'am?"

Grychn opened her eyes. The nandroid held a boy under each arm. They kicked and squirmed but could not break its hold. They still chanted, "We want Lady Blue."

"I'll just take them up to their room, ma'am and put them to bed. I'll stay with them and make sure they get to sleep. Everything will be fine in the morning." The nandroid carried the boys out of the room.

Grychn slumped into a chair. She felt terrible. She was ashamed of herself for losing control. She could have killed Craig. No, she couldn't have, she reminded herself. Nandroids were programmed to prevent pedicide. Before they had been so programmed, too many little Lords and Ladies had been lost. But she loved the boys. She did not want to hurt them. She wasn't crazy like the rest of them.

Or was she?

She had to talk to someone.

Who? She did not know how to reach Damiel. She had no friend she felt close enough to trust. Saraltr. They had once been close. Saraltr would listen to her.

Grychn stumbled outside and climbed into the skimmer. She did not trust herself to drive, so she told the compilot Saraltr's address and let the skimmer drive itself. She sat back in her seat and closed her eyes.

She opened them when the skimmer landed. She knew right away she had made a mistake: the pad was crowded with other skimmers. Saraltr was having another party. Grychn did not remember if she had been invited or not, not that it mattered. She had started feeling better on the ride over. Maybe a party would cheer her up even more. As long as she was here anyway, she may as well see what was going on.

She climbed out of the skimmer and went into the house.

As soon as a servbot came by she took two glasses of wine and a mnemone stick. She gulped down one glass of wine and sucked in a lungful of mnemone and began to feel even better. She circulated about the party, sipping wine, enjoying the mindless exchange of trivialties, indifferently looking for Saraltr.

She wandered past a room of dream-gamers.

The dream-game had not yet started; they were waiting for more players to arrive. Grychn went into the room and sat on the floor. Maybe she would play tonight. She looked around at the other players without speaking—it was considered impolite to converse prior to the game. She recognized some of their faces, but did not really know any of them. Dream-players formed their own fraternity and did not mingle much with non-players. They all had a certain gauntness to their faces and were lean enough to look malnourished. Not that bodily appearances meant anything to a dreamer. In the dream-game, only the mind mattered. Grychn tried to guess what kind of game might be played tonight—it would depend on the gestalt mood of all the dreamers. If she had known the players, she might have been able to tell. She was in the mood for a sex game. No real orgasm could compare with the duration and intensity of a dream-orgasm. In a dream-game, an orgasm was a combination of every orgasm you had ever had or imagined. Anything could happen in a dream-game. There was no sexual experience not possible. And it was completely casual—at the end of the game there were no feelings to get in the way.

Over the next half hour, players began to drift into the room and sit down. Finally there were twelve, the capacity of the dream-processor.

Each of them picked up a psihelmet and put it on. Grychn waited for the others, watching their faces go blank and their bodies slump over as the helmet dripped neuropeptide into their bloodstreams. She held the psihelmet over her head, pausing before slipping it on.

She could not.

She dropped the helmet and ran from the room, letting the dream-game start without her. She was afraid to play. She knew she would not want to stop.

Grychn ran down a hall and out on a balcony to get some fresh air. It was the same balcony where she and Damiel had sat the other night. The pool was directly below. Naked guests frolicked and splashed in the water.

Grychn pulled off her gown and tossed it on the floor. She slipped off her shoes. She was naked, except for her jewelry. The night air felt cool on her skin. She rubbed her hands along her thighs, over her buttocks, and up to her breasts. Thinking about the dream-game aroused her. Her skin tingled with vasodilatation.

She climbed and stood on the balcony's railing, weav-

ing back and forth for a moment before she caught her
balance. The people in the pool waved and shouted. She
flexed her legs and dove into the pool, barely clearing
the marble apron.

She hit the warm water cleanly and swam to the far
edge under water, before breaking to the surface and
treading water.

She felt fingers touch her buttocks and slide up her
back. At the same time, someone's head slid up from
her crotch, between her breasts, to break water in front
of her nose. A bearded man grinned at her.

"Gordon," she said, laughing, "I thought you were
down-under." "Down-under" meant the undersea colonies off the coast of Antarctica. Most of the inhabi-
tants were nereids—humans hybridized into marine
mammals—but there were a few true humans who lived
and worked in underwater bubble houses.

"I was down-under until yesterday," Gordon said,
"when I decided I had to get away from the seals and
back on dry land." He laughed. "Now I'm already back
in the water."

Gordon was Lord Gordon Ronmartha-Dandarl. He
was Grychn's half-brother, having been gestated from
one of Lady Ronmartha's gametes. His paternal gamete
was from the same lot as Lord George Dandarl, the interplanetary banker. Gordon was seven hundred years
older than Grychn, and being half-siblings meant nothing more than that.

He kissed her, pulling her tightly against him. Her
nipples pressed into his hard chest muscles. She kissed
him back, slipping her tongue into his mouth. She felt
his penis stiffen between her legs and she reached down
and inserted it into her.

Gordon pulled his face away from hers, looking surprised. "You're my sister," he said. "We can't do this
sort of thing."

Grychn laughed. "It never stopped us before."

As he thrust against her, Grychn could not help thinking of someone else. When he sucked her nipples, she
thought of other lips. When she climaxed, it was with an

intensity she had not felt for a long time.

Later they lay side-by-side under a tanning lamp.

"How is Sharlyn?" Grychn asked. Sharlyn was a friend who had been hybridized into a nereid, and was the reason Gordon had gone down-under.

"She's doing well. She is enjoying her new life."

"And you?"

"I'm not doing as well. A true human is out of place down-under. Seals are chauvinists and go out of their way to make a human feel uncomfortable. I will have to become one of them before I am accepted."

"Would you do that?" she asked incredulously.

"I've been considering it."

Grychn thought of her twins. They would have to become hybrids. She wondered if their feelings toward her would change afterwards. "How has the change affected her personality?" she asked.

"Tremendously improved it," Gordon said. "Sharlyn is the same basic person she was as a human, but she is no longer a borderline psychotic. The addition of xenogenes cured her of the mood swings she used to go through. She says she would have done it years ago if she had known how good it made her feel."

"It really made that much difference?"

"She says so. She thinks we have too many recessive genes that have made us prone to going crazy. Why do you ask? Are you thinking of hybridization?"

"Maybe." Grychn would not have, except for the twins. It might be easier on them if their mother became the same kind of hybrid. Grychn got up.

"Where are you going?" Gordon asked.

"Mingling."

"Will I see you later?"

"Maybe." Grychn leaned over and quickly kissed him, then walked into the house naked.

As she walked through the living room, a voice called to her. "Grychn! I've been looking for you." The voice came from a sofa across the room.

Grychn walked over to the sofa. Saraltr lay naked on it with a pedimorph. The pedi was kissing her breasts.

Grychn could feel its lips on her breasts in her mind.

"Grychn," Saraltr said, "where have you been? Come lie with me and my friend." Her speech was a little slurred, and her eyes were bright with peptide. "He's terribly expensive, but worth every penny of it. I didn't know what I would do with Alix gone." Her hand stroked the pedi's hairless penis.

"You did this with Alix?" She tried to sound shocked. She was annoyed at the envy in her voice.

"Of course. He was a talented little bugger."

"Your own son?"

"You needn't act so shocked. I've always envied you having the twins." She pushed the pedi's head lower, holding it between her legs. "The three of them were almost like brothers."

Grychn had a terrible suspicion. "What did you do when the twins stayed here with Alix?" she shouted. "What did you make them do?"

"The same thing you did when they all stayed with you." Saraltr laughed. "What else are little boys good for?"

Grychn leaped on the sofa, knocking the pedi away. She straddled Saraltr and hit her face with her fists. Blood poured out of Saraltr's nostrils and from splits in her lips. Grychn kept beating her.

The pedi jumped on Grychn's back. She felt it's fingers go around her throat and start squeezing. That did not matter. All that mattered was that she punish Saraltr.

Grychn's vision closed in around her. Her head began spinning. Blood roared in her ears.

Then blackness surrounded her.

When she regained consciousness, both Saraltr and the pedi were gone. Saraltr would be having a medroid repair her face, Grychn hoped. She felt her neck. It was tender, but not swollen. That figured. A pedi would know how to strangle without causing any damage. No doubt, such skills were part of their training.

Grychn got up and walked out to the skimmer pad. She did not bother to retrieve her gown and shoes. They were not worth the effort. She thought about Gordon and decided he was not worth the effort either. She climbed into her skimmer nude and told it to take her home.

As they flew over dark mountains, Grychn tried not to think about what Saraltr had said, but she did not succeed. She asked herself if the twins would have kept such a secret from her. They probably would have, she decided. She remembered when her father had been doing the same thing to her. She had been too embarrassed to tell anyone. She never had told anyone, not even Detrs. She had kept her terrible secret for over eighty years. She wondered what she should do. Should she try to get them to talk about it? Or would it be better to pretend she knew nothing? They would be leaving Earth tomorrow. She had made the right decision in that regard. The sooner they got away from Earth, the better. She would take better care of them now. Saraltr would not be able to get to them on Ceres.

The skimmer landed at home.

Grychn went into her house.

Before she went to her bedroom, she had to check on the boys. She opened their door and peeked inside. They lay sprawled on their beds asleep, with their blankets wadded up at their feet. Grychn tiptoed in and pulled the blankets over them. As she did, she admired their bodies, identical in every way. They were slender, with hands and feet a little out of proportion, prominent knees, elbows, shoulders, and ribs. Their body hair was still fine and white, not yet coarsening under their arms or at the base of their penises.

She turned to leave. At the doorway, she paused to look back. They looked so peaceful, asleep like that. No one would guess they were keeping such a grim secret.

Grychn could not help wondering what Saraltr had made them do. Would their penises stiffen? She supposed they would. Yes, of course they would. She remembered feeling one stiff against her. She remembered giving them baths herself, instead of letting the nandroid. When she washed them there, their penises had become hard in her fingers. But they would still be too tiny to give a woman pleasure. Maybe she just made them lick her. Or maybe she watched while they played with each other.

Grychn became aware that she was still naked. Sweat beaded from her skin. She felt tension in her groin, as her tissue engorged with blood.

She imagined Craig and Chris as grown men, standard humans, a way they could never be. She wished she could lie with them naked. She wished they could stroke her skin with their hands, kiss her breasts and lips with their lips. She imagined their hard penises. She would take one in her mouth, while the other entered her from behind, and both would spurt at the same time.

Soft laughter brought her out of her reverie. Her fingers were in her vagina. She jerked them out. A vague vortex of colored light hung in the air in front of her. She had recognized the laughter that had only sounded in her mind: it was the ghost of her father.

She left the room. The ghost followed her out.

"Will I have to put up with you haunting me forever?" she asked the ghost.

The ghost laughed again. "Only at night. I can haunt you only at night."

"I'll hire an exorcist to keep you away."

"Psiberwarps can be circumvented."

"Isn't it enough that memories of you torment my dreams? Why must you haunt me as well?"

"Even in the passionless gestalt, the memory of passion lingers. Even in the ascetic limbo of cybermind, the desire for lust persists. I'll eventually see you consummate this lust with your sons."

"Why won't you leave me alone?"

"I think you're beginning to understand," the ghost said and disappeared.

Mocking laughter lingered for a little longer.

5

Grychn spent the next day arranging things so they could leave. She had to be discreet, because she did not want cybermind to discover what was going on. She told her house computer that she and the boys were going down-under to visit Sharlyn—any calls or correspondence would be directed there. The house staff was programmed into a màintenance mode—they would keep up the place indefinitely. Lords and Ladies often left for extended periods of time. Nothing unusual about that.

She packed some baggage for herself and the twins— the sort of things one would take down-under. Nothing else mattered anyway, and besides, her other houses were already furnished. Money was no problem—most of her bank accounts were in foreign banks anyway, since her business interests were extra-terrestrial. Her legacy was held by Earth banks, of course, but it was a small fraction of her total worth, and was tied up in trusts anyway. She diverted as much electronic cash from her credcount to the RAM of her chargring as would be expected for an extended visit to Antarctica.

She called around and told her friends about bumping into Gordon and how she had decided to visit Sharlyn. It was a perfectly plausible story. She tried to call

Damiel, to make sure everything was still on with him, but there was no answer at his house and no message had been left for her. His personal holophone was not activated. Since he had not called or left a message, she took it to mean there had been no change in plans.

The twins moped around and pouted, secretly anxious to go to space, but mad at the thought of having to stay there. Grychn finally told them they could come back to Earth at the first sign of "growing up." The lie mollified their feelings, and afterward they could barely control their excitement. Grychn decided it would be prudent to wait until they were on Ceres before telling them the truth.

By late afternoon, everything was in order.

It was agony waiting around with nothing to do. They had dinner, but the twins were too excited to eat, and Grychn was too nervous.

The sun set and darkness settled around the house. Grychn loaded the skimmer with their baggage.

At 2030 they climbed into the skimmer and took off. Grychn flew manually and at altitudes below controlled airspace; there was no need for the air traffic computer to know where they were headed. She flew between the ice-laden peaks of the continental divide, relying on the skimmer's sensors to pick out the passes. A trip that normally took thirty minutes, now took sixty. It was 2130 before the skimmer settled down on the tarmac in front of the hangar that housed the *Kalispel Condor*.

Grychn and the twins carried their bags into the hangar.

Something was terribly amiss. The hangar was empty. The *Kalispel Condor* was gone. Surely Damiel would not have left them for being a half-an-hour late. Maybe he had already moved the ship out of the hangar.

Grychn went outside, telling the boys to wait for her in the hangar. There was no sign of the *Condor* anywhere. She walked toward the terminal, tuning her combracelet to the VOIR frequency. She listened to the terminal's computer talking to various departing and

landing ships' computers—there was no mention of the
Kalispel Condor.

At the entrance to the terminal there was a console
where private pilots filed flight plans. Grychn scrolled
through the day's list. The *Kalispel Condor* was not on
it. But then, Damiel may not have filed a flight plan.
After all, they were going to sneak past customs. But
how was she going to find the ship?

On an impulse, she scrolled backward through the
list. There it was, *Kalispel Condor*, filed for a direct
flight to Ceres. The ship had left last night at 2100.
Damiel had left a day early.

Grychn was stunned. Why would he lie to her? He did
not have to offer his help, so why would he and then
sneak off? He could have just told her she would have
to find another way to leave Earth. He did not have to
lie.

There was nothing she could do about it now.

She started walking back to the hangar.

She heard a peculiar, high-pitched whine. It was not
the sound made by a space craft. She looked up. A
shimmering blue sphere was hovering over the hangar.
Lady Blue! But she was coming too soon. Someone had
betrayed her twins.

Grychn ran toward the hangar. As she approached,
something dropped from the blue sphere and popped at
her feet. Noscamine filled her nostrils. She broke her
fall with her hands before passing out.

Lord Surgeon Edbryn observed the two boys being
unloaded from Lady Blue, which was no more than a
psiber-controlled ambulance with EMTroids. The blue
ionization field was a bit of whimsy Edbryn had thought
up himself. Normally, Edbryn did not personally supervise the hybridization of children. He had also seen to
the disposition of their cousin several days ago, making
sure he went into a zoanthrope tank. Alix had been a
special case. So were the twins.

He had been waiting for a set of twins for some time.

Corps Intelligence was short of path teams and twins made the best path teams—their psyches were already imprinted on each other. From the medical test that had been run the other day, Edbryn knew these two were perfect candidates.

He was glad Damiel had tipped him off that Grychn was about to flee Earth—he had sent Lady Blue out a little early.

He waited around until he saw both boys safely sealed in their own hybertank, reassured then that Entropy had not been cheated.

When Grychn regained consciousness, she was alone. Lady Blue's sphere was gone. The twins were gone. *Kalispel Condor* was gone. All that remained was the faint odor of noscamine.

Grychn had lost her boys. She would never see them again, or even if she did, they would not recognize her nor would she know them. Their memories and personalities would be stripped from them in the hybertanks, replaced by standard psyches known to be resistant to psychotic breakage. Their human form would be molded with xenogenes into the grotesque morphology of a combat hybrid. Hardware would be grafted into their flesh. Her lovely, sweet little boys would be no more.

Damiel had betrayed her.

But why? What possible reason would he have to betray her? He was no longer a Lord General. Or was he? Maybe his disaffection with Earth was just a ruse. If another rebellion occurred, cybermind would need spies. Maybe Damiel was a spy for cybermind. Grychn would have killed him if she could.

Maybe she could yet. Maybe he had not left Earth at all. Maybe he was home right now, laughing over the way he had tricked her. Maybe she could have the last laugh yet.

She loaded the baggage back into the skimmer. It broke her heart to think about the boys' things she would have to unpack. She opened her suitcase and took out a holstered hand pulser, setting it on the seat beside her. She told the skimmer to take her to Damiel's place. She would try there first. If he wasn't there, perhaps Edbryn could be made to talk.

The skimmer landed at Damiel's house on the Arkansas River. Only security lights were on. Grychn crept around the whole house to be sure none of the windows were illuminated. There were no other skimmers on the grounds. She holstered her pistol. She wanted to check out the house, but she could not break in without being zapped by the security system. Maybe she could bluff her way in.

She walked up to the main entrance. Lasewires scanned her and the door latch clicked open. Just as she had hoped, Damiel had not reset the ID file—her image was still in its memory as a friend.

Grychn wandered through the house. No one was home. The mechanical staff were in standby mode. She went through drawers and closets. There was nothing that told her anything useful: no letters, no notes, no holos. Nothing that would make the house any different than a hotel room. But then Damiel had not been back to Earth for several years. She wondered what had made him come back just then.

As she searched the house, Grychn's anger evaporated into depression. She already missed the boys. There was nothing else on Earth that she cared about.

She started weeping and could not stop for a long time.

She thought about killing herself—a clean burn behind the front teeth would be quick and painless. She would need more courage than she had right now to do it.

She rummaged through the pantry and found a bottle of wine—a decent vintage, at that. She poured herself a glass. Maybe when she finished the bottle she would be able to do the deed.

She had poured a second glass when the ghost materialized. The swirling lights appeared across from the table where she sat.

"How did you find me here?" she asked.

"You are not at all difficult to trace," her father's voice said. "Cybermind can keep track of all living beings on Earth. There can be no secrets from us."

"Then you knew all along what I was planning?"

"Certainly."

"Why didn't you let us go? What difference would two less soldiers make?"

"No difference whatever. But I could not let you humiliate me again. I knew what you would turn those two boys into—rebels, terrorists, just like you had been. You ruined my name once before; I will not let you do it again."

"Then I won't be allowed to leave Earth either?"

"Of course not. There will be another rebellion. Although I hate to say it, you do have a certain flare for terrorism. We will have enough difficulty suppressing this next rebellion anyway. Cybermind wants you where we can keep close tabs on you. Besides, we need more troops. You're young and healthy. You can have many more babies."

Grychn fingered the holstered gun.

"I know what you're thinking," the ghost said. "The trigger switch has shorted out on that gun."

Grychn drew it from the holster, pointed it at the ghost, and pressed the trigger. Nothing happened.

"You won't even give me that way out?"

The ghost disappeared without answering.

Grychn knew she was beaten. Edbryn had been right —cybermind was both pervasive and autocratic. She hoped the other Lords and Ladies appreciated the demigod they had created. There was nothing left to do.

She took the bottle and went upstairs to a bedroom, thinking she may as well spend the night there. She had no reason to go home.

She opened a window to let in some fresh air. She took off her clothes and lay in bed. A cool breeze blew in, raising her skin into gooseflesh. She shivered.

Rather than close the window, she looked for a pair

of pajamas she could wear. She began opening drawers. As she opened one, she stopped short, as though she was paralyzed. She stared into the drawer for a long time.

Finally she reached into the drawer and pulled out a dream-processor. She decided she would play one final dream-game. Just one dream. She hoped cybermind would allow her that much.

She carefully deactivated the processor's timer, so the dream-game would last until the processor lost power or her brain died. The processor was fully charged so it would run for a thousand hours. Without food or water, she doubted she would last that long. She set it for one dreamer. The dream would be hers alone, augmented and enhanced by the processor.

She put a psihelmet on her head. Tiny needles pricked her scalp; peptide burned into her brain. Muscles sagged; eyes stared blankly; face became lax.

She dreamed: *She frolicked naked with two young men, the twins grown to strapping manhood. Her beauty filled them with awe. Her sensuality filled them with lust. Craig lay on his back. Grychn straddled him. She took his penis into her mouth, pushing it in until her lips surrounded the root. Chris entered her from behind and began thrusting deeply into her. After a long time, the three of them came simultaneously, and their orgasms lasted forever.*

The woman's body was emaciated. Her eyes were sunken into a gaunt face, her arms and legs were spindly, her ribs stood out plainly. She lay in her own urine and feces, still connected to a dream-processor.

The medroids dispassionately disconnected her and placed her in a mummy stretcher, which automatically began rehydrating her and correcting her electrolytes. They flew her to Nyssa.

Edbryn shook his head as he examined her. There was no point trying conventional restoration—too much catabolism of tissue had occurred. She was a living mummy. She had probably burned out quite a few synapses also. Complete hybridization would be required.

He looked at a printout of her tissue analysis—the plasticizing potential was high. Her psychgram showed considerable latent schizophrenia—with perhaps a dozen suppressed personalities. She would be perfect to make into a chameleon.

He placed a plastic tag on her toe and watched as the medroids wheeled her away.

He briefly wondered why she had to become such a hybrid, and then forgot about her. He was not privy to the Prophet's precognition. Besides, he saw ten or twelve such dreamers every day. You could not wonder about them all.

BOOK TWO

DREAM-HUNTER

1

Pemont Byrd waited in the bar of the Little Bear Hotel, in the heart of downtown Ursus, the dome of which covered Callisto's largest crater. He sipped his drink somewhat nervously. He had good reason to be nervous, because he had a hundred thousand non-traceable cashier credits in the RAM of a credisk in his shirt pocket. He was waiting to complete a dope deal in which a hundred grams of pure peptide would be exchanged for his credisk.

The impending dope deal itself did not make him nervous. He had made too many of those. What made him edgy was that he was a vice-vark and did not have any backup. The deal had happened too quickly to arrange for any help to be present, and he was afraid if he had tried to stall for more time, it would have queered the deal. He had not even had time to go to the cybershop and get wired. And even worse, he suspected the two bad actors he was about to bust were the bunco team who had been hitting on dozens of the more prosperous members of Callisto's underworld, which meant they would be trying to get the drop on him. But when a voice like hers called you and told you to bring your money in fifteen minutes or forget about any deal, you took a chance.

Maybe things would turn out all right. He had a micro-holocam in the medallion he wore around his neck, so he could make a court-admissible recording of the transaction. The medallion was the Legion of Merit he had been awarded when he had been in the Corps, so it was reasonable that he would wear it at all times. He had a snub-nosed rapid-cycling autopulser tucked into a flesh holster carved into his left armpit—the slit in the skin was almost invisible, and he had put on enough fat so the bulge was hardly noticeable. A stun grenade was stuck up his rectum. But he would have felt a lot better with some decent backup.

Pemont was getting ready to retire from the Home Guard. He was fifty-five standard years old. That was too old to be working vice and bunco. In another year, he would have his twenty and a second pension. A man could live pretty comfortably on two pensions, even if he did have a girlfriend forty years his junior. Thinking about Luepin still made his cock stir: she was a sphinx, and sphinges were nearly double jointed. His friends teased him that he was going to have a heart attack trying to keep up with Luepin, but he did not care. He knew she loved him. In another year, he could spend more time with her.

His first pension came from the Foreign Legion. He had spent twenty years as a combrid in the Ghost Cavalry, finally making the rank of sergeant major. He had served on nearly every inhabited planet, moon, and asteroid, but had not seen enough combat to get himself killed. He had been lucky. The Hybrid Rebellion had already collapsed when he joined the Corps, so he saw only garrison duty, and the fire-fights were pretty few and far between. He won his medal in a brief, but bloody rebellion by the Marutes thirty years ago, when they would have overrun the garrison if he had not "held his post single-handedly against a superior number of insurgents until reinforcements arrived." The simple truth was he was scared shitless because he knew what Marutes would do to you if they took you alive. The way he saw it, he did not have a choice except to fight to the death.

Pemont had been born on Earth of human parents. Even though he had been given back his real memories when he retired from the Corps, they had dimmed now, so he did not remember much of his life on Earth. But it had not been a paradise, like it was for members of the aristocracy. Commoners had hard lives, cursed with pain, disease, hunger, and poverty. He had volunteered for foreign service, so he could escape the misery on Earth.

Now he looked like an ordinary middle-aged human, with graying hair, crow's-feet crinkling his eyes, and a developing paunch. He was almost an ordinary human. When he retired from the Corps, he had been demilled back to standard Terran morphology. Cosmetic surgery returned his appearance to standard human. Neurosurgery severed two of his three nervous systems. Orthopedic surgery unaugmented his muscles. Cybersurgeons ripped out various types of hardware. And the psychsurgeons gave him back his memories. When they made him into a combrid, they took away his former memories and replaced them with standard issue ones. Your human memories were stored as a psychcode and returned to you when you retired. For twenty years he had not known his real name, or where he had been born, or even why he had joined the Foreign Legions in the first place.

When he got his memories back, he realized he had no reason to return to Earth, so he stayed *up and out*, getting a job with the Home Guard on Callisto.

He had been a good, honest cop, despite working vice for most of his career. Promotion had been hindered only by his reluctance to keep up the paperwork, which was a serious shortcoming in the eyes of the bureaucracy. For that reason, he would retire no higher than detective, which suited him fine.

But first, he would have to get through this dope deal without back-up protection.

He ordered another drink, looking at the doorway, wondering what his soon-to-be business partners looked like. She had told him to wear sunglasses so they could recognize him and to sit at the bar. He was doing just that. He felt like an idiot wearing dark glasses inside.

He looked around the bar, wondering if they were already there, looking him over before making contact. They could be. The bar was crowded with almost every kind of hybrid: Martians, sphinges, sailors, miners, even a couple of Titanian Elves wearing methane masks. There were quite a few humans also, mostly business people and a few tourists. Nobody paid much attention to him. That meant they either weren't there, or they were professionals. On the phone, she had not sounded like a pro.

A nice-looking young couple walked into the bar. From appearances, they were tourists. They both wore shorts and tank tops. The man was about one hundred eighty cm tall, well muscled, with chestnut hair and thin lips. The woman was ten cm shorter, with long legs and nice curves, red hair, and a cute button of a nose. Pemont could not see their eyes because they wore dark glasses. They sat down at the bar next to him.

They did not beat around the bush.

"Do you have the money?" the woman asked in a soft voice.

"Do you have the stuff?" he countered.

"Not here. Do you think we'd be stupid enough to carry it around with us? This town is crawling with varks. We might get busted. If you don't have the cash, we walk."

"Relax. I've got it." He patted his shirt pocket.

"All of it? We don't take down payments."

"All of it."

"Did you come alone?"

"Just like you said."

"Do you have a gun?"

"Of course not."

"Do you mind if I check?"

"Be my guest."

She turned and kissed him like he was her long-lost sugar daddy, and at the same time patted him down. She missed the slight bulge in his left armpit. They must be tourists, he thought. Complete amateurs out to pick up a little cash. He would not need backup help to pinch these two. She felt his groin. She did not miss the bulge there.

"I thought you said you didn't have a gun?" she whispered into his ear. "He's clean," she said, turning to the young man.

"OK," he answered. "Let's go."

They all left the bar. Outside on the sidewalk, Pemont asked, "Where are we going?"

"Someplace safe, where we can make the deal," the woman said. "Now shut up."

She flagged down a cab, and they all climbed in. She told the cabbie an address, and he took them there. It was just a street corner. She flagged down another cab, and they went to another street corner. Pemont decided they were trying to lose a possible tail. He almost laughed. Amateurs! They repeated the ritual a couple of more times before they finally were let out back at the Little Bear Hotel. They went into the lobby and rode the lift-tube to the penthouse.

The woman unlocked the door of the penthouse and they went in.

"Peptide peddling must be lucrative," Pemont said. "Pretty fancy lodgings."

"The varks don't expect dope deals to take place in penthouses," the woman said.

"Where's the stuff?" Pemont asked.

"Let's see the money first."

He dug into his shirt pocket and pulled out the credisk, showing her its register. "Where's the peptide?" he asked. The micro-holocam had been running the whole time. If he did not hurry things up, it would run out of memory.

"In a minute," the man said. "First take off your clothes."

Amateurs, Pemont thought. He acted surprised, like

he hadn't been expecting it. "What for?" he asked with dismay in his voice.

"Just strip naked."

"Whatever you say." Next they'll probably make me have sex with the girl, he thought. Anyway, he hoped that was who they'd make him copulate with. You never knew with amateurs. He took off his clothes. His body hair hid the incision of his flesh holster. They did not notice how tightly his anus was pinched. They did not poke a finger up it either. Nor did they make him take off his medallion.

The girl had taken off her top and shorts and lay naked on the bed. Pemont almost laughed. Amateurs always thought varks couldn't actually have coitus with a suspect, that actual penetration was prohibited. As though there were still ethics and scruples in this day and age.

"Fuck her," the man said.

"Do what?" he asked. This time he sounded shocked.

"I said, fuck her. You know, the old in and out."

"What for?" Pemont asked. "No offense, young lady," he added.

"So we can make sure you're not a vark."

"I can't."

"What do you mean, you can't?"

"Look." He pointed to his penis, which dangled limp between his legs.

"Help him out, Risa," the young man said.

Risa got on her knees and took his penis in her mouth, sucking and licking furiously. In a minute, it was hard and stiff. Pemont never did have much will power. The girl lay back on the bed.

"Now, fuck her."

"OK."

He climbed on the bed, slipped between her legs, entered her, and began thrusting. Risa began to moan. Pemont was afraid he might lose control of his sphincter if he ejaculated, allowing the stun grenade to squirt out. Wouldn't that be a surprise? A real explosive orgasm.

She'd think he was the best fuck she'd ever had. But before either of them could climax, the man pulled him off.

"I guess you're OK," he said.

"I would have been a lot better if you wouldn't have made me stop." Nobody laughed but him. Pemont decided to be serious. "Where's the stuff?"

"There isn't any."

"What do you mean by that?"

"The deal is a little different than we told you on the phone. We keep the money; you keep your life. What do you think about that?"

"This." Pemont drew his gun from his armpit. "I have another deal in mind. I think this is a bust. I think twenty years at cyborg labor would be about right. What do you think now?"

"I think you're a brave man, but rather foolish."

The two tourists both laughed. Their images blurred and then came back into focus. Pemont knew they were not tourists. They were not even human. They definitely were not amateurs.

Pemont saw them change form into the creatures they really were. He was a brave man. He tried to press the trigger of his gun, but his finger would not move. The paralysis spread over his entire body. One of them grabbed his medallion, snapping the chain off around his neck. "Silly vark," was the last thing he heard before blackness closed around him.

2

Lady General Alelis Baxter-von Nakamura was in a sour mood. Her usually pretty face was screwed into a frown. She looked to be in her late twenties, but had a chronologic age of almost a thousand years. Her hair was red, her skin, chocolate and her eyes, black. Her features were vaguely oriental, a physiognomy out of style lately. She had long fingernails laquered red to match her hair. Her body was slim with small breasts, and she had shapely legs, which were shown off perfectly by her fatigue shorts. She was healthy, beautiful, rich, and powerful. But she was not happy.

Alelis had just spent an hour being on the carpet in the Supreme Commander's office. She did not enjoy being lectured by an old fossil who was several years past when he should have been interfaciated into cybermind. She did not like the insinuation that a change at the top might produce better results in her department.

Her department was Corps Intelligence. CI was responsible for the acquisition of extra-terrestrial data and the implementation of certain nonstandard remedies, such as torture, assassination, and kidnapping. Alelis directed over a hundred thousand chameleon operatives, each of whom might control up to a hundred local agents. The Long Range Terror teams and the WOLVES were also under Alelis's command. CI maintained a vast network of electronic listening posts that monitored both legal and clandestine transmissions, including all commercial data transfers. CI had the most powerful data-processing computers next to cybermind itself. They kept track of all the news publications, holovision broadcasts, spaceship passenger logs, police reports, and other official data banks, as well as a few unofficial sources. The intelligence data CI acquired was then fed directly into cybermind, the only data-processing facility with the capacity to process and integrate such volumes of random facts. Cybermind sometimes divulged its conclusions, but most often did not.

Alelis had been the head of CI for a hundred years, fifty years before and after the collapse of the last Hybrid Rebellion. She was next in line for a joint chiefship. You would not think one fugitive Marindian could jeopardize her entire career. But Geronimo had.

Geronimo was the name they had given to the war chief who had led the Marinidians in the last Hybrid Rebellion. They called him Geronimo because they did not know his real name or even from which tribe he came. He escaped capture when the Rebellion collapsed, and he had avoided capture for the past fifty years. One of Alelis' spooks had almost apprehended him six months ago, but when they sprang the trap, by blind luck Geronimo was gone. The operation had blown up badly. A WOLF went rogue and had not been found. An LRT team deserted. The commanding spook suffered a psychophysico break and had disappeared. Now they had no idea where Geronimo was.

Cybermind was convinced another rebellion was imminent. The newly formed Entropic Church was stirring things up as well. The Marindians were the key to a successful hybrid rebellion—if they revolted the Marabs, Asteroidians, Elves, and the other hybrid races would follow. Geronimo was the key to the Marindians—he was still the only leader who could unite all the tribes.

Without the support of the Marindians, a rebellion would fail. So cybermind wanted Geronimo captured and out of business.

Corps Intelligence had been ordered to accomplish the capture as soon as possible.

Lady General von Nakamura was pretty certain her career was at stake. If her head was to roll, she was going to make sure others rolled with it. Fortunately, she had a plan.

A tiny figure sprang up from the surface of her desk. The image of her clerk saluted and said, "Colonel Lomni is here, General."

"Send him in immediately." Alelis' face brightened considerably.

"Yes, sir." The corporal had a funny look on his face before his image melted into the desk.

When Colonel Dat Lomni walked through the door, Alelis knew why. Dat was in gynoid morphology, appearing as an attractive young woman, with black hair, dark eyes, ample breasts, and water-bottle hips. She was wearing an outfit that did not conceal any of her considerable charms.

"For cyber's sake, Dat, why don't you tell me what you're going to look like ahead of time, so I don't make a fool of myself in front of an EM. Why aren't you in standard morphology anyway?" Colonel Lomni was a chameleon with plastic flesh and could assume the shape of any of the nine hybrid races, as well as most any creature one could imagine. Changing from standard Terran male to standard Terran female was child's play for a chameleon.

"I was on a case when I got the call you wanted to see me. I didn't have time to change."

"I thought you lizards could change in a paper bag if necessary."

"We can. I could have changed my body back easily, but I did not have another set of clothes, and I wasn't sure you would want people to think you were seeing a transvestite."

"That's very thoughtful of you. You're quite lovely actually."

"You did not summon me here to compliment me."

"No. You're off whatever case you were on. I've got a little project for you." Alelis smiled charmingly.

"Your little projects usually end up with me nearly getting killed. You ought to be more careful of your best spook."

"What makes you think you're my best spook?"

"You told me once."

"Oh. A moment of temporary derangement. Besides, I wouldn't use you if I had any choice. You have had the new dual cerebrum neuro-mod?"

"I just got out of the hybertank last week."

"Do you think it will work? Can you fool a path team?"

"Maybe. How bad is it?"

"I want you to find Geronimo for me."

"Is that all? Most of the spooks on Mars have been trying to find him for the past fifty years. It would be easier just to wait. The poor guy must be seventy or eighty by now. In a few more years he'll be dead. Forget it. I'm good, but I'm not that good."

"We have a lead now."

"What kind of a lead?"

"An LRT team located him about six months ago. Ghost Cavalry raided the camp, but as usual, Geronimo was gone. They left the LRT team and a WOLF to track him, but something went wrong."

"What kind of something?"

"The LRT team went over."

"I didn't know a wild LRT team was a possibility."

"It wasn't, until now."

"I thought there were supposed to be hypnocommands to keep them from going over."

"There are. For some reason, they didn't work. We don't know why. Their spook commander had a psychophysio break and is not talking. As a matter of fact, she's disappeared also. But it gets even worse."

Dat groaned. "What could be worse than a wild LRT team?"

"A rogue WOLF."

"WOLVES go rogue all the time."

"This one was a pet of the Supreme Commander. He was allowed access to the master personnel files. We have reason to believe he knows his prehybrid psicypher codes, and he may know that about some other combrids, including the wild LRT team. But that's not important. What really matters is that this WOLF is apparently obeying his last orders, which were to track and follow Geronimo. If we can find this rogue WOLF, we can find Geronimo."

"You mean all the spooks and LRT teams on Mars haven't been able to find him?"

"I told you. He's no ordinary WOLF."

"How about other WOLVES?"

"They haven't been returning from the field."

"He must be one tough dog."

"I've got a plan to locate him."

"I was afraid you might. I suppose I figure into it?"

"Of course. You're never out of my thoughts. Do you want to hear my plan?"

"Do I have a choice?"

"No."

"Then tell me the plan."

She did. After she had finished, she asked, "What do you think? Will it work?"

"Maybe."

"Can you do it?"

"Maybe. Do you have any idea where this wild LRT team is now?"

"A vark flushed them on Callisto."

"And the broken spook?"

"Somewhere on Titan. Probably the Underground of Chronus."

Dat was quiet then for a while. "I guess it might work. But I'll be taking a lot of chances. I could get my brain fried."

"That's why you have two. Besides, if you succeed, there'll be a star in it for you."

"Spooks never make general."

"I need an adjutant. It may as well be you. A brigadier will do nicely."

"And if I fail?"

"I don't think I'll be your commander any longer. Of course, that won't matter to you in the state you'll be in."

"Of course. Do you have any other cheery thoughts."

"Don't fail." Alelis got up from behind her desk and walked over to a small bar. "Since we've got business out of the way, how about a drink?"

"OK. Whiskey and water. No ice. Ice bruises whiskey."

"I know what you drink." She brought Dat a glass without ice and sat on the sofa. "Make yourself comfortable," she said.

Dat got up from her chair and sat beside Alelis. She put her free hand on Alelis' bare thigh and sipped her whiskey. The Lady General put her arm around Dat's shoulders.

When Dat finished her drink, she set the glass on the floor, and turned and kissed Alelis. Alelis kissed her back and lifted her gown over her shoulders. Dat was naked underneath. Dat pulled off Alelis' tunic and shorts and began kissing her breasts.

Alelis cleared her throat.

Dat looked up. "What's the matter?" she asked.

"You know I don't like you like this."

"Like what?"

Alelis squeezed Dat's breasts. "Like this."

"Oh, I forgot. Just a minute, I'll change." She looked at Alelis. "Do you want to watch?"

"You know I do."

Dat closed her eyes. Her skin became loose and sagged, then fasciculated, as though there were millions of worms wriggling under it. Her hair retracted into her skull and grew out yellow and short. She grew several centimeters taller and her muscles became bulky. Her breasts flattened. A penis and scrotum grew from his crotch. "Do you like me better like this?" he asked. His penis stiffened.

Alelis said nothing. She was already panting and squirming with lust, excited by watching Dat's metamorphosis. She lay back and spread her knees. Dat crawled between them and entered her.

Later, they lay together in the glow of used love.

"Did you know the original KR-MR?" Dat asked. KR-MR was his psychcode.

"Kramr? Of course. He was under my command."

"Was he ever under you?"

"Maybe. I don't remember. It was a long time ago. Why do you ask?"

"I was wondering why you liked me."

"I like you for your body."

"But I can have any body I choose."

"I know." She started kissing him, then moved down and licked his penis.

"When do I leave?" Dat asked.

"In an hour."

"Do we have time for another?"

"If you hurry."

He did.

The Lady General's mood was considerably improved by the time he left.

Colonel Dat Lomni stood beside a hospital bed in Ursus, on Callisto. He did not like what he saw. He kept seeing his own face on the stiff in the bed. Not that he even knew what his own face looked like.

Like all combat hybrids below the rank of general, Dat had no idea who he had been before hybridization. Those memories were still in his brain, but they were locked up with a psicyper, so they could not be accessed. The Corps had found that combrids could be made more efficient if they were given standard psyches as well as standard bodies and uniforms. Corps psychsur-

geons picked out psyches that had been found to be particularly efficient, recorded them, and grafted them into
the minds of recruits during the hybridization process.
That way, they knew they would have brave, depend-
able, predictable soldiers. Combrids did not have to be
particularly nice or even sane. A crazy soldier was
sometimes better than a sane one.

Dat had a standard chameleon psyche, version KR-
MR. There actually had been a KR-MR in the Corps
about a hundred years ago. He had been killed on a mission before the end of the Hybrid Rebellion. Before he
had been killed, he had made some spectacular coups in
Corps Intelligence. His psyche had been recorded. After
a few modifications, it became a standard psych-type
for chameleons. KR-MR's memories were not particularly pleasant. The names had been erased, but he
had been born into the aristocracy of Earth. He had two
brothers. The three of them had been sexually abused by
their parents and their parents' friends, which warped
all three of the boys' minds. They played their own per-
verted games, mocking the depravity of their parents.
During one of these games, KR-MR killed one of his
brothers, resulting in his being sentenced to the Foreign
Legions. He became a spook.

Those were the memories with which Dat lived. His
nightmares sprang from that twisted childhood.

Sometimes he wished he had his own memories back.
No matter how depraved his childhood, no matter how
much hunger, pain, or squalid misery he had suffered, it
would have to be better than KR-MR. Nothing could be
as bad as the dreams he lived with now.

When he made colonel, they gave him his name back.

When he made general, he would get his memories
back.

The only other way was to make it through twenty
years of honorable service and retire. Then he would get
his memories back, but they would dehybridize him.
Dat had only served ten years.

Dat wanted to know what he really looked like. They
said a chameleon only reverted to his true physiognomy

when he was killed. Dat did not want to have to die to find out. If he succeeded on this mission, he would be made a general. Then he would know.

Dr. Robn Emde, Chief Psychsurgeon of the Tenth Mobile Hospital stood on one side of him, and Major Chasplat Patchout, Commander of the Home Guard, stood on the other. They were all looking at another member of the Home Guard, who was lying in the hospital bed with a lax expression on his face. The drool running down his chin appeared to be a major neurological accomplishment for him. The name on the bedside chart read: Pemont Byrd.

"Any progress in unscrambling his brain, Doc?" Dat asked. He was in cyrine morphology that day and wore Corps fatigues.

"None," the doctor answered. "Whoever did this was an expert. There is no structural damage; the derangements are all in software. But there are so many overlays it will take us at least a year to unravel things. His synapases are jumbled like a jigsaw puzzle. We've got to put them back one at a time, and if one goes in wrong, the whole thing shorts out."

"What are the chances of a quick fix—just enough to find out what happened at the end, if he learned anything useful?"

"His mind would never recover, and he'd end up in a permanent vegetative state."

"But would we get any information?"

"Probably not. There would be too many overlays to go through to get there. His brain would burn out before we could extract what you want. Like I said, an expert did this."

"What kind of expert?"

The doctor shrugged his shoulders. "I could have. Any good psychsurgeon could have—given a month's time and access to a K-bit psychprocessor and lots of neuropeptide. But I've got the only psychprocessor on Callisto, and this did not take a month."

"Where does that lead us?"

"I'm not a fool, Colonel. I went back and reviewed

our outpatient charts for the past month. Patients have been presenting with peculiar histories. They have been robbed somehow, but in such compromising circumstances they won't file a police report. They come to us with recurring nightmares or phobia or hysteria. On exam, they apparently have had minor, but very clever, psychsurgery. Only they have never seen a psychsurgeon before, and the synaptic rearrangements are not at all therapeutic in nature. The only other similar cases I've seen have been the victims of Long Range Terror. You, a full colonel in Corps Intelligence, arriving to investigate the matter of an ordinary vice-vark losing his mind, confirms my suspicions."

"Which are?"

"I said I'm nobody's fool. This must be the work of a path team. Since you're here, they must not be doing legitimate clandestine activities. They said it could never happen, but it has."

"What has happened?"

"A path team is on the loose. One has gone wild, hasn't it?"

"Thank you, Doctor. You have been quite helpful." Dat turned and walked away. The major followed him.

Dr. Emde shouted after them. "I'm right, aren't I? One of your terror teams is free. You better hope they never realize their true capabilities." His voice faded as Dat and Major Patchout walked down the corridor.

"Was he right?" Patchout asked when they were back in his office.

"Probably. A path team goes wild. The circumstances here fit that scenario. What can you tell me about your crime wave here?"

"Not much more than you already know. The victims are reluctant to report anything officially. Some of them still don't believe they have been robbed, and others have been robbed under circumstances that make them want to avoid discovery. Apparently some of the victims think they have killed someone, although we have been unable to come up with any hard evidence of murder. There must be many more we have no idea about."

"When did it start?"

"As best we can tell, six weeks ago."

"What was your vice-vark working on?"

"Unfortunately, he wasn't very good about keeping records. He was assigned to bunco, and apparently was working on a tip from an anonymous source."

"Who was the source?"

"We don't know. It could have been a holophone tip or something. He wasn't wired."

"What does the crime computer say? Has there been any similar series of robberies?"

"We ran a check just before you arrived." He read from a sheet of flimsy. "Marsport, about six months ago, lasting for just over a month. Five months ago in Piazzi; on Ceres, for three weeks. Scattered reports for the next three months: Pallas, Juno, Vesta, Hygeia, and most of the other inhabited asteroids, apparently random enough so that no pattern was noticed until now. And now Callisto. Where will they turn up next?"

"Ganymede," Dat said with sudden conviction.

"What makes you say Ganymede?"

"Just a hunch. They probably don't realize we're on to them yet. They will think your vice-vark found them by chance, which he did, and won't be able to talk for a long time, which he won't. So they will have no reason to be spooked and probably won't try to be too clever. Besides, I'm sure they think they can avoid either detection or capture. And from looking at your officer, I'm not sure they can't." Dat got up from his chair. "Thanks for your help."

"You're going to Ganymede?"

"Maybe."

"You think you can catch a path team by yourself?"

"Maybe."

"You're either brave or foolish."

"Maybe both."

3

Risa and I worked the penthouse of the Hotel Ganymede. Jupiter shone a baleful red overhead. Hydrogen clouds shimmered with starlight.

A woman hung naked in the center of the room, wrists and ankles each secured by silver shackles chained to magbolts. She was true human and was young and lovely; mahogany skin, gleaming almost ocher in jovelight; long hair shining like spun gold; eyes as bright as fractured emeralds. Her legs were long and lithe; her stomach was flat; her breasts were still tumid with adolescence. White teeth bit into her lower lip. Blood beaded along their edges. She writhed in her bonds, but could not pull free.

A man faced the woman, also naked. He too was of unaltered Terran stock, but could not be called lovely; radiation scars puckered his skin; one eye did not close completely. A skin cancer grew like lichen from his right cheek. His hair was close-cropped and once must have been black, but was now sprinkled with white from damaged melanocytes. Bulky muscles had become flabby with neglect. His name was Hitt.

The man used to ply an honest trade—gunrunning for the various insurgent hybrids of most of the Outer

Moons. When the Rebellion sizzled out, his gunrunning business slumped. But he had become quite wealthy from it. Now he had retired to enjoy the fruits of his labor.

The girl was a high-priced callbody. A deal with her broker was made a short time ago. So far, all had gone accordingly.

Hitt held an alphalash in his hand. Glowing filaments dropped like a horsetail of optical fibers. Protons dripped from their ends to bounce from the floor. The girl's eyes vibrated vertically, transfixed by the bounding protons.

Arm muscles flexed. Ionized air shrieked as the alphalash swung its arc. Ozone fumed into sharp olfactory tendrils. Shed sparks danced like dust motes caught in a moonbeam.

Breath whistled from the girl's nostrils.

The lash touched naked flesh; skin twitched into wrinkled blisters, then relaxed. Glowing lines burned into the skin where each filament of the lash touched. Energized protons became embedded in epidermis where they slowly shed their energy into pain receptors. Neurons then carried a symphony of hurt. No discipline was as painful as the proton whip.

The girl did not cry out from the first lash.

The alphalash descended again and again. Each time it struck, Hitt became more excited.

I was lounging across the room on a couch. Though Hitt could not see me, I looked like a true human: one hundred eighty cm tall, sturdily muscled, haughty gray eyes, aquiline nose, chestnut hair, lips that could be cruel. But I was not human.

Risa prowled like a cat through drawers and closets, collecting valuables into a bag. She was not human either. Her ermine fur had a silver sheen. When she smiled, sharp teeth flashed. Amber eyes with pupils contracted into vertical slits, glowed with their own light. She appeared standard sphinx, save the quivering tendrils above her head.

Though the callbody appeared human, she was not

real. She was an illusion, a figment of my imagination which only knew as much as I let it, a magician's image, conjured for pleasure.

There were no snoopers around. Both Hitt and I had made sure of that. Neither of us wanted witnesses to the night's activities. If there were any around, a ring on my finger broadcast a field that would confuse their sensors.

Risa discovered the wall safe behind a mutaholo. She glanced my direction and smiled. I nodded. She had found what we sought.

Hitt split into two images. One ghost continued thrashing. The other walked over to the safe and placed its palm on the sensing surface while staring into a retinal camera. Hitt would not remember any of this. Clever psychsurgery might be able to dredge it up, but not without damaging quite a bit of memory.

The safe swung open. Hitt fused into one figure again and continued whipping the girl. Risa looted the safe of its contents. She held up her thumb.

Time to end this psidrama.

By now the callbody was completely covered with ionic fire. Every square centimeter of skin was alight with a webwork of decaying protons. She did not scream nor beg for mercy during the entire ordeal. That made Hitt furious. He was even more brutal with his lashing. His face shone with demonic fire.

Hitt's reaction was predictable. His psychopathology was quite conventional. I envied him that. His motives were quite transparent to me. I wish I could be as sure of my motives. But I couldn't. My past had been constructed for the convenience of the Corps. My memories were synthetic. And even those pseudomemories were not intact—a gap existed in them, an amnesia caused by an event not remembered. Lately I had begun to doubt the validity of my memories, both pseudo and real, that had survived the amnesia.

But if I didn't know myself, I did know Hitt. His rage at the girl's silence caused the alphalash to whip with a frenzy, seeking tender places: face, breasts, groin. Her skin burned in an incandescent reticulum. I let the girl slump in her shackles, as though he killed her. Some dim sense of *déjà vu* disturbed me. I had an uncanny feeling I had seen all this before, as though we were repeating an old ritual. I pushed the discomfort away.

Even the girl's apparent death did not appease Hitt's anger. He slapped her across the face again and again. She did not respond. He suspected she was feigning. He kicked her. Her body rocked in its chains in synchrony with his kicks. Still, he was not satisfied. He stood behind her, pressed his penis between her buttocks and entered her anus. Her flaming skin burned a faint tattoo into his thighs.

Against my will, the girl's face was transformed into another's: rouge-red cheeks, white acrylic skin, poker-chip-blue eyes, curls of yellow yarn, button nose. A doll's face. The visage angered me. I did not know why it should. But I was furious at Hitt.

Protons fled the girl's anus, embedding themselves in Hitt's penis. He screamed and withdrew from her flesh. His penis flamed with ionic fire. He could not stand the pain. He grabbed a sonic knife and cut off his own member. But even that did not free him. Neurons remembered and sang with phantom pain. Hitt sank to the floor, moaning.

A ring glittered on Hitt's little finger. I had admired that ring all night—it was platinum and set with a singing sapphire of several hundred carats. It would look good on my finger.

I took the ring off Hitt's finger and slipped it on mine. It was too loose on my pinky, so I tried my other fingers, and it fit my middle finger. That was strange. Hitt's hands did not look any bigger than mine. I guess he had fat fingers.

Before we left, I sent one final scene into Hitt's mind: He hauled the callbody into the shower and cut it into manageable pieces, which he fed to the disposal unit.

Risa and I were safe. I took her hand and we walked out the door. Hitt's thought swirled after us, confused with pain. Yet within his unraveling mind tapestry, there was a locked weave. He kept some secret from us. No matter. We had beaten him.

Hitt would never report the robbery; he thought he had a murder to conceal from the varks. He would not want to bring suspicion to himself. Our larceny would never be investigated.

I had no reason to feel anxious.

Safe in our own room, we made love.

Risa lay beside me on a bed of wombskin in the Nyssa Suite of the Hotel Ganymede. There were eleven similar suites, each named after one of the ancient city-states of Earth. They formed a crystal duodecagon atop the hotel's main spire, which rose a thousand meters from the floor of Chalise Crater to protrude through hydrocarbon mists into clear, cold space. Overhead, Jupiter hung like an injected eye. Below, wisps of yellow fog lapped over the edge of the crater to swirl like wraiths across pocked terrain.

A room with a view, the desk clerk had said. It ought to have one for the grand a day the hotel charged. But the expense was necessary. We wanted to be in close proximity to the rich. The rich were the only ones worth pandering and preying upon. Besides, the varks wouldn't be expecting us to stay in a suite of the most expensive hotel in the system. If any vice-vark had followed us from Callisto, he'd be expecting Risa and I to hole up in some seamy icehouse in the Combat Zone.

But no one had followed. I'd made sure of that. The ferret who had made us in Ursus was now drooling and staring blankly at his toes. He'd been brave, but stupid. He hadn't been internally wired: no hardware in his skull; no cameras behind his eyes; no bugs in his ears. He'd been working naked, except for a simple external holocam without telemetry, which I had jerked from around his neck and smashed under my boot heel. Then the rest of his data was stored in software, including the only remaining evidence against us. A big mistake. It would take the psychsurgeons a year to bring his mind out of its autistic fugue. And each of their psionic manipulations would result in a few hippocampal synapses shorting out. By the time he awoke, he'd be lucky to remember his name, much less the identity of the path team that had once prowled his dream-time.

Risa and I would never be traced from Ursus to Chalise, then from Callisto to Ganymede. We had been here two weeks and had already made half a dozen decent scores. It was business as usual. Now, we'd scored big with Hitt, ten million alone in cash, not to mention the gems and drugs. Chalise was ripe for the taking; our prey was found anywhere perversions were pandered.

My hand stroked along her spine, smoothing ermine fur; she arched her back in rhythm. Static sparked blue between my fingers. With my other hand, I traced faint vibrations in her throat, lightly touching my fingers to her fasciculating flesh, smoothing away the contractions. Her eyes closed halfway; their irises caught and held jovelight like shattered amber. Instead of hair, silver filaments grew from her scalp, now quivering like fuzz on a thistle head. But they could lay flat and would then be mistaken for the mane of an ordinary sphinx. Her nostrils flared as she breathed.

She rolled over and kneeled above me, straddling my body with hands and knees. She bent to kiss me; a rough tongue slipped past my lips. Furry breasts pressed against my chest.

I closed my eyes. We wandered the psychic ether, riding updrafts of thought. Our mind's eye searched below for prey. I looked for Hitt. He should still be in his room above ours. But the room was empty. I expanded the search. His thought patterns were nowhere to be found. How could he hide from our psychic senses? Only the dead were safe from us.

Don't worry, Risa said in my thoughts. *Hitt no longer matters. We have other prey to seek.*

Is he dead?

No, just hiding. She laughed, almost a growl in my ear. *I'll explain later. Forget about him. The sea is filled with other fish tonight.*

She reached around to press my penis against her

labia, slipping the glans between them. She settled down, coupling, then rocked gently up and down. Her mucosal neurons interfaced with my cutaneous ones. My mind meshed tighter with hers—our psychic sensorium expanded. We flew as one over Chalise, soaring among bright tendrils of thought.

See how many fish?

Our talons plucked only the amber fibrils, bringing them close to our face. We touched our tongue to each shining filament, tasting fear, while our nostrils sniffed its acrid scent. We listened to terrified voices calling to an uncaring sky. Our eyes traced each filament back to its source, back to a living mind. The filaments unraveled there into a dream tapestry of a pathetic creature quivering with fright.

There was prey aplenty for dream-hunters.

Tonight's hunt is finished. Let's save prey for later.

We fell back to our room. Our sensorium contracted to include only our coupled bodies. Soft flesh yielded to hard flesh becoming just one flesh. We made love as one body: dual waves of pleasure synchronized into one rhythm; two hearts beat simultaneously; neurons sang one song, harmonizing into ever higher keys.

Finally we quivered with smooth muscle peristalsis, overcome with parasympathetic discharge. The climax could have come from one or both of us; no matter, it was perceived by both in unison.

We separated: two minds coalesced out of one; two bodies lay close without touching.

Risa slept.

I watched her eyes roll back, her tongue dart in and out quickly between her lips. I envied her the ability to fall asleep so quickly, like an innocent animal. I was jealous of those genes. Sleep did not come as quickly for me.

Her breathing slowed, became deeper and regular. Soon her eyelids fluttered with fasciculations of REM beneath. She dreamed.

I wished I could dream her dreams. How wonderful they must be, from what little she would tell me: animal

dreams filled with moving air and warm sunlight and
the smells of Earth. As a pathic gestalt, we could share
our thoughts, but for some reason not our dreams.
Perhaps it was for the best. Some secrets were needed.
One must have something to call one's own.

Later, I finally dozed.

Images rose in my sleep-lulled brain: three young
boys cavorted naked with a nude woman. The woman
held an alphalash in her hand and used it to prod the
boys. She made them suck each other's penis while she
watched. Then she made them suck her nipples and lick
her groin and anus. If they hesitated, they felt the sting
of the lash. After hours of tormenting the boys, the
woman finally fell asleep. Those images dissolved, replaced by others: a baby suckled at his mother's breast,
contentedly, only to open his eyes to find he was really
clinging to a wire manikin with a rubber nipple protruding through the mesh; ghost children argued over a
doll, pudgy hands tugged on plastic arms and legs until
they were disjointed, and the doll's torso and head fell
to the ground; doll's eyes swung back and forth in
mechanical nystagmus, conjuring dreams out of their
hypnotic rhythm.

I woke with my skin afire. Protons danced on my body
like angry corposant, as though I had dived into a boil-
ing geyser. I thrashed about on the wombskin, trying to
put out the fire. Risa woke also. She pinned me down
with her hands and began licking me with her tongue.
With each rough stroke, a little fire was extinguished.
She started with my face and worked down my body.
Gradually, I relaxed. The rest of the psychic fire went
out without her tongue's help.

You can stop now. I realize it was only a dream.

Just a little longer. She laughed. *I like the salt in your
sweat.*

OK.

Her lips made their way between my legs.

Hey! I thought you said you liked the taste of sweat.

I like salt—wherever it's found.

I did not argue.

Eventually she was finished. We lay side by side.

"I dreamed again of being alphalashed. A spook officer was doing it to me. I couldn't see her face, but I think it was Kaly. I don't remember being flogged in the Corps. They knew better than to try that, so why do I dream about it? Because of guilt over deserting?"

"That would be the conventional interpretation."

"And why do I think it's Kaly?"

"Because you are afraid of her."

"I suppose," I looked at Risa. "Tell me about your dreams?" I asked.

She closed her eyes. This was a nightly ritual with us.

"They're hard to describe. I don't think they're supposed to be described since they originated in nonverbal minds. There are images, quite vivid, and odors and scents and tactile sensations."

"Do I ever appear?"

"Sometimes." She laughed. "I pounce on you and eat you alive. What do you say to that?"

"I guess that's the best way to be eaten. Do you ever dream of Major Kaly?" Kaly had been our spook commander when we were in the Corps. Now she was probably looking for us.

"My dreams have forgotten her."

"I wish mine had. Do you ever dream of the alphalash?"

She didn't answer.

"Have you dreamed of the lash?"

"Sometimes," she said slowly. "Sometimes I have a dream of three boys being flogged by a woman to make them perform sexual tricks for her."

I almost gasped. That was one of my dreams. "Do you know who they are?" I asked.

"No. One boy is older. The other two are brothers, maybe twins. They look like I imagine you must have looked when you were a child."

"I have had the same dream."

"Then maybe I have shared your dream-time."

"Maybe. That must be it."

Eventually the room lightened with Ganymede's artificial dawn. With the shadows gone, I could sleep undisturbed for a little while. But night always waited.

Hitt lay naked on a wombskin bed in a pool of blood. Blood still oozed from his severed penis. Pain still burned in his groin. He remembered killing the girl with remarkable clarity, cutting up her body, and feeding the pieces into the disposal.

But he knew none of it had really happened.

They were good, this path team. Their illusions were first class. An ordinary brain would have been completely fooled. But Hitt did not have an ordinary brain. Only the top layer of gray matter was susceptible to psionic manipulation; the deeper layer was insulated with a buffered neuro-bus. His other psyche had been able to peep inside the path team's mind as they peeped him.

The control codes were missing from their psionic operating systems—somehow they had become erased. He did not know how because a certain amount of ordinary memory had also been erased. Something had happened to them on their last mission that produced memory loss. But without the control codes, they could not be brought back to the service. Capture would be extremely difficult. It might even be impossible to kill them, without using tactical weapons and taking out a few thousand innocent civilians.

But they could be fooled. They might sucker for their own deception. They could be manipulated.

Hitt began changing. His skin fasciculated as though worms were wriggling beneath it. His scalp hair withdrew into its follicles, producing a bald pate. His facial features remodeled themselves. His penis grew back. Inside, his outer brain rearranged its synapses. New memories were recorded.

Hitt disappeared.

So did the blood stains that had never existed except in software.

An entirely different body and persona left Hitt's

room and went to another in the same hotel.

A new game began.

Risa began to purr.

We had spent the day in our room making love, then dozing intermittently with the troubled sleep of nocturnal creatures. Now it was night again. Our time had come. We shunned daylight, even the artificial kind. Illusion was harder to maintain in the light of day.

Not long ago, we had made love again, sharing pleasure as only a path team could, not knowing whose orgasm had come first. Now we lay in the lethargy of ebbing passion. In the hiatus beyond both desire and spasm, Risa purred. She knew she was safe.

A wry thought amused me. Risa never purred while we were making love. Always afterward. I imagined the sensations produced by a vibrating throat would be quite interesting. I wondered if she would purr a little earlier for me.

Not likely. Her teeth flashed stars from their points as she laughed.

Why not?

I only purr after I'm pleased.

And you're not pleased when we're making love?

Only afterwards. She smiled. *There are two kinds of pleasure. Fire and ice. Only one makes me purr.*

Which one? I imagined a furred creature about to pounce.

That would be telling.

Risa was a xenohybrid; her recombinant DNA had been derived from several other biotypes: cat, dog, bird, insect. I envied her diverse ancestry; each species brought along its own racial memories.

I was an allohybrid. Although my DNA was still entirely human, it had also been blended by genosurgeons. My dreams were human dreams, but were not pleasant ones. I cared too much for Risa to want her to glimpse my dream-time.

Neither of us had dreams that were really our own; our real memories had been wiped out by psychsurgeons. We had been given the essential synthetic persona to replace our own—and a childhood was not essential. Our real memories began when we were born out of the hybertanks, after conscription into the Corps. The synthetic memories of the time before had been stolen from someone else and were now no more than dim nightmares for me. For Risa, they had not faded as much.

I can't remember how many times I'd asked the chameleon officer who commanded us to tell me who I really was and what I'd really done to deserve a hitch in the Corps. Kaly always refused, laughing, saying it was better for morale that I not know. Besides, she insisted she did not know the psicypher code that would release my latent memories. And now I'd never have a way to find out the truth.

"Do you ever wonder about who you really were before?" I asked Risa, already knowing the answer. Sometimes words were needed.

"Occasionally."

"How much do you remember?"

She hesitated. "Not much more than you. A few fragments, a few bad dreams. A few glimpses of a place on Earth where I once must have lived—a little town in the mountains called Telluride. I think I might have been a boy in that other life. Why, I don't know. But a certain face sometimes bothers me in dreams. Not often now. Usually my dreams are quite pleasant now."

"You don't want to know more about yourself?"

"Not now. That self no longer matters because I am no longer her and can never be her again. I don't have to be sorry for what she did. I don't have to feel guilty for her crimes. I'm someone else now. I have another past with different ancestors. I have dreams of soaring in the air, prowling in the moonlight, stalking prey, mating with uncomplicated passion."

"Is that enough?"

"It's enough for me. My animal genes have brought dreams enough. I have better instincts now—from my cat genes."

"What do your cat genes tell you to do now?"

"They make me want to prowl at night."

She leaped from the bed and landed lightly on the window sill across the room, balancing herself in front of the window. Her eyes watched the pleasure domes of Chalise far below. Stroboscopic reflections winked from her pupils. Psitendrils quivered as they probed the psychic ether.

Overhead, night deepened. I closed my eyes. Specters rose from hippocampal graves, disturbed by circadian winds. They thought the dream-time was close. They couldn't frighten me now, not while I was awake. Ghosts could only frighten sleeping children. Terror only came in the dreams. I didn't sleep at night anymore. Demons were easier to take in the light of day.

I snapped a mnemone stick and sucked its vapors deep into my lungs. Euphoria burned in my mind. Wraiths melted into mists which evaporated away.

I got up and stood behind Risa. She continued to peer out the window, crouching on all fours. I kissed the back of her legs, nuzzling soft fur with my lips. I moved upward, rubbing my cheek against her rump. She remained tense, caught up in the hunt.

I knelt behind her, cupping fur-covered breasts in my hands, and entered her. She wiggled her bottom, to more deeply receive me, then rocked it up and down. Mucosal surfaces contained more induction neurons than cutaneous ones, since they were no more than modified tactile receptors. Mucosal contact produced the best pathic gestalt. I lay my head between her shoulders and joined the hunt.

Myriad thoughts swirled through the ether, like a million gleaming threads wafting in the wind. We moved among them, watching, listening, sniffing each in turn. Then we found the scent for which we searched. We crouched low to the ground; the fur bristled along our back; our tail was held upright with only the tip twitching back and forth. We followed the mental scent back to its source, slowly and cautiously, so not to spook our quarry.

We'd hunted thus too many times. Fear was easy to find and easier to foster. The simple superstitious tribesmen on Mars had been helpless to resist our sophistication. We terrorized their dream-time; their chiefs and shamans had prophetic visions of doom that completely demoralized them, so they were helpless when our combrid troops attacked. But now Risa and I hunted for ourselves.

We had been together for just a year—six months in the Combrid Corps as an LRT team on Mars and now six months as a free-lance path team. Something had happened to us on a mission, something with enough psychic trauma to induce amnesia about it and several weeks prior to our running away. Technically we had deserted from the Corps; we hadn't bothered to muster out. They did not just let you leave the service anyway. A discharge from the Corps included debriefing and demilitarization—the Lord Generals didn't want civilians running around with full military hardware or software; they tended to become mercenaries in future rebellions. But the Lord General didn't want to pay idle soldiers either. Their solution was simple: D & D— debre and demil. Debre wasn't bad—psychsurgeons wiped out both Corps hypnotraining and all memories laid down since conscription. Demil was more unpleasant—cybersurgeons ripped out any removable hardware and snipped through muscle and nerve tissue to bring a combrid down to standard Terran. Then cosmesurgeons gave you back your original appearance—approximately.

But Risa's and my military tissue was mostly gray matter. On the outside, save her almost normal mane, Risa looked like an ordinary sphinx. I appeared to be standard Terran. Only our insides were different, primarily our brains. So D & D for us meant a little neurosurgery to disrupt classified synapses. Then a spot in a vegetable patch. No thanks. Even being a hunted fugitive was better than that.

Besides, it was kind of fun to match wits with the

vice-varks. We'd been afraid the spooks of Corps Intelligence would come after us, especially Kaly. After all, we'd been assigned to work under her. Spooks made me nervous. They were chameleons—they had plastic tissue and could change both shape and appearance at will, becoming any other hybrid or individual they wanted. The perfect disguise. Quite useful when you wanted to infiltrate the enemy. But what made them even more dangerous, especially from a path team's viewpoint, was that they also had incredible control over their thoughts. When a spook assumed a cover, he organized his mind into the identity of the cover, with a complete set of memories. His own psyche was buried so deep and linked so tightly with limbic nuclei, he would die before any incongruous thoughts could give him away. There had even been talk of a new neuromod, where they gave a spook a dual brain, so they could maintain twin psyches. Even a path team could be fooled by a spook.

But in the six months we had been on our own, we had yet to encounter a chameleon—just dim-witted vice-varks. Hardly the match of a trained Long Range Terror team, a pair of fear hunters late of the First Psyche Division. Risa was the empath—she peeped minds to discover what primal terrors lurked in their dream-time. I was the telepath who sent those hippocampal fears back to the cerebral cortex and magnified them beyond the endurance of even the strongest mind. Quite demoralizing to be tormented by the one thing you fear most, be that ghosts, goblins, snakes, rats, fire, wind, water or what not. Mere illusion? Maybe so. But the demons I conjured out of racial memory were more terrifying than if they had been real. They evoked an instinctive fear that a rational mind was helpless to defend against, simply because the fears themselves were irrational. I only wished I was not cursed to have to remember all the fears myself.

But Risa could seek out other feelings. And I could create illusions other than fear.

Her flanks began quivering beneath me. Something besides starlight gleamed in her eyes. We had located our quarry. He was quite near and was unsuspecting. We could surprise him. Fear was only one of the many perversions that could be pandered.

4

We again hunted close to home tonight.

The door to our suite opened into a small foyer, across which was a lift-tube. We stepped into the down-tube and dropped slowly, holding hands to keep from getting separated. Our prey was still in his room. We followed his chanting thoughts, entered his mind, and examined his memories. Nothing had changed. Our plan could continue.

Several floors down, we switched to the up-tube, although no living eyes saw this. Our images still drifted down. Those same living eyes saw a child dressed in a blue satin gown floating up the other tube, carrying a white cat in its arms.

Only Risa and I knew otherwise.

The child stepped out of the lift-tube at the 249th level into the foyer of the Ophir Suite, which was directly opposite our Suite. The child touched a finger to the annunciator. A few seconds later, the door dilated open. The child stepped through. Before the door closed, Risa and I also entered, darting through as quick as specters.

An Entropist monk sat in a lotus position on the floor, facing the door. He stopped chanting. He wore only the lavender robes of his order. His shaven skull gleamed with oil; his eyes shone with their own green fire. He wore a silver band around his head. Though he had taken personal vows of poverty, this monk was hardly destitute. He was a money courier. The Entropic Church had been founded by a man named Marc Detrs. It was the first new religion to start in the past one thousand years. (The past millennium was noted for its agnosticism.) Marc Detrs was supposed to have a precognitive ability. The authorities thought his clairvoyance was contrived and dismissed him as a charlatan. But he had attracted quite a following among the hybrid races. One of the reasons was that one of the tenets of Entropism was rebellion against Earth.

Marc Detrs was one of the most wealthy men in the System. The bulk of his wealth now belonged to the church. It was rumored that the Entropic Church was financing most of the residual, smoldering rebellious activity against good old Mother Earth. This monk was delivering a fortune to one of those rebel groups. He was to make delivery later tonight, after his amusement was finished. The spooks of Corps Intelligence would have loved to have the proof of this sedition. But Risa and I were not about to tell them. I doubted the information would win us amnesty. Nothing would do that.

The child bowed low. The white cat leapt out of its arms and began to prowl about. "You desire comfort tonight, Brother Monk?" The child asked formally.

The monk nodded his head.

The child touched its fingers to opposite shoulders, and the blue gown slipped into a pile on the floor. It stepped out, placing one hand on its hip and the other over its head with index finger pointed down, and spun about slowly.

It appeared to be an ordinary human child of about ten years of age, a little long of leg and somewhat potbellied. Its features were androgynous—upturned button of a nose, rosy cheeks, eyes sapphire blue, short curls of flaxen hair. It completed its spin and faced the monk, then advanced closer, stopping a few centimeters from the monk's crossed legs. It spread its knees and thrust its pelvis out. A tiny boy's penis dangled there. Then penis and scrotum retracted, becoming immature female genitalia—a hairless mound, undeveloped labia, rudimentary clitoris.

A figment of my imagination? Hardly. An illusion, yes. But the image was based on reality. The child was a pedimorph—a child surrogate hybridized into an hermaphroditic creature whose development was arrested in preadolescence. It could have been fifty years old or fifteen; its physiologic age would always remain prepubescent. Pedimorphs were indentured by their parents to the Guild for twenty years—after that they could buy out their contract and be brought back to standard Terran to complete normal endocrine development. Most didn't. Most spent their entire lives as pedies. Which usually wasn't all that long—the suicide rate was quite high.

The pedi stood motionless, extending its hairless penis and scrotum again. A pink tongue darted out to wet its lips. "Am I acceptable, Brother Monk?"

"Quite so," the monk answered. "You may begin."

The monk pulled off his own robe, although he imagined the pedimorph did it. The pedi stood behind him, massaging his taut shoulder muscles.

The ritual was beginning to disgust me. After all, my imagination was creating the images in the monk's mind. Pedies were an acquired taste. But this illusion was necessary for our larceny to succeed.

Risa left and entered the bedroom. A valise of money was suspended in mid-air within an alarm beam. She plucked it from the beam.

A ruby on the monk's finger began flashing and beeping. He did not notice. The pedi now stood in front of him, with its ankles caught between the monk's crossed legs. The monk's face was pressing into its groin.

Risa returned from the other room carrying the valise. She waited by the door.

The monk's hands cupped the pedi's slender buttocks. His fingernails cut deep into tender flesh. The
pedi screamed in pain.

Suddenly, I was angry. Rage narrowed my vision into
a blurred tunnel. My reaction disturbed me. I'd seen
worse in other minds. Why should this scenario bother
me?

The pedi's hands encircled the monk's neck. Thumbs
gouged deep into carotid arteries, then flattened
tracheal rings. The monk's eyes bulged; his lips turned
blue. Spittle drooled down his tongue. He did not resist.
This was still all part of the ritual.

He lost consciousness.

I should have relaxed the spasms in his neck now and
released his diaphram from its paralysis. But my rage
was too strong. The pedi continued to squeeze.

I had the overwhelming urge to strangle the monk. I
wanted him dead. A rational island in my mind was
puzzled. I had never killed before, even in the war. Why
now? What compulsion had overcome good judgment?

Anger burned even hotter. Now my fingers did the
squeezing; I closed my eyes.

A voice whispered in my ear. Soft lips nuzzled my
cheek. Strong arms wrapped around me; supple fingers
kneaded my flesh. A warm body pressed against mine.

The monk's mind was almost dead. But there was
serenity instead of panic, as though death was prefer-
able to life. Dreams unwound like a raveling tapestry;
scenes of war, combrids going into battle against a
dozen different kinds of hybrids, seen through rebel
eyes, making love to a dozen different kinds of partners,
then cutting each lover's throat, sticking knives into the
backs of sentries looking the other way, leaving bombs
behind.

Risa's cool thoughts flowed over my fire, extinguish-
ing the flame.

I opened my eyes.

I stood before the monk. My hands strangled him. I
let go. His head slumped forward while his body remained erect, locked upright by his lotus posture.

Dreams unraveled, weaving back together. I sensed disappointment.

Risa relaxed her embrace. She picked up the valise and started toward the door. The monk's mind tapestry faded. But a melting image lingered to disturb me; a doll's face with its features twisted into rage, its teeth bared, lips snarling.

I stumbled out the door after Risa.

We were again safe in our suite.

When the monk recovered, he would not report the theft of his money—that would direct suspicion toward him. He would instead try to locate a certain pedimorph himself. His search would prove futile since this pedi did not exist except in memory.

I sat near the window staring out at the glistening domes of Chalise. Risa padded over to join me, rubbing against my side. Static sparked between us. A rough tongue licked my neck. I let her pull me over to the bed. She climbed on top and began undulating slowly. Risa was never one for prolonged foreplay.

No stray dreams disturbed our lovemaking. I blanked my mind, concentrating only on delicious friction.

Later, as I held Risa close, the troubled thoughts came back.

I remembered a dissolving image.

Did you notice anything unusual about the monk? After all, she was the empath.

The memories were a little strange for a religious person. He seems to have had an interesting life. There was an area I couldn't probe. Her thoughts resonated. I touched her throat. She purred. *Probably church secrets. Rituals. Memories I would have to kill to extract. Such protected zones are common among monks.*

Something was wrong. *Didn't Hitt also have such an area?*

She nodded involuntarily. *He was a smuggler and a gunrunner. It's to be expected he would pay a psychsurgeon to seal up a few secrets.*

It seems odd that two in a row should be protected.

A coincidence.

She seemed sure of herself. I let it go. She was the empath. I trusted her ability. *There was something peculiar about our encounter with the monk. I wondered why I got so angry?*

Her thoughts were silent.

A realization struck. *Why did I get angry? You know, don't you?*

She waited for a while before answering. *I know.* With finality.

What is it? Why?

An unconscious memory bothered you.

What kind of memory? A memory of what?

That is hidden even from me.

You won't tell me?

I don't know.

She was not quite convincing.

But what could I do? She was the empath. I couldn't see into my own head, much less into hers. *OK. As long as it doesn't matter.*

Not to me.

She sought me again, as though in proof.

The monk sat in lotus.

His neck still hurt. The bruises were real and would not fade until he rearranged his tissues. The little bastard had almost strangled him. There had been so much irrational anger in his mind.

Why would he get so angry over a scene with a pedimorph?

The monk thought about the telepath's psyche. He reviewed the memories that remained.

Of course. He did not know. The same amnesia that had erased the control codes had produced a self-delusion in his mind. The empath did not suffer from the same delusion, but she was playing along with it. Why? What was her game?

He laughed.

It did not matter. He knew now how to play his. He knew now what he had to do. He would use K-11 pseudomemories. That would be easy. All spooks had a set of those. He would turn the delusion against the telepath. This would be simpler than he had imagined.

His body remodeled. His mind rearranged itself.

A female sailor left the hotel. She went to the spaceport, rented a spaceship, and made a few other arrangements.

The game continued, but the rules had changed a little.

Demons haunted my dream-time.

I was paralyzed and could not move a muscle. Rat teeth nipped my flesh, gnawing my fingers away. Snakes slithered around my neck, gradually tightening their coils, while fanged faces watched mine, tasting my fear with cloven tongues. Birds also hovered about my face, pecking at my unblinking eyes. Bats fluttered about, then landed, using sharp teeth and lapping up my free-flowing blood. Flies buzzed lazily, depositing yellow spawn in my wounds that soon hatched into wriggling maggots. Then I heard water flowing. Cool wetness touched my skin. The water climbed higher and higher, until it lapped about my neck. For some reason, I did not float. And I was still paralyzed. The water rose—over my mouth, over my nose, then over my eyes. I held my breath until it seemed my lungs would burst. I could hold it no longer. Bubbles streamed out my nostrils. I gasped for air, water filled my lungs instead. I tried to scream. Images darted out of my mouth and floated away.

A radioactive doll glowed in the darkness, luminescent tears dripped from its eyes.

The woman sometimes let her friends enjoy the three boys. She would supervise, using the alphalash if they balked. If they screamed too loudly when men entered them from behind, she would quiet them by paralyzing their throats with a few deft strokes of the lash.

• • •

I awoke with sweat cooling on my skin. Risa sat up in bed beside me holding her head between her hands.

"I was sending." I didn't make it a question.

She nodded. "I'm afraid so. A shame you sometimes broadcast with REM sleep. You've given me quite a headache. Most of the other hotel guests have had bad dreams, not to mention half of the rest of Chalise. In a few days, after casual conversations, they'll begin to realize they all had the same nightmare."

"Then varks will start snooping around. We'd best move on."

"No, not yet." I missed the cunning in her voice. "We have time for one more."

"You've found someone?"

"Yes. She looks very interesting. Just your type. We'll sting her tonight."

"You're sure there's enough time."

"Of course, I've searched all of Chalise. No one is suspicious yet. And I've located a perfect mark. I can't resist this one. You'll enjoy it. She's a demilled veteran of the Corps."

I lay back and closed my eyes. Yes, this next sting would be enjoyable. We veterans all had something in common; in our pseudomemories, we'd committed some atrocity, some capital offense that had gotten us sentenced to the Foreign Legions instead of death. Demilled veterans were given back their real pasts. That was the law. Since I was an outlaw, I didn't have my past. But I still held the naive hope that I would find some common theme in the backgrounds of other combat hybrids that would enable me to guess my own.

I dozed off.

A doll's face cycled out of its hippocampal tomb.

Ganymede's artificial day had faded.

Risa stood before the window. I followed her gaze; she watched white hot plasma spewing from the fusion fountain of a night club perched below us on the rim of Chalise crater.

Another hunt began.

We strolled the streets of Chalise. If any cameras recorded our passage, the captured images would show only a true human and a sphinx walking together. Not so unusual by today's standards. Hardware was difficult to fool. We'd have had to have been chameleons to fool cameras. Not so software. The living eyes that saw us, "saw" two merchant sailors on shore leave. We were two among many, for Chalise was a maritime city. Two sailors were even less likely to be remembered than a sphinx and a standard human and attracted no immediate notice at all. We appeared to be quite ordinary sailors; two meters tall; naked save our capes and the sonic jewelry on our fingers, toes, noses, and ears; skin as black as obsidian and shining with protective monomer; supple fingers and toes equipped with tree-frog suction cups; nictitating membranes covered our eyes and other sphincters protected nostrils and ear canals; bald skulls with scalps that were convoluted into ridges by subcutaneous cyberwires. Two common cybernetic hybrid sailors. Nothing at all to attract attention.

I was pleased with my attention to detail. You couldn't be too careful in our line of work.

We passed all the usual diversions found on the Outer Moons; peptide parlors, simulacrum arenas, isotope wrestling, mnemone dens, deformity brokers, and mind casinos. Pedimorphs leered at us from open doorways, tempting us with their tongues. We showed polite interest, as sailors would, but declined. I concealed the revulsion I felt. We had a different game to play.

We slowly made our way to the ice cliffs that lined the crater wall. A thousand meters above the crater floor, a permaplastic dome covered the wreckage of an ancient fuship. It had crashed there ages ago, before nuclear energy was supplanted by radiacrystals and gravsails. But the old fusion thruster still throbbed with life, plasma spewing into space from the old jets, forming a thermonuclear fountain that threw bright tendrils a hundred kilometers out—all leading back to a night club called *Critical Mass*.

Tonight's quarry awaited us there.

We came to the crater wall. A lift-tube dropped from the rim to the Chalise dome. That presented only a minor problem. Risa and I would have to ride the lift-tube up—I could not survive outside. Sailors would never stoop to riding lift-tubes. They would show their disdain for the airless void by climbing up the outside of the tube, clinging to its polished walls with their suction cup digits, protected from the cold vacuum by brown adipose and sealed sphincters. They could laugh at the stinging hydrocarbon mist at minus two hundred degrees. I was not so fortunate.

We stepped into the lift-tube. No one saw that. What anyone watching saw was an empty chamber rising up the transparent tube, while two sailors clambered up the outside through swirling methane snow. A simple illusion. But effective.

We entered *Critical Mass*. A hostess greeted us and pinned a radiation badge on our capes. I smiled at this cunning touch of realism. She showed us to a table.

A transparent dance floor formed a disk pierced through its center by the thruster chamber. Tables were placed along the periphery. A dim blue glow emanated through the walls of the magnetic bottle. A low throb beat from each solid surface. Audiocrystals hung overhead. Tendrils of optical music exuded from their facets to swirl in mid-air over the dance floor, before slowly drifting down into tangles among the dancers.

Risa smiled. To other eyes, a sailor's lips curled upward. To my eyes, furred lips separated to reveal sharp white teeth. Music glinted from their points. Her eyes gleamed a sulfur green. Silver fimbriae quivered about her head.

"Let's dance," Risa said.

"Is she still here?"

"Let's dance." She touched my hand with her finger, moving the tip in a circular motion. Induction neurons set up their transcutaneous field between us. A tingle ran up my arm; an image darted into my mind; an old lioness watched two young lions courting. Resentment smoldered in her eyes. She bared toothless gums in a grimace of hate.

"You're right. Let's dance." I picked up Risa's hand and led her out to the dance floor.

We danced as sailors danced—with wild abandon, yet also graceful; elegant, but with leaping pirouettes that took us almost to the ceiling.

When we returned to our table, someone was waiting there. Her face was obscured by shadow. A finger wearing a ring set with a huge singing diamond tapped nervously.

"I admired your dancing," she said, lowering her eyes briefly in false shyness. "I wonder if I might speak to you for a moment. If it's no bother . . ."

"Certainly," I said.

"No bother at all." Risa giggled.

We both sat down.

I saw her clearly now. She was almost beautiful. The cosmetic surgeons had done a good job when she had been demilled. There were a few tiny scars around her eyes and nostrils where sphincters had been removed. Hardly noticeable, unless you knew where to look. I knew there could be other scars through which hardware had been salvaged, but they were concealed by her gown. Full breasts pushed out against a gold-trimmed bodice. A necklace of singing pearls rested on them. Her hair was straw-colored and cut as short as wheat stubble, but was thick enough to hide the white lines where cyberwires once had been. Her eyes were the green of jade.

I placed my hand on Risa's. An electric tingle tickled my palm. We entered her mind together.

"What do you want to talk about, Lady Johan?" She was once again a Lady from Earth, now that she was no longer a lance corporal in the cyrines.

"How do you know my name?" She looked at me, afraid for an instant. The face she saw was open, pleasant, laughing. She relaxed. "If you know my name, then you know my story as well. You know what I want you to tell me." She smiled. A waiter arrived with a vase of mnemone tubes and a glass of Earth wine. "I took the liberty of ordering for us. I hope I got it right." She reached for the glass and sipped its wine, rolling the liquid around her mouth with her tongue.

Risa and I snapped open mnemone tubes and inhaled the vapors into our lungs.

"I want you to tell me about the blue empty," the Lady said. "If that wouldn't be too much trouble. I'll pay you for your time." She drank down the wine in one long gulp. A drop ran down her chin. "My yacht is moored at the spaceport." She smiled slyly. "We could be more comfortable there. I think it's important to be comfortable when telling stories, don't you? Shall we go?"

I nodded. Telling stories of the blue empty was the code phrase used by sailing fans to sailors when they meant they wished to purchase our favors. But the Lady's schemes went beyond the usual. I could hardly wait. Risa had been right.

Three bodies sprawled on a wombskin pad in the main cabin of a blue space racer: Lady Johan and her two new sailors. All were naked. Two sailors lay on their backs, head to head. Lady Johan sat near them, holding a small vial between thumb and forefinger. She dipped her tongue into the vial, then leaned over a sailor's face, lowering her protruding tongue until it touched his eye. Blue peptide flowed across his cornea. She repeated the ritual with the other eye. Then with the other sailor. The vial contained a mixture of endocaine and endrogen—speed and sex steriods.

Soon our bodies mingled into a confused mass of torsos and limbs. Tongues licked. Fingers probed. One penis slid into a series of moist places. A peptide frenzy slowly built. Flesh slapped against flesh. Sweat shone from skin. Breath whistled out of nostrils. Low moans escaped clenched teeth.

The bodies form an oral-genital triangle: mouth to vulva, mouth to penis, mouth to vulva.

Risa finished plundering the yacht—a meager haul for a member of the aristocracy: a few mediocre jewels, a little cash, two uninteresting *objets d'art*. But that was all right. I was more interested in the mind of this particular mark than in her loot. We had explored her mind thoroughly.

She had been a young Lady of one of the old families on Earth, amusing herself with the usual diversions. While under the influence of too much endocaine, she had caught her lover with another. In a fit of jealousy—mainly because she had not been invited to share her lover's lover—she grabbed an antique sword from the wall and decapitated them both. That had been her ticket to the Foreign Legion. She had become a cyrine. While in the Corps, she found another lover—a sailor. Their ship took a hit and depressurized. She lived, he died. That explained the next part of her ritual.

Sex steroid burned like fire in the minds of the sailors. The Lady was on her hands and knees over the female sailor, their tongues probing each other. The male sailor stood behind the Lady, and entered her holding tightly to her breasts. His thrusts set all of them rocking.

The Lady had a unique perversion. She had set her ship's computer to automatically blow open the main airlock at a preprogrammed time. That time was right now. Of course, Risa reset the computer so the lock would not open unexpectedly. Empathy had certain advantages.

We were ready to leave, so we pulled on space coveralls and used 02 clips to form bubbles of oxygen around our heads. We entered the airlock and closed the inner door.

The Lady must not be disappointed. Otherwise she might inform the varks. So I let the hatch blow in her imagination; warm air suddenly rushed out of the cabin, replaced by thin wisps of hydrocarbon at minus two hundred degrees. The sailors reacted instinctively—one ran for an emergency sealing kit, while the other placed his lips over the Lady's mouth and nose. Their respirations synchronized. The sailor had oxygen stored within his brown adipose—a little diffused back into his lungs and his exhaled breath—enough to keep the Lady alive, if not conscious.

The airlock cycled and the outer door dilated. Risa and I stood in near vacuum, protected by space coveralls and breathing recatalyzed oxygen. The inner door remained sealed, the cabin warm and pressurized. Except in the Lady's mind. She sank into a pseudohypoxemic coma.

Risa turned to face me. I leaned toward her until our O_2 bubbles fused. Our lips touched; our tongues slipped past themselves.

Beyond the inner door, a mind tapestry unraveled—images unwound from the fabric of memory. The Lady was playing her endless ritual, seeking something lost to the blue empty, all recapitulations of when her lost lover had not been saved by her because she chose to flee instead of staying to help him; scenes of war flashed by, then staccato glimpses of a sword flashing an arc through the air, biting through muscle and cartilage, with blood spurting high. Then I saw another pattern hidden within the weave of the other. Ghost dreams came back to haunt me; an alphalash swings its terrible arc, a doll strangles a naked monk. Memory threads stopped unwinding; their strands were held by a locked weave whose pattern was amorphous gray.

But I had seen enough already. I understood the Lady's deception.

I willed her heart to stop and for her lungs to cease breathing. My thoughts couldn't penetrate her basal ganglia. Those parts of her brain were protected. I tried to open the inner door, to let in the real vacuum, but it was locked from inside. No doubt another preprogrammed order in her ship's computer. She was safe from me. All I could do was buy a little time for Risa and me. I depolarized a few more cortical synapses so she would remain unconscious for a little while longer.

Risa had been wrong. It was more than coincidence that our two previous marks had part of their memories protected. They had been bait, to keep us occupied while help arrived—all disguises of the same person, the same Lady. She was no ordinary vark, that was certain. Varks could not change both their appearance and persona at will.

But she had made a mistake. She had blown her cover. We knew who she was now.

I shivered.

If we were lucky, Risa and I could still escape.

I took her hand and we ran through methane snow.

5

Lady Johan slowly regained consciousness. She had never lost her inner consciousness, but her inner thoughts could only control her brainstem; they did not have motor control. She had to wait for her outer brain to repolarize before she could move.

Her plan was working splendidly.

Both of them thought she was Kaly. They would let her approach now—at least the telepath would. He thought she could tell him something. He thought he could get his memories back from Kaly. He could. But she was not Kaly.

She went to the control room and sent a coded message on the radio. The Lady General would be pleased their plans were succeeding so well. Dat Lomni would get his star.

She would have to be careful during this next encounter. This was the critical scene. This was where the telepath discovered who he really was. Poor little bastard. She almost felt sorry for him.

Lady Johan changed. Her skin became black again. Nictitating membranes covered her eyes. Her scalp convoluted into ridges, as though cyberwires were implanted beneath the skin.

A cyrine major left the ship.

This game was almost over.

Our bags were packed; our loot safely hidden in concealed niches. We were ready to go. A gravship sailed for Titan in thirty minutes. We had already booked and confirmed passage.

A bellmech came and picked up our baggage. Risa prowled back and forth in front of the door. "Hurry, Nate!" Her voice was an impatient hiss. "She wakes. We must leave at once." I seemed to have no ambition left. I was numb. Nothing mattered, even escape. Memories of dreams kept dancing in my head; skulls with yellow teeth clicking; bats fluttering; rats scurrying across bedclothes; demons howling with glee. They were my dreams, glimpsed in the Lady's mind tapestry. Gray ghosts coalesced into unfamiliar faces. I knew what was wrong.

"We can wait no longer." Risa came over to tug at my arm. With her touch, I too sensed the Lady waking. Dream filaments unraveled, weaving back into memory; a million children screamed in terror at the night, huddling beneath their blankets as specters shrieked their taunts.

I knew what was wrong. The dreams unwinding were my own. The Lady shared my dreams, knew my nightmares. There was only one way that was possible.

"We have to go now!" Risa shouted.

I pulled free of her touch. "I can't leave," I said. "She knows who I am."

"So do I."

"Then tell me."

"We don't have time."

"Tell me."

"I can't." Her eyes held the wild fear of a creature trapped.

"Then I'll wait for the Lady."

Risa's hand struck out, slashing me across the cheek.

Four lines stung my face. I touched my finger to the wetness on my skin, then licked the blood from its tip.

Risa's eyes shimmered wet. She turned and ran out the door.

A doll's face leered at me where she had been, with eyes that could not cry.

I stood alone in the penthouse, staring out one of its facets. A gravship rose out of clinging mists and whispered outward: Risa was leaving. Part of myself was also leaving. We had been imprinted on each other and had worked together for a year. You couldn't be a path team without an empath. I had lost my eyes and ears, my taste, touch and smell. But that was a less immediate problem. I'd made my choice. I might not get another chance to exorcise myself of my dream demons. I could no longer bear their taunts. I had to know who I had been.

The door opened. Someone walked into the room. I turned to face her, and stared into the muzzle of a hand pulser.

"I knew you would be waiting for me," she said. "Even though I'd blown my cover. You need something from me."

She wore one of her myriad disguises, but this one I recognized—a cyrine officer named Kaly.

"Are you really Kaly?" One could never be certain with spooks.

She laughed. "This time, yes. I remember you well. It's taken me a long time to find you, but it wasn't hard to trap you once you were located."

I must have looked surprised.

She laughed again. "If I hadn't, someone else would have. Your MO is too stereotyped. All I had to do was set up the right personas as bait, and you came to me like a moth to a candle. You should have been more ambitious. With your abilities, you could rule an empire, instead of committing petty larcenies concealed behind obvious fantasies. But you couldn't help yourself, could you? We knew one of your kind would eventually escape undemilled from the Corps. We made sure you would be incapable of causing much trouble." She looked around. "Where's your little pet?" I didn't like the nasty inflection she put on the word. "Where is the 'Cat Corporal'?"

"Gone. She doesn't like unpleasantness."

"But you had to stay, didn't you? You saw something in my thoughts that was irresistible. You had to find out more." She laughed again, but not with the smugness you might have expected. Her voice was tainted with something else. "A shame you're not more cunning. You shouldn't let yourself be so easily manipulated." She motioned for me to move by flicking the pistol back and forth.

I stayed put.

She gestured again.

I smiled.

She said some gibberish. The words were meaningless to me, but I guessed they must be control codes. They did not work. If they had, I would have fallen unconscious. "It was worth a try," she said. "Too bad the control codes didn't work. Now I'll have to shoot you."

This time I laughed. "Go ahead, try to shoot."

I'll give her credit, she tried. Her finger would not press the firing stud. Then her wrist slowly twisted until the gun was pointing at her own head. She strained to turn it away, the muzzle did not waver.

"You want to shoot someone?" I taunted. "Go ahead."

Her finger now slowly tightened against the stud. Her eyes stared at the gun's muzzle, waiting for a quantum of light to flash out and burn a crisp hole in her sweating forehead. The button moved.

"OK," she gasped. "You win."

Her hand opened abruptly. The gun clattered to the floor.

"What is it you want?" she asked. But she was not yet totally defeated.

"I want to know about myself. Everything you can tell me."

"Fair enough. But is there any need to be so formal?"

I let her cross the room. She waved a hand through a

laser beam; a circular bed rose from the floor. I let her lead me to it and lay with her on the wombskin. Our clothes came off and dropped to the floor. I would allow her one more ritual.

"Let's not talk just yet," she said, smiling. Her lips began nibbling my skin. I knew she was stalling.

"Tell me first," I said.

"There'll be plenty of time for talking later."

I sharpened knives in her mind.

"OK, OK." She brought her head up to look into my eyes. "What do you want to know?"

"Why the nightmares? Why are my genodreams of terror?"

"Telepaths were harder to engineer than empaths. I ought to know; I was once a genosurgeon for Corps Intelligence. Empaths were easy. There were lots of species with latent empathic abilities—dogs, cats, raptors, certain insects. Those genes were easily isolated. We found sphinxes were ideal hosts for those genes. But there were no known animal telepaths—just a few psychotic humans that did not live past puberty. And they were rare. None were in existence when we needed them. So we had to create a telepath." Her voice caught for the first time.

"And how was this done?"

"Only a human brain was complex enough, and it had to be one that had not yet developed non-telepathic synapses—habits, if you will. Telepathic brains are extremely rare. We weren't monsters; we only did what we had to."

"Which was?"

"Millions of fetal brains were set up in vitro. All motor efferents were severed—the brains were physiologically paralyzed." She laughed the eerie laughter. "Then it was just a question of providing the right stimuli and waiting for something to develop."

I visualized millions of tiny brains floating in bubbling culture media, with thousands of fine wires running to each. "What kind of stimuli?" I asked. "What kind of dreams?"

She smiled slyly. "Oh, you know that. Night terrors. Childhood fears. You gave them visions of your own choosing, from your own dreams. The terrors themselves were quite abstract—pure fear, if you will. Our computer merely stimulated the right limbic nuclei. The fetal brains had to develop in a milieu of terror and could do nothing about it, in a conventional way, with their motor efferents cut." She smiled in a funny way. "They withered and died from fright."

"Except one."

"Except one," she agreed. "One brain developed differently: TXP-333. Its motor cortex convoluted in a strange new way, and lashed out at its tormentors the only way it could—telepathically. I'll always remember the images it sent into my mind. I'll never forget those dreams. Anyway, we'd found our telepathic brain. The potential had always been there—only the right conditions were necessary to bring it out of its latency. It was routine genosurgery to isolate the responsible genes."

"Those genes were given to me?"

"Of course. But we couldn't separate telepathy from night terrors. The one predisposes to the other. Only a fearful mind is a telepathic one. Because of that, the brain must not ever completely mature. If it grows out of night terrors, it would also grow out of telepathy." She winked at me. "That's why your morphology was picked. It was easier to make do with what we had."

"What do you mean?" I suddenly felt confused. "What's so special about me?"

"Don't tell me you believe your own charade? A magician who is fooled by his own tricks? How amusing." She thought for a moment, then kneeled over me, waving her breasts in my face. I took a nipple in my mouth. She settled her pelvis on my groin, and my penis entered her. She arched her back, pulling her nipple out of my lips. She rocked up and down on her heels as I slid in and out of her. "Of course. That last night before you deserted. Was it really that traumatic? Was Terle that bad?"

I did not know what she was talking about. I felt confused. "What about me? Why was I sentenced to the Foreign Legions? Why were my memories stolen from me?" Panic touched my thoughts.

"You killed a man," she answered simply. "You murdered a customer." Sweat shone from her skin. Her breasts bobbed up and down. Her eyes gleamed with more than jovelight.

"A customer? What's that supposed to mean?"

She laughed wickedly. "You broke the most sacred covenant of your Guild. No punishment was too severe for your kind. Besides, I already told you we had to make do with physiotypes that were already hybridized. Only immature brains could be made telepathic. We needed brains that couldn't mature. Your kind did nicely."

She began changing in front of me. Her honest cyrine face lost its black sheen and protective bony ridges around nose and eyes. It became a glob of congealed plastic. Another face grew out of the ruins of the first. I knew what creature she was becoming.

"Stop it!" I shouted.

But the change was complete. A child straddled me. A child with a doll's features; upturned button of a nose, rosy red cheeks, eyes the blue of robin eggs, soft curls of yellow hair. Not a child, either. A pedimorph. Another penis rose between our bellies.

"Stop it. Change back to something less disgusting. I'm no pederast. I can make you change into something else."

"Like you changed yourself?" The voice was high-pitched, with childish inflections. "Haven't you guessed what creature you are? What you always must be?"

"No!"

A hand intercepted a laser beam. A ceiling holomirror sprang to life overhead. I saw two naked dolls locked in an obscene embrace. Both had identical features. I knew it was no illusion. Illusions were of my making.

The chameleon lifted upward until my penis pulled out. Its penis had become erect. It leaned over and guided its penis to the slit below my scrotum and entered me.

A doll's face came close; doll's lips began kissing mine.

"Stop it!" I screamed. My hands circled its neck; my fingers squeezed tight.

"Haven't you ever wondered how they demill chameleons?" she forced out before her larynx was crushed. An unpleasant image darted into my mind; a woman being skinned alive by sharp scalpels.

I kept squeezing. Eyes bulged. The head slumped back, flaccid with paralysis. I must kill the foul creature. Drool ran between its cyanotic lips; blood dripped from its ears and nostrils. I suddenly remembered killing once before. He too had wanted to stick his smelly penis into me. I would not let him, even though he was a customer. He had wanted to copulate and had used an alphalash on me, trying to force me to agree. I would not give in, even though I hated the lash. He whipped me until I was paralyzed with pain and could not resist, then took me by force. Despite the pain, I had an orgasm, my own orgasm. I was furious. I did not want to come that way. I did not want to be taken by force. I turned pleasure to pain. I hurt him instead and then I killed him. It had been worth it then. It would be worth it now.

Then I remembered another night with Kaly. She had whipped me with an alphalash then, trying to hurt me enough that I would lash back at her telepathically. But I had fooled her then. I could fool her again, but it would be more fun to kill her. Why not? I was on the run anyway. They could only fry your brain once.

A voice whispered in my ear, soothing, calming. Strong fingers tugged at mine, pulling them away one by one. Lips kissed my cheek.

Risa!
I couldn't leave you.
I'm glad you came back.
So am I.

I almost killed the spook. We looked into her mind. I could not do that alone. We both gasped in surprise. A strange psyche lay out of psionic grasp. A psyche we had never seen before.

She is not Kaly!

No, she's not Kaly. Let's find out who she really is and who sent her. We probed her mind, none too gently.

We could see the pattern in the spook's mind tapestry. The gunrunner, the monk, and Lady Johan had all been real covers used by the spook. She had really lost her lover, twice. I saw endless cycles of friendships broken, lovers betrayed, of hiding behind disguises, never allowing either true visage or persona to be seen. And then I heard the cries of a million children, frightened to hysteria by the demonic images carried by wires to their brains. Those were standard pseudomemories. Kaly had those. All spooks had them. There were a few real memories also. This spook had his own name: Dat Lomni. He had been sent to terminate us with extreme prejudice by the Lady General von Nakamura herself. He would become a general himself if he could kill us. He would never get his star now. Some memory registers were protected. We could get into them, but it would kill him. He had some information we wanted. Maybe he would talk.

We brought him back to consciousness. "You are not Kaly," we said.

"No," he agreed. "Not your Kaly, anyway."

"Where is Kaly?"

"I don't know."

"This can be easy or difficult. We know you know. If we have to go in and get the information, it will cost you some brain cells."

We convinced him.

"On Titan someplace," he said. "That was the last place we tracked her to. We haven't found her yet. She suffered a psychophysio break shortly after you two deserted."

"Does she know what happened to us on our last mission?"

"She did. She had you bugged. She saw and heard everything, but she failed to make a recording. We have no record of what happened. It is all in her software. Who knows if she still remembers?"

"She's the only one who knows?"

"The only one."

We knew he was not lying. Only Kaly could tell us what happened to cause our amnesia. For some reason, it was important we know. We would have to find Kaly.

But we had to take care of this spook before we could look for Kaly.

The barriers were down. The spook's mind was unprotected.

There's an easier way than death, Risa reminded me.

There was. I flooded his hippocampal gray with peptidases; neurotransmitters were dissolved from synaptic pathways; dreams spun out, their filaments melting like cobwebs in sunlight, never to be unraveled.

The chameleon would remember nothing of us, or of anything else since childhood.

Risa and I left together.

When he was sure they were gone, Dat Lomni woke up.

His outer brain had been almost entirely erased—lucky for him he kept duplicate files. He pipped a few over. Gray matter worked better if it had a little data stored.

He went to the spaceport and took off in his cutter for Titan. The path team had taken a commercial vessel. He would arrive ahead of them and have a few days to get ready for his next game. A shame it had to get rougher; he was enjoying playing with them. But Entropy must be served.

BOOK THREE

DREAMS UNWIND

In a cabin in a gravliner, Risa and I made love.

Jupiter dwindled astern, its moons no more than bright stars. Ahead lay Saturn with its brilliant rings and other moons, one of which was Titan. Kaly was someplace on Titan. Risa and I would have to go to Titan to find her. We would catch up to our baggage somewhere along the way.

Our images were reflected from burnished brass: a lithe cat-woman entwined with a doll. As our bodies moved toward love, a mind tapestry raveled. I saw a strange melding of imagery, as though seen through both our eyes, of our life together on the run, then the war. But there was still a missing section. I did not know what had happened on Mars to make us desert. There must have been a lot of psychic trauma, enough to induce amnesia in both Risa and me, enough to cause my mind to fool itself. I saw my own delusion of my appearance, of the illusion I projected to others. What could have happened? Kaly knew. We would make her tell us.

Then new dreams unwound: I saw endless images of myself performing a pedimorph's ritual, being whipped with an alphalash, being raped, all ending in the same murder of my client. I remembered ten years of cold, hunger, and misery, living in the slums of Denver. I saw myself sold to a child broker, so the rest of my family could survive a few more years. I remembered my siblings. I was chosen because I was the fairest child. I remembered my parents. Their only sin was being poor and having too many children to love. I loved them all again. I forgave them. Night terrors rose, but could no longer frighten. I remembered myself again, but the memories were the standard pseudomemories of an N-10 telepath. There really had been an N-10 once, but he had not been me. I had my synthetic past back, now I wanted my real one even more.

My pseudomemories weren't taken away.

Not completely. Only hidden. A mental defense mechanism of some sort.

And the delusion. I remembered orgasms I had never had.

Mental self-defense. So you wouldn't have to kill again.

But you knew all the time?

Laughter. Warm and pleasant. *Of course. What can be hidden from me?*

I had another thought. *Do you remember what happened on Mars?*

Her thoughts seemed sad. *No, I've forgotten that also. We must have been synapsed at the time for both of us to suffer the same amnesia.*

I believed her. *And you don't mind? About me? About what I am?*

More laughter. *We've been imprinted together. I love you as part of myself. The way you are. All of you.*

Why didn't you tell me about my self-delusion?

I was afraid you would want to change if you remembered you were a pedimorph. I knew how you felt about it. You could have had your endocrine arrest reversed. You could stop being a pedimorph. I was afraid you would. Then you would neither want nor need me. I would lose you.

Another realization struck. *Then you knew about the*

chameleon all the time. You let her play her game with me. So I could find out about myself without you telling me.

A cat-face grinned. *Yes. Are you angry?*

Not now. I let a thought curl about the edges of my mind. *I do have more than enough money to buy a little endosurgery. I could grow out of this doll's body. I could have real sex.*

Risa's mind was guarded; she kept her feelings hidden.

But then I would no longer have the gift. Or you. And we still have to find Kaly to find out what happened on Mars.

I kissed her. She knew what that meant and kissed me back. Bodies were unimportant, merely to be looked upon. I could have any body I wanted, be any beauty to living eyes. Pleasures were just as fine no matter in whose neurons they first originated. Telepathy was a rare gift, not to be given up lightly. Being part of a path team was even more wonderful.

And the spook had been right—we could be more than petty thieves. That was a phase out of my past, which had now been exorcised.

I looked out the port. There were worlds to conquer out there. But first we needed to find Kaly and find out what had happened on Mars. Then I wanted to find out who I had really been before hybridization.

Risa and I touched. Our bodies moved to love, driven by resonating thoughts, rather than tactile stimuli. Beyond both the desire and the spasm, we remained touching, basking in the warmth of ebbing love.

I've saved the best for last. Her thoughts were sleepy. *I no longer have to guard anything from you.* She dozed.

Dreams unwound: I sail high above the ground on outstretched wings, riding summer thermals. I howl at a moon of night. I charge across dry veldt, my terrible roar paralyzing my prey with fright. Talons slash. Claws rend. Fangs tear open throats. Tongues lap warm blood. My mate runs beside me, proud.

Lost amid these bright images were dimmer ones; ghost boys suffered the sting of the lash, the shame of sexual abuse.

We took the penthouse of the Hotel Titan in Chronus. Old habits die hard. Besides, the spook who had been on our trail was out of commission now, and we were going to be hunting for just one victim. We registered as Lord and Lady Dexter-Smyth and listed our business as import-export. We were in Chronus to buy radiacrystal at the upcoming auction. No one would think to verify our credentials—they were utterly convinced of our authenticity. We looked like a Lord and Lady: I was tall and handsome, with green eyes and short blond hair; Risa was lithe and lovely with curves in all the right places. We appeared to be in our twenties, but could have been a thousand years old. We had just the right touch of refined arrogance. We tipped generously.

Chronus was known as the Queen City of Titan. It had been built in an ancient crater, within which a volcano had subsequently risen and died. A dome twenty kilometers wide and one kilometer high covered the crater and kept Titan's minus-seventy-degree hydrocarbons from mingling with the warmer oxy/nitrogen that Terrans favored. Chronus had been settled nearly a thousand years ago by expatriated Terrans and had maintained a Terran flavor, becoming an island of homeland surrounded by hostile foreigners. Even a lengthy seige by the endogenous Titanian Elves during the Hybrid Rebellion had not changed the colonial lifestyle. Even Chronusians twenty generations removed from the original Terran settlers still considered themselves Terrans, as did the government of Earth.

Stately mansions sprawled on the slopes of Mount Erubus. A pleasant lake, surrounded by parkland, lay in the west end of the crater. Juniper, oak, and cypress grew on the crater's and the volcano cone's slopes, and maples, elms, and sumacs in the flats. One could hear the sounds of country leisure living all around: the pounding of the hooves of polo ponies; the baying of hounds on a chase; the rustle of flushed partridges followed by gunfire; the thunk of racquets hitting balls across grass courts; and the tinkle of ice in tall glasses amid laughter on verandas. Chronus had remained like the Earth of a thousand years ago—an Earth that no longer was.

Downtown Chronus was the best free port in the System. Sailors would save their pay for months if they knew they were stopping at Chronus. The lazos were open night and day, as were the restaurants, gymnasiums, and specialty shops. Well-bred Chronusian girls would sneak downtown to play with sailors, to the shame of their parents.

But there was another side to Chronus, a seamier side: the famed Underground. It was literally underground, having been built in the abandoned tunnels of the mines that honeycombed the nickle/iron matrix upon which Chronus sat. Every perversion was pandered to in the Underground: sex, pain, euphoria, philosophy, greed, death. There were brothels: human, pedi, hybrid; mnemone dens and peptide parlors; muticlinics and cancer tattooing; churches and temples; and casinos, where one could bet anything of value, including the infamous mind-casinos where the dream-game was played.

If Kaly was on Titan, she would be in the Underground. Risa and I knew where to look. Now we just had to find her.

I thought it would be easy. I was wrong.

We spent night after night synapsed in a pathic gestalt, prowling the psychic ether, searching for Kaly's dream-trail. We could not locate it. Then it occurred to me she had suffered a psychophysio break. She was not the same Kaly we had known. We would need help finding her. So we hunted other dreams, haunted other dreamers until we found someone who knew something about Kaly.

Lady Jain Maure lived in a mansion on the summit of Mount Erubus. Her house was built on the edge of a sheer, thousand-meter cliff, with a balcony overhanging thin air. Jain and her guests sometimes gravglided from the balcony.

She had once been a famous cosmetic surgeon. People had come to her clinic from all over the System to have themselves made into someone else. Her work could still be seen in the faces and bodies of the ultra-rich. But she no longer practiced medicine. She had discovered other pursuits.

For several nights, we had probed her dream-time. We knew she knew something about Kaly, but her dreams were too confused to allow us to figure out just what it was she knew. We would have to get closer.

It was not hard to implant a suggestion in her dream-time. She called Lord and Lady Dexter-Smyth and invited them to a party at her house.

Jain Maure greeted us at the door herself. She appeared to be of unaltered Terran stock: her hair was long and as black as spun carbon; her skin was the usual burnt amber of Earth aristocracy; she was slim waisted with long legs and full breasts not quite concealed by the spidersilk gown she wore. She had a striking beauty that made one wonder if it had been purchased, with perfect eyebrows, long eye lashes, high cheekbones delicately hollowed underneath, and a nose too symmetrical to be natural. Her eyes shone like polished copper pennies. She wore ten carat singing ruby earrings and another one of at least a hundred carats around her neck as a pendant.

She took us around and introduced us to her other guests, who were mostly native Chronusians and fawned all over us, thinking we were nobility from Earth. We spent most of the evening making up stories about Earth and the aristocracy. The other guests were enthralled. You could tell they wanted to hear more, but at exactly 0200 people started saying goodnight, and by 0230 everyone was gone except Jain and us. No doubt they were following some arcane colonial party protocol.

Jain saw the last of the other guests off and closed the

door. She dropped to a sofa, allowing her gown to slip up on her thighs, showing me a lot of skin and a glimpse of her crotch. "It's about time," she said. "I thought they would never leave."

"Maybe we should be leaving too," I said.

"No, not you. I meant the others. I want you to stay. We can start enjoying ourselves now."

"What do you mean?"

Jain held up a small vial. "We could do some peptide for a start. Then let things go from there."

"Am I included in this party?" Lady Dexter-Smyth asked.

Jain leered. "Of course, dear." She lay back on the sofa, showing me even more of her naked groin. "You can do me first, if you please." She held the vial out to Risa.

Risa went over to the sofa and took the vial. She unscrewed the top and dipped her tongue in it, then lowered her still protruding tongue to let the peptide drip into Jain's eye. She repeated the ritual with the other eye. Jain's body went into spasms for a few seconds after each dose. It must have been pure, uncut peptide.

When she stopped seizing, she lost all modesty, and pulled off her gown. Her body looked like it was expensive to maintain. "Your turn now," she said to both of us.

Jain thought we stretched out on the sofa as she dripped peptide into our eyes. She thought we took off our clothes. She imagined the three-way sex and later, being shackled and thrashed with an alphalash. Not that it mattered. I'm sure it was just as good for her, and I know it was considerably easier on me.

The three of us lay naked on a wombskin bed. Jain thought the Lord and Lady had just licked out the fire in her skin. She lay on her back, contented.

"Who are you?" she asked.

"Dexter-Smyth, who else?" I answered.

"I mean, who are you really? There is no Lord Dexter-Smyth. You obviously have never met the names you dropped tonight, much less know them.''

"What makes you say that?''

"Then you would have remembered that I am really Lady Jain Maure. I really did come from Earth. I really am five hundred years old. You two are imposters. Very delicious imposters, but fakes nevertheless. What do you want?''

I had known all that, of course. Just as I had known she knew we were a phony royal couple. I licked my hand to improve conduction, and placed it on Risa's behind. "We're looking for someone. We heard you might be able to help.''

"Who are you looking for?''

"A broken chameleon named Kaly, Major K-11.''

"There must be a thousand spooks of the K-11 type. What makes you think I know one?''

It was too late. We plucked the thought-tendril from her mind. We knew what had happened to Kaly and why we could not find her. I felt sorry for Kaly. I would not have wished her fate even on her.

I put Lady Jain to sleep. We did not need her anymore. But since she had been so cooperative, I made sure she would think she spent the rest of the night performing various sexual excesses with the fake Lord and Lady, resulting in the two of them accidentally falling off her balcony a thousand meters to their deaths. After hours of embarrassing interrogation by the police, no charges were filed. She would even remember seeing the newscasts. In a few days, she would wonder why none of her friends knew anything about it. But in a few days, Risa and I would be long gone.

We went to the Underground that same night. I had been right, Kaly was in the Underground. The reason we had not found her was that she was dream-gaming—her mind was trapped within the circuits of a dream-processor. No dream-tendrils were escaping into the psionic ether.

Kaly had gone to Lady Jain for some reason. Jain did not even know why. Apparently, Kaly had once known

Jain, before she had been hybridized. Jain did not recognize Kaly, but she had taken her in and made her into a dream-player. Lady Jain had one of the largest stables of professional dream-players in Chronus. There was no more despicable a business.

A week ago, she had entered Kaly in a dream-marathon in one of the casinos. A marathon was a dream-game that continued until all but one of the players had died. A marathon would usually last for a couple of weeks—death resulting from dehydration. Marathons were strictly illegal, but then so were most of the diversions in the Underground.

Risa and I floated down a drop-tube, supported by a partial p-grav field. We had to go to the lowest level. No living eyes saw us descend. We passed portal after portal. Creatures of all kinds stood on each portal: pedies, prostitutes, priests, pissers, peppers, and others, hawking their wares to each passerby.

At the lowest level, we walked through twisting tunnels that branched repeatedly, following a mental map we had stolen from Lady Jain. Our path led to an amphitheater, a huge chamber carved out of solid rock with a central dais and seats rising all around. We walked past the door guard unnoticed and sat down.

Twelve dream-players lay naked on cots on the dais, each wearing psihelmets. They all were wanton and wasted. I could not tell which one was Kaly; she could have been in a guise I had never seen. Not that it mattered—her mind was in the circuits of a dream-crystal. Lasewires connected the dream-players to a central dream-processor—a K-bit psichip—and also filled the amphitheater, connecting monitors to the dream-processor. Bettors could make wagers on the outcome of a dream-game, and by putting on their own psihelmet, vicariously follow the action. The casino was not very crowded yet; it would be another week before dreamers started dying. Then the big betting would begin. A sparse crowd suited our purposes.

We needed to be synapsed tightly. Risa sat on my lap, and I entered her.

We hovered over the dream-crystal for a moment, then folded our wings and dove in, crashing through a thousand thought filaments. The severed ends spewed out images. Never had we seen such images of despair. We sorted through them, until we found the one we sought. We followed it back.

A woman frolicked naked in a green meadow with two men, also naked. She was slender, with a narrow waist, fine breasts, and nice legs. Her hair was short and white and contrasted against nut-brown skin. The two men were identical with yellow hair, steel-gray eyes, thin lips, strong, smoothly muscled bodies. Their images made us uncomfortable, in an undefined way. We shrugged it off.

They looked up as we approached. The two men faded away.

"You took away my playmates," the woman said. "Did you come to play? You look nice and strong." She lay down and spread her legs, opening her vulva with her fingers. "Come play with me."

"Do you know who we are, Major Kaly?"

She recognized us. "No!" she screamed. "Don't take me back. I don't want to go back."

We looked into her eyes. They coalesced into a black hole. We reached in and pulled out a tightly woven rope. She screamed with each tug, as though we were pulling out her soul. Finally the rope would come out no farther. It lay in coils around her feet. The end began unraveling. Dream filaments untwisted.

Dreams unwound . . .

2

Images began to fill our minds; images a code sequence had made Risa and I forget. But Kaly still remembered . . .

Sunlight ebbed through our barracks window, shining on Risa's fur as she lay on her bunk. We had just finished making love, and she still purred in contentment. I lay beside her, feeling the vibrations in the wombskin beneath me. The sphinx lifted her head from the pillow, turning it toward the west for a moment, then lay back again. I knew what that meant. I got up and stood naked beside the window and looked outside. A cold, distant sun was setting. High above Olympus Mons, ice storms played amid the fire of day dying into night.

Specks danced on the horizon, as though buoyed on the shimmers of a mirage. Red dust devils swirled into tall vortices above the Arcadia Planum. The specks darted through the columns of dust. I looked closer, squinting my eyes. The motes came nearer, visible only by the particles they displaced as they passed through the dust storms. On a clear day, they would be impossible to see.

Ghost Cavalry returned from their patrols.

Before long, the whine of gravturbines became audible. Huvies slipped through the garrison's force field, visible only by the corposants that sparked around them as they settled down on landing pads. They disappeared again when the static discharged as their struts touched ground. Hatches opened, disgorging ghost troopers, seemingly from thin air. In their camoarmor, they appeared only as vague outlines, looking as insubstantial as the wraiths that were their namesakes. But there was flesh and blood inside; invisibility was just good camouflage.

A shackled tribesman was hauled out of a huvy and escorted over to the spooks' office. He looked like a Marajo. I hoped he could convince the spooks he was an innocent herder. Because if he could not, Risa and I would have to work on him.

Risa pulled me away from the window, back to her bunk. Furred lips kissed mine; a rough tongue probed my mouth. A penis that was not entirely mine rose hard between us; Risa's hand guided it into her. She began to moan in unison with my thrusts.

I let my mind drift out and watched. A pedimorph and a sphinx made love on a wombskin bunk. The cat-woman sprawled beneath the child surrogate, writhing with the obscene pleasures of pederasty.

The sphinx appeared to be standard Asteroidian, with short blue fur, as fine as sealskin, except for the black mane of longer and coarser hair; she had long and supple arms and legs, a lithe build, pointed ears, sharp canines, a twitching prehensile tail. The pedimorph seemed typical for its kind: short of stature with the gangly androgynous body-build of preadolescence, blond curls, blue eyes, upturned button nose, pudgy fingers.

Sphinges had been one of the first hybrid races to be bioengineered—their kind had built and populated the low-G settlements, both on the asteroids and the free-standing space stations such as New O'Neil. They had prospered and now were one of the most numerous hybrid species, with a population estimated at half a billion. Pedimorphs were not one of the hybrid races—

the genetic engineering that produced our hermaphro-
ditism and arrested development had been accomplished
entirely with human DNA. Besides, we were not true-
breeding, since breeding would ruin our purpose. Pedies
were sold as children by their parents. After the Guild
had made the necessary modifications, we spent the rest
of our lives pandering to the jaded desires of certain
members of the Terran nobility.

Hey, voyeur. Can I watch too? Risa's psimorph
joined mine in the air above her bunk.

Who's minding the bodies?

Basal ganglia can take care of what they're doing.

We watched together as our bodies continued their
motions of love. From the detached perspective of a dis-
embodied persona, their undulations seemed silly—
thrusting pelvises, rocking torsos, protruding tongues.

Come back with me, Risa said. *I don't want to miss
our orgasm.*

I let her psimorph draw mine back to our bodies.

We were more than what we appeared. Risa and I
were not just a pederastic cat-woman buying the favors
of a pedimorph. Ordinary sphinges and pedis were not
psionic. Back inside our bodies, we were overwhelmed
with the spasms of our orgasm. The neural impulses
originated in Risa's basal ganglia, as pedis could not
have their own orgasms, but the sensations were shared
by both of us while we were in a pathic gestalt,
resonating between our brains, and were just as intense
for me as real ones would have been. Since the neural
messages were in assembly language, my basal ganglia
translated them before they reached cerebral cortex.
Risa's vaginal contractions became spurts of my penis in
my mind, spurts that continued longer than physiologically possible for a male. When the parasympathetic discharge subsided, I collapsed limp on top of Risa.

Ghost troopers began to file into the barracks. Shedding camoarmor, the combrids beneath became visible:
one hundred eighty cm tall, sturdily muscled, bald
scalps convoluted into ridges with implanted cyberwires, eyes hidden behind nictitating membranes, skin

as black as coal with antirad granules. More and more of them lounged around naked, smoking mnemone, 'balling peptide, or drinking propyl.

Without looking at the ID tattoo, you could not tell them apart, as though they had been stamped from the same mold. And in a sense, they had. The hybridization tanks turned out identical clones. Hypnotraining gave them identical memories. There were two models, however. The Lord Generals had discovered that troopers fought better if their libidos were left intact. So there were male and female combrids.

In combat mode, you could not tell one from the other. But under the influence of various intoxicants, they quickly went out of combat mode. Pelvic sphincters opened, allowing external genitalia to descend. Brown adipose thickened with edema, forming perfunctory breasts. Monomer ducts began secreting sex pheromones—soon the barracks would reek with their musty odor. Before long, the combrids were on their bunks in pairs, òr in threes or fours, and the air was full of the sounds of flesh slapping against flesh.

Risa pulled the privacy curtain around us with her foot.

She began licking me with her tongue, already recycled and ready to make love agian.

A voice interrupted, "Sorry to disturb you two lovebirds, but Major Kaly wants to see you. On the double." The voice belonged to Corporal J-20, the spook's orderly. "Did the message get through?" The privacy curtain shook.

"All right," I answered. "We'll be there. You don't have to wait." Risa kept licking me. I pushed her head away. "Save it for later," I said. "We don't want to keep the spook waiting."

"But I don't want to wait either," Risa whined. Sphinges liked immediate gratification.

"It'll have to be later, I tell you."

I pulled on a set of fatigues. Risa did the same. I opened the privacy curtain and with Risa's hand in mine, ran out the barracks quickly, pulling her with me.

If she got a good whiff of synpheromone, she might get uncontrollable.

Static sparked around us as we went through the barracks barofield, going from a comfortable pressurization of four-hundred torr to an ambient atmospheric pressure of one-hundred torr. I felt like someone had kicked the wind out of me. I snapped an 02 clip to my nasal septum: a field-effect oxygen bubble formed around my nose and mouth, letting me breathe comfortably again. The temperature had dropped about thirty degrees also. Fatigues would keep me from freezing for the brief time we would be outside.

Only the garrison's buildings were pressurized and heated. The force field surrounding the garrison was strictly defensive. They could have easily brought the entire volume inside it to four hundred torr and twenty-five degrees. But heat and pressure were considered luxuries by the military. And I was one of the few soldiers who had not been hybridized to be resistant to both. Why bother making me comfortable? I dreamed about there being a slow depressurization while I was asleep and waking up with hypoxic sickness. Sometimes I even slept with an 02 clip on. I had always had a fear of suffocation.

The spooks had already strung up their Marindian captive—he was shackled to the crucifix in front of their office. They called it "softening" him. They would leave him that way without food or water for a few days before having Risa and me interrogate him. It made no difference to us if he was "softened" or not—we could get as much out of him either way. Marindians were not "softened" much anyway by such treatment. They did worse to themselves as a rite of passage to manhood, hanging for a week by hooks dug into their pectorals. The only real reason for "softening" a prisoner was the spooks' sadistic pleasure in tormenting their prisoners.

The Marindian glared at us as we walked by. He was not very soft yet. I wondered if he knew what awaited him. Probably not. He would have chewed off his arms and legs if he suspected.

Corporal J-20 sat behind his desk with his feet propped up. He waved us into Major Kaly's office. The door was open, so we walked in without knocking. The door closed behind us.

Major Kaly looked up from her desk. She was in standard Terran morphology today. With spooks, you never knew how they would appear; they were chameleons and could assume the appearance of any of the nine hybrid races. She was a brunette, with hair as black as spun carbon, green eyes, fine features, breasts as large as neutron bombs.

We did not bother saluting—military decorum was lax in Corps Intelligence. A Terran wearing Corps fatigues without insignia sat across from her. He was pretty average in appearance: one hundred eighty cm tall, seventy kilos weight, short straw-colored hair, aquiline nose, gray eyes. He stood up as we entered the office.

"Sergeant N-10, Corporal R-6, I'd like you to meet Lieutenant T-11, of the WOLVES," Kaly said.

The WOLVES were an elite terrorist unit composed of zoanthropes—shape changers. They also had short-range psionic ability. On Mars, lycanthropes were mostly used. I looked closely at Lieutenant T-11. From appearances, one would never have guessed he was a werewolf.

We shook hands all around.

"Nate," I said, "and Risa," giving him our nicknames.

"Terle," he answered.

"Lieutenant T-11 has just come in from a terrorist tour of duty. The particular band of Marjuns he has been entertaining may know something about the whereabouts of Geronimo. We would like a little long range intelligence before going in with ghost troopers. He will direct you to them tonight." She looked from me to Risa. "Any questions?" she asked.

We shook our heads.

"What time do you normally start dream-hunting?" Terle asked.

"Around 2400," I answered.

"Lieutenant T-11 will join you in your operations room at 2400," Kaly ordered. "If you discover anything germane, report it to me at once." She started reading some reports on her desk. We were dismissed.

The three of us got up to leave.

"Sergeant," Kaly said, looking up.

"Yes, ma'am," I answered, stopping.

"I want to talk to you for a minute. Alone."

Risa and Terle went out. I stayed. The door closed. I knew what Kaly wanted.

"I'd like you to report to my quarters at 2000." She smiled for the first time. "Don't keep me waiting."

Just as I had suspected. Another "private briefing." But what could I do? Kaly was my commanding officer and a spook at that. I had no choice.

I saluted, turned, and walked out of her office.

Terle and Risa were waiting outside the building. As I went to join them, I glanced at Corporal J-20. He was grinning wickedly. I'd get even with him someday.

3

It was 1800 hours. To kill a little time, Risa and I took Terle to the NCO club. Since he was not wearing insignia, nobody knew he was an officer.

We sat down at a table and ordered drinks, specifying ethyl rather than propyl alcohol for the base. Only cyrines could drink propyl without going blind or crazy or both. In an NCO club, it paid to be cautious.

There was not much going on in the club—it was early enough that most troopers were still unwinding in the barracks and their NCO's were helping them. A couple of cyrine gunnies were playing combage. A sergeant major was watching a replay of the lasoccer finals on the holovision over the bar. An E-4 company clerk was feeding tokens into a slot-computer, playing various games of chance. No one paid any attention to the three of us.

"What's it like being a WOLF?" I asked. "We haven't had any at this garrison before."

"It's not bad," he replied. "Especially the wolf part —sensory input is enhanced, so everything seems brighter, sharper. There are wild feelings that are impossible to describe. We usually go out in the field in pairs, male and female. Female werewolves do not have a cyclic estrus; they are sexually receptive continuously.

There is no better sex than when in wolf form. WOLVES have an unwritten rule that they will not have sex with each other except as wolves." He finished his drink and ordered another. "But there is a price to be paid."

Risa smiled. "What price?"

"We suffer from the same psychophysio strain that affects chameleons—probably a little more, a little sooner, because their changes are all superficial and their neuroendocrine system remains human. You know what happens to spooks?"

"They eventually go crazy," Risa said laughing. "Corpsmen haul them off in restraints to be demilled."

"I can look forward to the same fate, eventually."

No one spoke for a moment. Demilling was not a pleasant fate.

"How long were you out in the field?" I asked, to change the subject.

"Six months. My mission was indeterminate in length. As a wolf, I could live off the land indefinitely. But six months is as long as a lycanthrope can be in wolf form before he starts shedding lupine virus. If that happened, you would see a werewolf epidemic. I roamed about a large free-terror zone containing hostiles and sympathizers, terrorizing them at will and collecting intelligence. My mission would terminate early only if I discovered a certain type of intelligence."

"Information about Geronimo?"

He nodded.

"Do you think your intelligence is accurate?"

He shrugged. "Who knows? I obeyed my instructions. I came in from the field as soon as I discovered anything about Geronimo." He smiled at Risa. "I guess it's up to the little lady to find out how accurate my information is." I did not like the way he looked at Risa. He glanced at me. "With your help, of course."

"Are WOLVES' memories the same as the rest of ours?" I asked.

"What do you mean?"

"Do you remember any of your own memories, or are they all standard issue?"

"Standard issue, of course. Generals are the only ones with their real memories."

"Do you ever have glimpses of something else?"

"Sometimes. Especially when I'm changing. But the images are blurred and indistinct. I can't make much of them. Why do you ask?"

"No reason in particular. I seem to be obsessed with wanting to know who I really was before, why I happened to become a combrid. I suppose it's just part of my present persona—the psychsurgeons probably had a reason for putting it in."

"No doubt. They have reasons for everything they put in a persona."

"Where is your she-wolf? You did have a partner, didn't you?"

"Certainly. She stayed out in the field to finish out the six months. Only one of us was needed to bring back the intelligence."

"So what are you going to do?"

"About what?"

"About sex. You said nothing was as good as wolf sex."

"Make do with second best, I suppose."

I did not like the way he leered.

"All this talk is boring me," Risa interjected. "I want to dance." She took Terle's hand. "Come dance with me. Nate doesn't like to dance." She led him out to the dance floor. As they stepped on it, optical music swirled around them. They began to dance amid the shining strands of sound.

I ordered another drink and watched Risa and Terle dance. I did not like to dance because I was so short; my head only came to Risa's chest.

Risa quite frequently danced with other troopers when we went to the club—she was strong and graceful, smooth and lithe. Normally, I did not mind her dancing with others. But there was something in the way Terle put his hands on her that I did not like at all. And there was something about the way she laughed that bothered me.

They danced for an hour, only stopping briefly for another drink. This time Terle asked Risa to dance.

"Do you mind, Nate?" she asked. "We've been ignoring you."

"Certainly not," I lied. "I enjoy watching. Besides, I've got to go. It's 1930. Kaly's expecting me at 2000. I'll meet you at the ops room at midnight." I got up to leave.

They were already dancing before I left the room.

At exactly 2000 hours, I knocked on Kaly's door. She opened it and ushered me into her quarters.

The senior officers had their own individual houses. The only officer more senior than Kaly was the Lord Brigadier himself. Kaly had her own furnishings: sonic sculpture, mutaholos, furniture made of real leather and wood, olfactory tapestries, antique rugs woven out of animal hair. Everything was real and imported from Earth and expensive.

She was still in standard Terran morphology, but was wearing a diaphanous gown of spidersilk, instead of fatigues. She went barefoot and obviously wore nothing beneath the gown. She had a single strand of singing pearls around her neck and a pearl earring attached to each ear.

We sat down on her couch, and she poured me a glass of real Earth wine.

"So nice of you to come," she said.

"It was nice of you to ask me," I replied. *As if I had a choice,* I thought to myself.

"I do enjoy our talks."

"So do I."

"I need someone who understands me. You do understand me, don't you? You know what I need?"

"I think so." I understood her better than she realized.

"I'm lonely. I can't talk to anyone else. They would misinterpret friendliness for weakness. But I can trust you, can't I?"

"Of course you can."

We went through the same ritual each time. I had it memorized by now. I got up and wandered about the room, looking at its expensive furnishings, wondering if I had ever had enough money to afford the same. One never knew. I might have been a Lord myself before hybridization. I left an image of myself on the couch talking to Kaly.

"Have another drink," she said to the image, pouring its glass full.

"Thank you," my image said. It drank the wine and held out its glass for more. Kaly filled the glass again.

"This is very good wine," the image said, with slightly slurred speech. It burped and giggled at its indiscretion.

"I'm glad you're enjoying it. Have some more." Kaly filled the glass again.

My image drank unsteadily, spilling wine all over itself, and laughed.

"Here, let me help you," Kaly laughed. She pulled off my image's fatigues, leering at the naked boy's body. The wine had soaked through and stained the skin. "I'll clean you up." She began licking the stains with her tongue, moving it across my image's chest and belly. When the wine was all licked up, she moved lower to lick its smooth scrotum and suck its hairless penis.

I watched all this from across the room. I'd been playing the same trick on Kaly for weeks, ever since the first time she had tried to seduce me. I took pride that she had not yet noticed the deception. I knew there would be hell to pay if she did. I wished I knew why she singled me out for her attentions. I wished I could peep into her mind to find out the nature of her psychopathology; most neuroses were programmed in by the psychsurgeons for their own arcane reasons, but some persisted from prehybridization times. Kaly's fascination with me might be because of a lingering neurosis from when she was human.

I wandered about her house, examining various objects, poking into drawers and closets. While I did so, my image continued to let itself be ravished by Kaly. She was becoming frenzied with sex steroid. She had taken off her gown. Sweat glistened on her naked body. My image was licking her groin now.

I had not yet found anything new or interesting. I searched Kaly's quarters each time I was there, but had not found anything helpful. I suspected Kaly knew who I had been and the circumstances under which I had been conscripted into the Corps. Once I had asked her, but she refused to tell me anything. I had been tempted to peep into her mind when in gestalt with Risa, but if we were caught it would mean demilling for sure. I hoped I might find some clue in her house, but there was never anything of use, no papers or notes or diary. Spooks were trained to not leave footprints.

I went into her bedroom. A set of fatigues lay crumpled on the floor. Perfume and cosmetic bottles stood on her dressing table. I was about to go on when I noticed something. There was a smudge of dust on the dressing table. I looked closer. Not dust, but the remains of a self-disintegrating flimsy. Kaly had neglected to brush away the residue. I could still make out some of the words.

They were difficult to read. Something about Lieutenant T-11 being the key, that he had been the adjutant to the Supreme Commander. The rest was smudged. It did not look like Corps flimsy. It was not signed.

I decided it was not much help. A shame the residue had diffused enough to make most of it illegible.

Kaly and my image were bringing their party into the bedroom.

My image lay on the bed. Kaly picked up a vial from her dressing table and straddled what she thought was me. She opened the vial and dipped her tongue into it, then leaned close to my face, letting a drop of peptide drip into my eye. It was a mixture of endocaine and endrogen—speed and sex steroid. My little-boy penis stiffened and grew ten centimeters. Kaly reached around and inserted it into her. My image licked and sucked her breasts as she rode him. Sweating bodies slid against each other. Teeth nipped nipples. Kaly moaned with each thrust.

She wanted more. She always did. She rolled off my

image and reached under her pillow, pulling out an artificial penis thirty centimeters long and five in diameter. She placed one end over my image's penis and lay back, spreading her legs. The image climbed on top of her, inserted its new club into her, and thrust in and out. She shrieked with delight.

Kaly had a half dozen orgasms over the next hour. You'd think she'd have been satisfied. But she wasn't. She never was.

My image and she lay side by side, naked and sweaty. Kaly pulled the artificial penis off and held it in place over her groin. Dermycelia attached it firmly to her flesh. She kneeled above my image.

"Now it's my turn to return the pleasure you gave me," she said.

My image screamed and kicked her away. It rolled off the bed and ran out of the room. Kaly chased it, with her new penis bobbing up and down in front of her.

She finally got me cornered in the living room. She pinned me down and tried to enter me with her penis. She seemed surprised when the artificial penis met resistance, and pushed harder.

I, the real me, was getting tired of the game.

My image groped about with its hand, finally finding a gold statuette in convenient reach. It hit Kaly on the head, knocking her unconscious.

Actually, nothing at all that crude happened. I merely stimulated a few critical cerebral neurons, triggering a seizure. She would sleep for an hour or so.

I had no choice, really. I mean, I'll be damned if I'd let her bugger me, even if it was only pretend.

I had time for a quick shower. May as well use Kaly's.

As I showered, I wondered briefly how Risa and Terle had amused themselves.

4

Risa and Terle were waiting for me in the ops room.

They were already dressed in psisuits. I shucked off my fatigues and pulled one on. Psisuits were polymer body stockings containing thousands of induction coils on their inside surface, which interfaced with the specially modified induction neurons in a psipath's skin. Thousands of tiny holosequins studded the outside surface, projecting 3D lasewires outward, which would interface with the ones projected from another psipath's suit. A technological way to form the gestalt. Sexual contact was more efficient, but was not "professional," and the psisuits amplified the signal, allowing long range capabilities.

Risa and I put on psisuits and prowled the dream-time nearly every night. Sometimes we were dream-hunters, looking at the dreams of the natives for intelligence. Sometimes we were dream-terrorists, planting dreams of our choosing in the natives' minds. Long Range Terror was particularly effective against the superstitious Marindians, who put great stock in dreams. We could manipulate those dreams from a hundred kilometers away.

Tonight we were dream-hunters.

"Ready?" I asked.

Risa and Terle nodded.

"Suits on," I said. We each touched the sensitive dots over our sternums. Tiny red light wires sprang out in all directions, touching each other in mid-air.

The gestalt formed.

We drifted out of body, rising high above the garrison, floating in the ether. We were one mind: our canned memories were shared, insignificant as they were, but also, the racial memories carried in our xenogenes were experienced by all. We remembered being a great hunting cat, hunching down, belly in the dust, tail flicking, waiting for the charge, the slash of claws, the terrible bite at the throat. We remembered running with the pack and the silent communion of the hunt and howling at a moon of night.

We were hunting again.

We stalked our prey. They were everywhere below, scattered about the plains and plateaus, huddled together in their villages, sleeping, thinking they were safe. But they dreamed. Their dreams rose from their minds like smoke from a fire. Currents in the ether swirled the dream filaments, twisting them together into a confusing weave.

We hovered over a particular village, plucking dream filaments at random, following them back, letting their images unravel: hunting bison on horseback, stalking deer, pounding gold into sheets and making jewelry, making love with your friend's wife.

Dawn was near. Sunlight disturbed the ether, disrupted the dream-tendrils. Dream-hunters hunted best at night, resting during the day. Prey was less wary at night, their minds less guarded. We retreated before the advancing day, floating back the way we had come, dropping back to the garrison, going back to our bodies. Lasewires flicked off. The gestalt was broken.

I stood unsteadily on my feet for a bit, getting used to being in my body again. Risa and Terle were a little wobbly also. After a few minutes, I felt normal again. I took off the psisuit and put my fatigues back on. Risa and Terle did likewise.

"Did we find out anything useful?" Terle asked.

"Who knows?" I shrugged. "Only spooks know what is useful to them. I doubt we found out anything about Geronimo. See the holostuds on the wall over there." I pointed at one wall. "A computer monitored and recorded everything that happened in our minds. The spooks will spend all day analyzing the data. Who knows what they'll glean. They don't bother to tell Risa and me. But at least this way we don't have to go through the bother of being debriefed."

"Good. I could use a drink."

"The club doesn't open until 1500."

"I've got a bottle in the barracks," Risa said. "Let's all have a drink."

"Sounds good to me," Terle said.

I would rather have had Risa to myself, but said nothing.

We left the ops room and walked across the compound to the barracks. Sunrise already stained the eastern horizon. Ghost troopers left their barracks and filed into huvies, which rose with a faint hum and streaked away in different directions, carrying out their various missions. They would not return until dark.

Our barracks was empty, as it usually was in the morning.

We sat on the edge of Risa's bunk and drank ethyl out of plastic cups. Risa sat between Terle and me. After my second glass, I began to feel better. I did not have much body mass, so alcohol affected me quickly.

"I like to make love after a dream-hunt," Risa said. She said it for Terle's benefit, as she knew I knew her proclivities. "I always feel close after a hunt. The after-effects of the gestalt, I suppose."

Terle looked at me with an uncomfortable expression. But I could tell he wanted Risa. He wanted me to tell him it was all right. As if I could tell Risa what to do. I stared back at him with what I hoped was a blank expression.

Risa pulled off her fatigues. She then took off mine. Terle's came off next.

We sat naked side by side. None of us made a move to advance things further. Terle was too uncertain. I was too stubborn. Risa was waiting in amusement.

"I want to make love to both of you," she said finally. And, to be sure we did not misunderstand her intentions, she added, "At the same time."

She kneeled on the floor, alternately licking our penises until both were ready. Then she pounced on me, pushing me back, and kneeled over me, sticking my member into her vagina.

She looked at Terle. "I want you from behind."

He stood on the bunk above us and leaned over. I felt him enter her rectum; his penis pressed against mine through thin tissue. With Risa between us, we synchronized our thrusts. She screamed like a wildcat. I closed my eyes, thinking of nothing but delicious friction.

Fingers touched my scrotum, feeling the slit between it and my anus. I opened my eyes and pushed Terle's hand away.

I did not like what I saw in his eyes. I had seen the same look in Kaly's too often.

The three of us lay in Risa's bed. With the peace of the animals they partly were, Risa and Terle slept. My DNA was entirely human. Sleep was not as easy for me.

I knew Risa and Terle as well as it was possible to know others—as well as I knew myself. Secrets were not possible in a pathic gestalt. But all I really knew about the three of us were artificial memories—memories I could just as easily have looked up in the Corps Personnel Manual:

N-10, Sergeant, Standard Telepath. Morphology: child surrogate. Xenogenes: none. Cybernetics: none. Specialized software: central nervous system augmented with telepathic neurons derived from TXP-333, including limbic system enhancements and peripheral induction neurocoils. Psychological operating system: standard CS-5 pseudomemories—lived first ten years with his family in abject poverty in the slums of Denver, before being sold to a child-broker and bioengineered into a pedimorph, to spend the next twenty years working in various pediparlors, until killing a client, which resulted in conscription into the Foreign Legions.

R-6, Corporal, Standard Empath. Morphology: sphinx. Xenogenes: various, mostly feline. Cybernetics: none. Specialized software: central nervous system augmentation with empathic neurons derived from various non-human species and peripheral induction neurocoils. Psychological operating system: standard S-7 pseudomemories—grew up on Ceres, apprenticed to the Microwave Fitters Guild and advanced to Master, working throughout the Belt, became involved with crystalyst smuggling and was caught, chose conscription over cyborg time.

T-11, Lieutenant, Standard WOLF. Morphology: lycanthrope. Xenogenes: lupine and plasticizing. Cybernetics: none. Specialized software: low-grade psionic neurons and peripheral induction neurocoils. Psychological operating system: standard W-8 pseudomemories—middle class childhood, graduated from college with a liberal arts degree, became a scriptwriter for a laservision production company, developed an addiction for peptide and killed his actress girlfriend while in a peptide frenzy, volunteering for military duty rather than the Antarctic prison farms.

The memories had once been real. There once had been an N-10, R-6, and T-11 who had lived those lives. The Psyche Corps had recorded the memories of all the soldiers to serve in Earth's Foreign Legions and its computers kept track of subsequent military performance. The psychological profiles of the best soldiers were found. New soldiers were given those psychological profiles, rather than take a chance on their own. Different psyches were blended in each squad, but the squads were all the same. The psychodynamics of a platoon, company, battalion, and division were predictable and reproducible. There was no desertion or mutiny or other surprises in the modern Corps.

The memories I had been given would make me a better soldier. But they were not my memories.

Terle had awakened. He was looking at me. "You seem troubled," he said.

"Does it bother you that you don't know who you were, that your memories are someone else's?"

"Not really."

"It bothers me. I want to know who I really was."

"What does it matter? One set of memories is as good as another."

"Not to me. I want my own."

"You still have them. They're still in your hippocampus."

"Then why can't I remember?"

"Your prior memories are encoded with a psicypher. Your conscious mind is denied access to them. If you knew the code, you could unlock your previous life's memories."

"How do you learn the code?"

"There's only one way you'll ever learn it."

"How's that?"

"Serve your twenty years and be demilled. They give you back your real memories then."

"Then the code's on file someplace?"

"Sure. On Luna. In the central data bank of the hybridization complex. When you crawl back in the tank, you'll get your memories back—if you're one of the one percent to survive twenty years in the Corps. There's also a copy at the Cybergon. The lord generals have access to them. Meanwhile, I'd be careful to whom I mentioned this obsession."

"Why?"

"If the psychsurgeons think they had a bad take, they'll recyle you back to the hypnotanks. You'll lose all the new memories you have."

"I keep thinking my life may have some importance, some meaning."

"Forget it. You weren't important. If you were important or your life had any meaning, you wouldn't be here. Your past only differed in minor details from any of the standard memories. You lived a squalid life. You were forced into a desperate act. You were so miserable, you chose conscription to an honorable punishment. What difference does it make if the details are off a little? The essential facts are the same for all of us. If I knew my psicypher code, I wouldn't use it. I would rather not know who I had been. I would rather not have to re-live that kind of misery."

"I have a feeling that I'm different, that I'll make a difference."

"You won't."

"Why do you know so much about all this?"

"I was once the adjutant to the Supreme Commander."

"Why aren't you still?"

"We had a falling out."

"Do you know your psicypher code?"

"I might."

Risa opened her eyes. "Some of us were trying to sleep." She rolled over on top of me. A furry face kissed me. "Now you'll have to make me sleepy again."

I did not have time to ask Terle more questions then. But I would soon. I had a feeling he knew more than he was letting on.

My private briefing with Kaly came early that day. Corporal J-20 came over to the barracks in mid-afternoon and told me Kaly wanted to see me in her quarters right away. I had to leave in the middle of another three-way sex party with Risa and Terle. Though I hated to leave Terle alone with Risa, in a way, it was a relief. Risa's libido was insatiable, and I was tired of pushing away Terle's groping hands and questing penis. Bisexuality was OK, I guess, but it was not for me, thank you. It would be a relief to play mind games with Kaly.

But when she opened the door to her quarters, I knew I was not going to get a respite. She was in combrid morphology that day.

Instead of a voluptuous Terran with critical-mass breasts, a gynoid combrid greeted me. Her head was bald with its scalp wrinkled with ridges. Her muscles were lean and hard. Her eyes were hidden behind nictitating membranes.

Kaly's personality changed with her different guises.

As a cyrine, she liked her sex on the rough side. She beat up my image a little and made it perform various degrading acts. Then she shackled it to the wall and used the alphalash. I did not care much for it, even if it was only happening in her imagination.

In my pseudomemories, I had killed a customer. He had wanted coition with my vagina. I didn't care for that and refused. He had whipped me with an alphalash until I was too weak to resist, then forced his penis into me. I had my first and only real orgasm then. But I felt my body had betrayed me. I had not had another orgasm of my own since. A neurosis? Certainly. But what could I do about it?

Anyway, I got tired of being whipped, so I put Kaly to sleep a little early. I had to hang around, so she would not get suspicious. She might have had somebody watching her place.

I hauled her into bed and lay down beside her. If I had to kill time, may as well take a nap.

Kaly's screams woke me.

She lay on her back with the sweat pouring off her face.

"A nightmare?" I asked.

"I've been having them for some time. I can barely

remember what happens, the images fade as I wake. I seem to be having sex with two young boys, apparently twin brothers. I have a terrible lust for them, but at the same time, I am repelled. If they misbehave, I tickle their bottoms with an alphalash. I don't know why I should feel so ashamed. You know how much I like boys." She smiled. "You know what they say about nightmares?"

"What do they say?"

"They say they're our previous memories trying to recycle, our old lives trying to surface."

"What do you suppose it means?" I was disturbed. Her nightmare was similar to one of my own, except I was one of the twins, and there was another boy in the party. Why should Kaly's and my nightmares be similar? Why were our dream-times connected? "Who do you suppose you were in your previous life?" I asked.

"I don't know." Tears streamed from her eyes. Combrids were not supposed to cry.

I held her in my arms. The real me, not my image.

She made love to me then. For a change, it was almost tender.

5

The tribesman lay spread-eagled on Martian permafrost, hands and feet shackled to stakes. But at least
they had taken him down from the crucifix, for however
brief. He had hung there all night and all day without
food or water.

Tonight's session would just be preliminary question-
ing to decide what topics to discuss in more detail later,
when he had become even softer. If he were smart, he
would relate everything he knew immediately, and convince Kaly he knew nothing of importance. But it would
not be that easy—Marindians played the game by their
own rules.

He did not look very soft yet. Behind nictitating
membranes, his eyes were still as cold as carbonic snow.
His face was as immobile as a mask: aquiline nose,
proud cheekbones, thin, haughty lips. He wore only a
breech clout—the red kind his tribe wore when they
went to war. His body was still smeared with ceremonial
paint, and bits of feathers clung to his hair where they
had been woven into his long braids. He certainly
looked like a guerilla—I doubted he would convince
anyone otherwise.

A night and a day without food or water was no hard-

ship to him. He had been trained from his early childhood to fast ten times that long just to have the proper
visions before going off to war. Night-time temperatures that dropped to minus fifty degrees did not chill
his naked flesh—brown adipose and a hyped metabol-
ism kept him warm. Three more days of the same would
not make him any softer. Tonight's session was unnecessary—Risa and I would get just as much out of
him without it.

I had told that to Kaly before. She did not care. So
why should I? What did it matter to me if the spooks
had their own rituals? If they played the game by their
own rules? If it made them happy to needlessly torture a
captive, what business was that of mine?

Pain would not make a tribesman talk. They could
tolerate any pain Kaly could administer; the captive expected that. Torture had been refined to an art among
the perpetually warring Martian tribes. Stoic bravery
under physical torture was a test of manhood. Bravery
was the only way a Marindian could hope to eventually
be rewarded with an honorable death by his enemies.

But our captive had not fallen in with honorable
enemies.

His torture tonight was just for Kaly's amusement.
He would not be rewarded with death.

Risa paced back and forth in front of me. The
tribesman watched her impassively, not even letting his
eyes follow her movements. We both wore psisuits. If he
knew what that meant, he would have been worried.

Kaly stood beside us. She was a cyrine major still.
She held an alphalash in her hand. Dripping protons
sizzled against the permafrost.

She spoke to the captive in the gutteral sing-song of
his native tongue. He ignored her. She spoke to him
again. He stared ahead, oblivious to her. Kaly smiled.
She looked at me. "Are you and the corporal ready?"

I nodded.

Kaly swung the lash. Blazing filaments splayed across
the Martian's body. He did not even flinch with their
sting. From his reaction, Kaly could have been splashing

him with warm water instead of energized protons.

Risa sat down in front of me. We were about ten meters away from the prisoner. Psychic antennae quivered from her head. She watched the captive dispassionately, the reflected images of decaying protons tracking across her eyes. From her expression, I could guess what was going on in the Martian's mind.

May as well know for sure, I thought. I pressed the spot on my chest. Invisible lasewires sprang between us. Our minds fused into one—we sailed in the air on outstretched wings.

From out-of-body, we watched Kaly lashing the Marindian. His skin glowed with trapped protons. Every cutaneous nerve sang in agony. He should have been writhing from the pain. But a warrior knew how to deal with sensations as inconsequential as pain. He had spent all his life perfecting that simple mental manipulation. His consciousness had already gone to that place in his mind where bodily messages could be ignored. As the pain increased, he shifted his sensorium to a deeper level, thought filaments began winding back as he retreated ever deeper into hippocampal recesses.

We could have followed him in, like a ghost slipping through a closing door, and rummaged about his secret mental drawers. But we did not. Kaly had given us orders not to sneak into his mind. We were just supposed to watch for stray thoughts. She did not want to be cheated of her fun.

And, Kaly had a lot of fun. She was a master with the alphalash, working it over every square centimeter of the Marindian's skin, until he glowed like a radioactive zombie. I imagine she was a little disappointed her captive did not shriek and writhe in agony. He lay passive. His mind was protected from the anguish of his peripheral nerves, insulated by layers of protective software. He had learned how to control his perception of sensations. He knew the pain was there, but it did not matter. It could not intrude enough to bother him. Deep inside his mind, he laughed. He thought us fine enemies, to inflict such exquisite torture on him. He would not think so highly of us, if he knew of the treachery to come.

Even though she was cheated of the pleasure of watching her victim suffer, Kaly continued thrashing the Marindian. With each swing of the whip, arcs of bright protons flew through the air.

The scene sickened me a little. I did not care much for the discipline of the alphalash. That quirk was built into my psychological operating system, and was one of the reasons the original N-10 had killed his client. The other reason was to avoid being buggered. Now I shared those two phobias of my genosibling. I knew I could kill again, under the right circumstances.

I joined my psimorph and Risa's, and we sailed high overhead, soaring on psionic wings in the psychic ether, like a hunting raptor. Everywhere below us was the spoor of our prey, dream-tendrils twining together in inexplicable patterns. We could pluck one and follow it down to its source and insert dreams of our choosing into a defenseless mind. Or we could tug on the dream-filament and pull out other secrets attached to it. We did neither. Not tonight. Tonight we were hunting closer to home.

We fell back to Mars.

Kaly was through. The alphalash hung limp in her hand. The Marindian lay still, skin burning with ionization, like a specter settled to ground. Kaly kicked him in the side a couple of times, then walked away, leaving him for us.

We waited.

The glow ebbed from the Marindian's skin. His eyelids fluttered with REM sleep. A dream-filament rose from his head.

We plucked the filament, letting it tangle in our feet. We did not even look at the streaming images—his miserable existence did not interest us. We had better prey to hunt. But as we flew away, his life's dreams trailed behind.

I reported to Kaly personally. In her quarters, of course.

She had changed into human form, becoming again a voluptuous Terran, with blue eyes, amber hair, wet lips, and fine, white teeth. In this appearance, she called herself Saraltr. She wore a satin jumpsuit sheer enough that you could see nipples and labia through the fabric.

"Did you find out anything from our friend?" she asked. "Did I pry anything loose from him?"

"Yes, I think so."

"What?"

"I think Geronimo may be in the camp of this fellow. We only got a glimpse, but I'm pretty sure it was Geronimo."

Kaly's eyes shone topaz. "Let's find out." She grabbed my hand, pulling me toward the door.

I pulled out of her grasp. "Not tonight. It would kill him."

"That's OK."

"It would kill him before we learned enough."

"Oh."

"Tomorrow night will be soon enough. Besides, we wouldn't want him to spoil our fun." I let a mental image of myself go over to her and kiss her, opening the seam of her jumpsuit. Fabric tumbled about her feet. An imaginary tongue started licking her.

As my mental image occupied Kaly, I noticed the alphalash lay on a table. Things were going to get rough. Kaly would want me to whip her tonight. I was glad it would only happen in her head. Clever me.

We went through the ritual. In her mind, I worked the alphalash over her body as handily as she had whipped the Marindian. When her body glowed with imaginary fire, I strapped on an imaginary dildo and buggered her while she shrieked with both pleasure and pain. We went through the same ritual each time after she interrogated a prisoner. She always assumed the guise of Saraltr when she wanted to feel the lash. I suppose the ritual assuaged her mind of some inner guilt, but I often wondered the reason she was always Saraltr. Since it was her mind that wanted punishment, I thought it clever of me that only her mind was punished.

But I wasn't as clever as I thought I was. Or Kaly was more clever than I'd thought. I failed to notice the holocamera lens stuck to the ceiling.

After the fun and games with Kaly were finished, meaning she was finally in a post-ictal coma, I went to the NCO club for a drink. I needed to relax.

The club was crowded.

Optical music spewed from the ceiling over the small dance floor, concealing the dancers behind shimmering filaments. Every stool along the bar was occupied, as well as every chair at every table.

I pushed my way over to the bar and squeezed between two cyrine gunnies to order a drink. The gunnies glared at me, but did not start any trouble. They knew better. The last cyrine to take a swing at me broke his own jaw with his own fist, as well as making a mess in his pants. The word had gotten out in a hurry that I did not fight fair.

But why should I? I did not have any combat modifications. My reflexes were standard human, not triple speed. My skin was not reinforced. My bones were not augmented. My muscles were normal strength. I was half the size of a combrid and slight of build. All I had to fight with were my telepathic abilities, so why shouldn't I use them? No reason at all, as far as I was concerned. But I was not very popular with the cyrines. I had no real friends at all on base. Just Risa. And, she could not help herself—we had been imprinted on each other. If not for the sex, we would have been like brother and sister.

I took my drink and tried to find a quiet corner where I could stand and drink it.

There weren't any.

I went back to the barracks. Risa and Terle were making love. I should have been mad, but I was feeling too sorry for myself. I needed my friend, even if she was sleeping around on me. Sometimes I wished the geno-surgeons would have left out the feline morals when they gave Risa the genes of a cat.

She was delighted to see me. "You got through with Kaly early," she said. "Come and join the fun."

I did. What else could I do? Sometimes Terle and I took turns, sometimes we both had her at the same time.

I finally fell asleep.

I woke when a cold nose touched my crotch.

A wolf lay in bed with us, sniffing my groin.

"If he licks me, I'll kill him," I said.

"Relax," Risa said. "He's harmless."

"He's changed for you before?"

"Certainly. I think he's kind of cute."

I got up.

"Where are you going?"

"For a walk."

"Nate, I never knew you were so prudish."

"I draw the line at this. I won't watch my girl copulating with a dog, no matter how cute she thinks he is."

I walked out of the barracks. I did not see what happened next. It was just as well.

6

The tribesman hung from his crucifix, suffering his third evening in our captivity.

Kaly stood before him, holding an alphalash—it was time for another interrogation session. Normally this one would have been for her amusement, like the first had been, rather than to seriously obtain information. But since she thought the prisoner might really know something about Geronimo, Kaly had instructed Risa and me to probe deeply tonight, using all possible means. That meant she did not care if the captive died or became a vegetable as a result of our efforts—as long as we extracted everything useful from his mind.

The Marindian did not look any more concerned now than he had last night. An alphalash was a mild form of torture for him after all; it did not maim or mutilate. He stared straight ahead. His face showed no emotion, let alone fear. His lips were grimly straight, his jawline set. But his eyes betrayed him a little—they vibrated in vertical nystagmus, following the whip's protons as they bounced off the ground.

Risa and I went into the pathic gestalt before Kaly started whipping the Marindian. We wanted to be sure to get into his skull before his consciousness retreated too deeply. Lasewires surrounded us, we went out-of-body, our eyes became dull with autonomic control.

Kaly had been watching for that signal.

She swung the whip.

At its touch, the Marindian began reeling in thought tendrils. We grabbed a winding filament and let it pull us into a hippocampal tapestry, where we blended our pattern into the wave—a ghost image of a raptor, lost among more vivid dreams. Soon all his mental fibers had wound back and his sensorium was safe within deep mental recesses. He would feel no pain.

He thought his dreams were safe now. He was secure in the knowledge that now no secrets could pass his lips.

He was wrong.

Dreams unwind.

Pari Tunavurur awakes in darkness.

Protons still glow in his skin, but their light has faded to a blue spiderweb. Each strand of webwork sears across his skin like a hot wire, and more pain still lingers in spinal roots, but pain can be ignored.

Pari is ten years old. He has been riding with the war party of the great war chief for two years. Marindian boys become men at the age of eight and can go to war then. He is the son of Cuthair, chief of the Cebrenian band of Marutes. Since he is young, he is also foolish. The troopers caught him on his way back from a liaison with a Marajo herder girl. He still thinks she was worth the risk.

He opens his eyes and glances around.

He is no longer outside, neither shackled to the crucifix nor staked to the ground. He is inside one of the buildings, lying on a metal table. He is naked. The room is empty, except for him.

Interrogation instruments lie on a bench beside the table: neuroprobes, peptide vials, EEG leads, evoked potential transceivers. Pari does not know if they are through with their interrogation attempts or about to begin.

But his shackles are off! They do not expect him to

regain consciousness so quickly. He has a chance to escape.

He rolls off the table, landing on all fours. His joints creak and are stiff and painful with movement. He moves about the room, checking it out carefully.

There is but one door and no windows. He can see no lasewires or other scanners, but that is no guarantee he is not being monitored, so he waits before the door for a moment, listening.

At first, he hears nothing outside. As his senses become more alert, he hears the shuffle of combat boots and the sound of quiet breathing. He listens carefully, hearing nothing more. There is only one guard outside the door.

He imagines the scene outside, constructing images in his mind, making his plans, rehearsing each move meticulously. He cannot afford to make a mistake.

He crouches by the door, waiting for the right moment. He holds a neuroprobe in his hand.

Finally he hears the sound he has waited to hear, that he has to hear before he can act: the snap of a mnemone tube being opened.

Pari presses the stud. The door slides open. He stabs with the neuroprobe at the place his ears had told him the guard's face would be, not taking the time to visually confirm his target, because even a few milliseconds delay would be enough to allow the guard to protect himself. He has guessed right—the guard's visor is up, a mnemone tube fumes at his lips. His face is unprotected. Pari's aim is true. The probe slips into the guard's eye, and he slumps noiselessly to the ground.

Pari picks up the guard's weapon and glances around. There is no alarm, no sound of rushing feet. So far, so good.

He is outside. The cold air feels good on his skin. The building he has just left is in the center of the garrison. He slips from shadow to shadow like a coyote wraith, unseen and unheard by other sentries, until he crouches before the garrison's force field. He times the passing of bored sentries, until he knows the pattern of their patrols. When both guards have passed and it will be thirty seconds before the third comes by, Pari darts through the field easily—it was designed only to keep intruders out—and scoots across the buffer zone walking backwards, brushing away his tracks with his hands. He lies behind a jumble of rocks, waiting for the clanging of alarms, the whine of huvies rising, the criss-crossed beams of searching lasers. Nothing happens. All stays quiet. His escape remains undiscovered.

Pari crawls through jumbled rocks and brush until the lights of the garrison can no longer be seen. Then he runs swiftly, frequently backtracking, jumping from rock to rock when he can. He wants to escape, but he wants even more to be sure he is not being followed. They will soon find the dead guard and begin searching for him. If a huvy flies overhead, its sophisticated sensors will easily find him. He wants to be far away before the search begins.

He is lucky. With the coming of dawn, he has made ten kilometers of distance and no search craft has flown overhead.

He finds an overhanging rock on the margin of a ravine and excavates beneath it by scraping the loose dirt out with a flat rock. He digs until he has made a small chamber a meter deep. He then uproots some bushes and peels their bark until the branches are sticky with aromatic sap.

He crawls into the hole under the rock and scoops dirt back until only a small opening remains. He pulls the uprooted bush into the opening. He should be safe now. He is out of sight from surveillance satellites. The rock overhead should shield his body heat from thermosensors, while the pungent sap confuses chemosensors. A search party would have to stumble across him to find him now.

He does not notice a gray bird soaring in circles overhead.

Inside his burrow, Pari is tired, thirsty, and hungry. He cannot do much about food and water; they will have to wait. He closes his eyes and goes to sleep.

When he awakes, it is dark again. He listens carefully, but hears nothing unusual. He pushes the bush out and peers through the opening, but does not see anything alarming. He enlarges the opening and crawls out, stretching cramped muscles for a few minutes.

Then he is moving again in the compact run of a Marindian, loping across the chaotic terrain at a steady pace.

In the bottom of a steep ravine, he pauses to scrape hoar frost off the north side of a rock face. He lets it melt in his hand before sipping the water through parched lips. In a few minutes his thirst is slaked, and he continues his run. At the top of the ravine, he discovers a patch of thorn berries. Shriveled berries still cling to the vines, so he quickly picks a handful and gobbles them down. Soon after, his stomach begins to cramp, but the pain does not slow him. He finds several other patches of frost before morning.

He is lucky and finds an abandoned wolf den in which to spend the daylight hours. There are old bones with bits of marrow still inside that he sucks and tatters of skin and gristle to chew. A pallet of matted hair provides comfort as he sleeps.

The next night he reaches the breaks of the Vallis Marineris.

The following night he locates the sinuous canyon he seeks. He waits until daylight before going up it.

Deep within the canyon, hidden beneath overhanging cliffs, is the camp of his war party. Sentries watch him approach. He signals them the pass sign, and they allow him passage.

The camp is excited by his safe return. Dogs bark. Horses whinny. Warriors shout their greetings.

Pari staggers into camp and collapses into the arms of his war chief. He faints, secure in the knowledge he could not have been followed.

When he opened his eyes, the tribesman saw Kaly again standing over him with a dripping alphalash still in her hand. Risa and I stood apart, no longer synapsed with lasewires. He struggled in his shackles. They were secure. He realized what happened to him. His composure broke, sending his screams stabbing through the night. He had not screamed from the pain of the alphalash. Betrayal was a deeper pain from which there was no escape.

7

Kaly debriefed Risa and me. That consisted of the three of us watching a holomonitor play back the little dream-drama we had constructed inside the Marindian's head. Risa and I pointed out any discrepancies in the tape, if there were any; there weren't.

Kaly was in cyrine morphology. She grinned, obviously pleased. "A clever ruse," she said. "Simple, but clever. Use his own dreams to betray him. Let his own memories lead us to the others." She smiled at me. "If you continue with this kind of work, you'll have quite a career with the Corps." She got up from behind the monitor and paced back and forth. "We'll do a little search and destroy at dawn. Maybe a company or two of Ghost Cavalry. I'll want you two to go with them, to identify Geronimo." She looked at Risa. "You can go now, Corporal."

Risa padded out of the room.

Kaly looked at me with a leer on her face. "I feel the need for a private briefing."

I should have guessed.

"Let's go to my quarters and celebrate a successful interrogation." It was not a request.

● ● ●

We walked to her quarters together and went inside.

"Make yourself comfortable," Kaly said. She picked up a tray of mnemone sticks and held it out to me. "Help yourself," she said.

I created an image of myself in her mind reaching for one.

Kaly said something.

I did not have time to recognize the word before passing out in a grand mal seizure.

I knew what had happened as soon as I regained consciousness. Kaly had spoken the control command, triggering a hypnotically implanted reflex to cause a seizure, which had scrambled my thoughts and released control of her mind. My game was over.

"I don't know if you were messing around with my perceptions just then or not," Kaly said. "I don't have enough psionic capability to sense intrusion into my thoughts. That was just a warning so you'll realize I'm still in control."

I also knew what had gone wrong with my little game with Kaly. A hololens glittered from the center of the ceiling. Red laser beams criss-crossed the room. The other night they had not been red—they had been invisible. But they had been there, I realized, with a sinking feeling.

"I think red is much more passionate than infrared. Don't you agree?" She smiled wickedly. "I made a recording of our interlude the other night. I thought it might be amusing to be able to enjoy our games vicariously. It was the first time I'd thought of using a holocamera. I set it to infrared, because I didn't want to upset the spontaneity of the occasion." She snapped open a mnemone stick and stuck it under my nose. I inhaled the vapors, suppressing an urge to cough. Kaly sucked another into her lungs. Her eyes clouded momentarily. "Imagine my surprise when I played back the recording. I just sat around with an idiotic expression, while you rummaged about the place. That's not at all like I remembered. Why do you suppose that is?"

"A faulty memory?" I tried to laugh, but could not.

"I don't think so. I think a certain telepath has been playing mind-games with me. I think certain pleasures we've had have been imaginary."

"What difference does that make? Imaginary pleasures feel just as good. Probably better."

"Not to me." She slowly undressed me. "I want my pleasures to be real. I want my memories to be authentic."

I stood before her naked. She watched me as she took off her own fatigues. I did not like the way her eyes examined my body.

Soon she too was naked. Cyrine gynoids were not bad looking: obsidian skin, lithe musculature, taut belly, flat breasts with areolas the size of daisies. Kaly looked typically cyrine, but it was all cosmetic, her body did not have cyrine cybernetics. Spooks were all software. They were easier to kill than real cyrines.

As she stood before me, her breasts swelled with edema. Her pelvic sphincter opened, allowing labia and clitoris to protrude. Sex pheromone droplets glistened under her arms and between her legs. She was out of combat mode. Too bad. It would have been better for me had she stayed battle-ready.

She had an unpleasant leer on her face. She nodded in the direction of the ceiling. "I switched to red light so you would know about the holocamera. It's going to record everything that happens here tonight. You're a little too clever. I'm going to compare my memories with the recording of our little sojourn. If there are any discrepancies, you'll be shackled to that crucifix out there. I don't think you would tolerate it quite as well as a Marindian. Do you understand?"

I nodded.

My game was up with her. I was no longer going to be able to play mind-games with her. Now the sex would have to be real.

Kaly placed her hand on my chest and pushed me over to the couch. I sat down on it. Kaly knelt beside me. A vial dangled from a chain around her neck. She ran a finger down the center of my chest. "Do you do it with the cat-corporal?"

"You mean Risa?"

"Of course. R-6. Do you do it with her?"

"Yes."

"How do you do it?"

"What do you mean?"

"How do you do it when you're hunting, and you need a tight synapse?"

"The usual ways. You should know."

"From behind?"

"Sometimes."

"Does she pant?"

"Sometimes."

"Does she shriek?"

"Sometimes."

"Can you feel what she feels when you stick it in her?"

"Sometimes."

Kaly laughed. "Yes, I bet you can remember how that feels." She stroked my penis; it stiffened in her fingers. "How does this feel?"

"OK, I guess."

"Just OK?"

"Fantastic then."

"We'll see about that." She leaned over and took my penis in her mouth, making it even harder with her tongue.

After a bit, she looked up and smiled. "Do you trust the cat-corporal?"

"Of course."

"Do you trust her like a sister? Would you trust your life to her?"

"I think so."

"I wouldn't."

"Why not?"

"Cats are not to be trusted. They have no loyalty. What would you say if I told you I've had private briefings with her?"

"I don't believe that. She would have told me."

"See what I mean? She's not to be trusted. It's true. I've had her several times. You know how she purrs with it down her throat . . ."

I slapped Kaly's face.

She grinned at me. "Touch a nerve, did I? Here's another. What do you think your cat is doing right now?"

"I don't know."

"Maybe she's fucking a dog."

"Maybe she is. So what?"

"Maybe she'll like dog-fucking better?"

"Maybe she will."

"Have the three of you copulated together?"

"Maybe."

"I've had Terle also. Both ways. I like him as a wolf. I like the feel of his dog penis. Have you had him yet?"

"Of course not."

"Maybe I'll get all of us together later. Would you like that?"

"Suit yourself."

"I'll have to think about it. Actually I like you better than the cat and the dog. Do you know why?"

"Suppose you tell me?"

"I like your little boy penis. But I think the cat prefers a real man."

"I'm man enough for her."

"Are you?" She started sucking my penis again, running her tongue furiously over the tip, taking it down her throat.

A half hour later she looked up. "A real man would have come by now."

"I never come that way."

"I've never had a 'man' I couldn't make come."

"You've had your first."

"We'll see." She unscrewed the lid of the vial around her neck. "Nobody can be trusted. I've learned that, and you will too. You can't let them see your real self. But you have no real self to reveal, do you? I don't trust you at all. Don't forget. The recording better be exactly as I remember things."

She stuck her tongue in the vial and withdrew it. A drop of blue peptide hormone hung from it. She bent over, bringing her face close to mine. The drop of peptide fell into my eye. The ritual was repeated with the other eye. Soon synthetic passion burned in my blood as I was overcome by a testosterone storm. And, there was a brighter fire: endocaine.

Kaly lay on the floor and spread her legs. I entered her and began to thrust. Ten minutes later, Kaly shrieked with her first orgasm. She shrieked for another ten minutes before I rolled off and lay on the floor beside her.

"Tired already?" she asked. She stroked my penis, which was still stiff. "But you haven't come yet. You have no reason to be tired yet." She leaned over me again with peptide on her tongue and dripped it into my eyes. Sex steroid and speed burned along every nerve.

Things got a little confused.

At some time, Kaly metamorphosed into a Terran disguise named Saraltr. I missed the actual transformation.

Saraltr strapped on her artificial penis and chased me around the room. She finally cornered me, held me down, and was about to bugger me with it. Unwanted images rose in my mind. I pulled one hand free and groped around, finding an alphalash.

I beat her off me with the lash, then continued thrashing her, as she writhed on the floor. I whipped her with it until her body glowed as bright as a flourescent tube. With each stroke she howled, but they were not wails of pain. She kneeled in front of me, exposing areas of skin not yet on fire: face, breasts, inner thighs. I played the lash over those areas. She bent over, spreading her buttocks.

I climbed on top and entered her, ramming my pelvis viciously into her bottom, trying to bruise our flesh. Fire burned in my skin where it touched hers. I thrust for a long time. Her orgasmic shrieks did not dissipate the passion in my blood. I needed something more.

I began licking the fire. My tongue was seared with

each lick. Acid sweat burned in my mouth. I worked my
way down her body: face, neck, breasts, belly, thighs. I
buried my face between her legs and began sucking her
clitoris. It grew in my mouth and elongated. Labia
swelled into a scrotum. Soon I was sucking a penis—
real, not artificial. I could not stop sucking. The penis
grew larger. I wanted it within my body. I needed to feel
it there.

I pulled my mouth away and straddled the body that
lay on the floor. "Go ahead," Kaly laughed. "Give it a
try."

I held Kaly's penis vertically and lowered myself on it.
To my surprise, it slipped in easily. I had not so used my
vagina for a long time, as I considered myself male. I
rocked up and down. The hardness felt wonderful inside
of me. Mucosa stretched deliciously. I wanted it deeper.
Kaly's penis obliged and grew longer. I bounced up and
down. Moans escaped my lips.

"Do you like that?" Kaly asked. "Do you like the
way it feels? You pleasured me well. Now I'll do you.
You can share the pleasure."

"Yes, yes," I moaned, overcome with pleasure.
"Fuck me. Please fuck me."

A clockwork almost burst its warmth inside. Then the
images rose again; I remembered other nights, long ago,
when there was more pain than pleasure. I remembered
I was the master of illusion. I could not be fooled so
easily.

I circled my hands around Kaly's neck, squeezing
with my fingers. She beat at me with her hands, but her
blows were feeble. Her eyes bulged. Her lips turned blue
and drooled spittle. Soon her muscles became lax.

I released my hold before any permanent damage was
done.

I stood up, letting the limp penis pull out of me. Kaly
lay still on the floor.

I searched her quarters and found the holographic recorder. But Kaly had been smarter than I had thought.
The recorder was locked in a safe. I could not get to it
by myself. With Risa, I could have peeped the combina-

tion from Kaly's mind, but I did not have Risa. I would have to make do with what I did have.

I went into Kaly's unconscious mind and erased the evening's events. I also erased the memory that she planned to record this evening's "private briefing," and the suspicions that led to the thought. I left her with a memory of a perfectly satisfactory "private briefing" that had never happened. I made sure she entirely forgot about the camera and recorder.

I would be in good shape as long as she did not find the recorder and play it back.

My clever trick did not bring peace of mind to me. I left Kaly's quarters, knowing I had left behind a time bomb.

8

Dawn barely lit the eastern horizon, sparkling from ice storms in the upper atmosphere.

Ghost troopers filed into the open hatches of huvies, grim and silent. They were always that way in the early morning before a mission—a combination of fatigue and fear, with a little headache and hangover thrown in. Jocularity came easier after the fire-fight—then you knew you had survived another day.

Eight huvies warmed up that morning—enough for two companies of Ghost Cavalry. Two hundred troopers should be enough to roust a rag-tag band of Marindian guerillas, even if one of them was Geronimo. Any more huvies leaving on a mission would attract attention—Marindian spies always observed the comings and goings of the garrison. The spooks did not want their quarry flushing wild.

Risa and I waited on the tarmac for Terle. Kaly had decided he should come with us. I don't think she entirely trusted either Risa or myself. Terle was late.

The door to Kaly's quarters opened. For a moment, I thought she had decided to accompany us. A figure dressed in camoarmor came out and trotted over to the field. Lieutenant's battle embroidery were on the collars. Terle's face smiled from behind an open visor.

I looked toward Kaly's quarters. "A 'private briefing'?" I asked with a sneer in my voice.

Terle laughed. "Just some last minute instructions from the major," he said. "She doesn't want Geronimo getting away. She wants me to track him if he manages to slip away. She said I'd better not come back without him." He laughed again, less enthusiastically. "She said I'd take his place on the crucifix. I'm not sure she was joking."

"I'm sure she was not," Risa said.

"Then we better make sure he doesn't get away," he said.

We climbed into the lead huvy and strapped ourselves into our seats. The hatch closed, and we rose into the air and lazily drifted toward the north, the opposite direction from our true objective. We flew in formation, gradually increasing our speed, making a wide circle over the Arcadia, slowly turning toward the south.

We dropped to within a few meters of the ground and streaked southward at Mach .5, hugging the west flanks of Olympus Mons and circling around the great cone, before darting into the jagged peaks of the Tharsis Montes. Our altitude never exceeded ten meters from the surface.

It was quite a ride. I was glad I was strapped in. Despite the huvy's internal gravity buffers, my stomach felt like it was bouncing between my head and feet. A few more minutes of it, and I was going to be sick. The combrids acted like we were out on a leisure drive. Of course, they had the inner ears and cerebellums of bats.

We skimmed over the Marineris Breaks—steep, twisting, interconnecting canyons that were tributaries to the Valles Marineris. The Marineris Breaks had been badlands since the first settlement of Mars over a thousand years ago, hiding outlaws, renegades, and now guerillas. The terrain was too rough for surveillance satellites or reconnaissance flights to be of any use—the only way to adequately search the Breaks was with mechanized troops, and it would take a couple of divi-

sions to do the job. There was only one division of
Ghost Cavalry on Mars, and they had to man a hundred
garrisons, so they were spread too thin to do more than
a few perfunctory patrols of the Breaks. That was why
the Cavalry had to rely on Corps Intelligence to direct
their activities.

Because of Risa's and my efforts last night, the
Cavalry knew exactly where to go. Pari Tunavurur had
an accurate map in his head—most Marindians did. The
topography below was just as he remembered it. We
knew exactly which was the right canyon.

As we approached our target, huvies began peeling
out of formation. Four flew in a circle, disgorging
troopers in an airborne assault. Two flew down the canyon, only a meter off the canyon floor. While door
gunners sprayed the canyon walls with detonation
beams to stun the guerillas with ultrasonic bursts and
dazzle their eyes with light flashes, troopers jumped out
the back, rolled with the impact, and came up firing.

The two remaining huvies streaked up to a thousand
meters, where their troopers set up mortar and artillery
positions in mid-air, supported by p-grav platforms.
They were for backup, in case unexpected reinforcements should arrive.

Once empty of troops, the huvies began making tactical runs on enemy positions, dropping canisters of
nerve gas and smoke.

Risa, Terle, and I stayed in the huvy with the CO, a
Major B-8. I knew Bates slightly. He was not much different on a mission than he was off-duty—he seemed to
take things too seriously all the time. We were not combat troopers and would have only got in the way in a
fire-fight.

We caught the Marindians completely by surprise.
Only their sentries managed to get off any return fire,
and they were quickly suppressed. The others were captured in their lodges, still wrapped in sleeping robes,
largely without a struggle.

Within an hour, the camp was secure, and all the
Marindians were either dead or in shackles.

Our huvy landed and we climbed out. The camp was just as Pari had remembered it. One canyon wall was a sheer cliff. Thermal erosion had undermined the base of the cliff, carving out a series of shallow caves, completely hidden from the air. The Marindians had pitched their lodges inside these caves. Ground water bubbled from natural springs and there was good feed for their stock on the canyon's floor. Supplies could be brought in by horseback and not attract much attention.

We inspected the dead first, to be sure Geronimo had not been accidentally killed. He had not. None of the six dead warriors even remotely resembled the image I had extracted from Pari's mind. Next, the ghost troopers paraded each living warrior past Risa and I. There were twenty of them, but still no Geronimo.

Baker was about to have a fit. "Are you sure he's not here?" he screamed.

"Of course, I'm sure," I answered, as patiently as I could. "None of the dead or captured look like the Geronimo Pari Tunavurur knew."

"But are you certain? They all look the same to me. Maybe he's wearing a disguise."

"I'm sure the Marindian we're looking for is not here. But to be certain, we'll have to peep each one. That will take a little time. Why don't you send out some patrols to search for him—he might be hiding somewhere close."

"Alright. I guess that makes sense. Kaly will skin me alive if we don't find Geronimo. You know how she is."

I did indeed know how Kaly was.

Risa and I spent the rest of the day in a pathic synapse, peeping each Marindian's mind. Geronimo was not among them, unless he could disguise his thoughts as well as his appearance, and I was not willing to admit anyone but a spook could hide his thoughts from us. The other Marindians were as surprised as us that Geronimo had not been captured. His image was similar in each memory. The search parties had not found anything either.

"He must have slipped away last night," I told Bates,

"without telling anybody where he was going. Apparently he did that every once in a while. Maybe he has a woman he visits. His horse is also missing. It was bad luck he left right before our raid."

"Bad luck! You try telling Kaly about bad luck." He paced back and forth. "I guess I better get it over with and radio her the bad news." He disappeared inside the command huvy.

He came out carrying three field packs.

"What are those for?" I asked.

"Kaly says you, T-11 and R-6 are to get on his psychic trail, track him down, and find him. You're going to be resupplied in the field for as long as it takes to locate Geronimo. I don't think Kaly was too amused by our failure." Bates smiled for the first time all day. "You're supposed to call when you find him. The rest of us get to go back to the garrison."

I knew better than to argue with Kaly's orders.

Besides, she was right. We might be able to track him, since he had only left camp last night, and since I had a fairly accurate composite I'd extracted from the other Marindians' minds. With Terle's help, Risa and I might be able to follow his psychic trail.

The three of us stood together and watched the huvies depart.

There was nothing else we could do but try.

We made a field camp in the remains of the Marindian camp. Their lodges and other belongings had been taken back to the garrison for lab analysis, and their livestock had been run off by the battle. We would have to begin the hunt there anyway. We would have to wait for dark to start, since sunlight masked faint psychic emanations that were already eighteen hours old.

We built a fire and sat around it eating field rations.

The fare was about as good as you got back at the garrison, although if any of the spooks heard you say such blasphemy, you could count on eating garbage for a week. But field rations were not that bad. They came in compression pouches, squeezed down to one percent

of normal volume by the membrane-effect force field of
the pouch, and weighed practically nothing, thanks to a
wafer of p-grav built right in. A five course meal with
wine was about the size of a package of illicit tobacco-
smokes. A trooper could easily carry a hundred in his
pack—enough food for a month, even with giving some
away. The pouches were self-expanding and ther-
momatic—both warm and cold—and disintegrated to
dust an hour after they were opened. There were ten
basic menus, patterned after traditional Terran meals,
from French nouvelle haute cuisine to Australian billy-
beef. If you only liked quiche and bean sprouts, you had
to do a little trading. But on the whole, they were quite
palatable.

When we finished our trays, we threw them into the
fire. We each still sipped at the half-liter of wine that
came in each pouch.

"Do you think it wise to have a fire?" Terle asked.

"Why not?" Risa countered.

"There might be more guerillas in the vicinity. I
always kept cold camps and tried to be as unobtrusive as
possible on WOLF missions."

"You were vulnerable to attack," Risa said.
"Besides, the activities today would have scared off any
guerillas."

"You mean you aren't vulnerable to attack?" Terle
asked.

"Not Nate and I together. We could become invisible
to any living eyes for clicks around. We could paralyze
everyone as far as you can see, or make them cut their
own throats. Nothing living could sneak up on us,
awake or asleep."

"You have such power?" There was awe in his voice.

"Of course. I thought you knew. All that is easy.
Dream-hunting is the challenge."

"I could have used you two in the field."

"The spooks don't normally let us go out in the
field."

"Why not?"

"There are not very many path teams. The psigenes are rare and hard to get to take."

"There's another reason," I said.

"What's that?"

"I don't think the spooks like us to get too far away. I think they're afraid they'll lose control over us. They keep us close enough so they can always give us the control command."

"The control command?"

"Don't play dumb. A post-hypno command word that will render us unconscious, should we ever go berserk or mutinous." I looked at him hard. "I think you know the command."

"Me? Why should I?"

"I think Kaly sent you with us to watch Risa and me. I think you're our control."

Terle said nothing in reply.

"Well?" I asked

"I have my orders, same as you."

"I would say they're a little different."

"Not really. They're just orders. Do you think I enjoy being a lacky for the spooks?"

"I don't know. You might. I've heard worse of better men."

"Well, I don't. I just do what I'm told."

"And what were you told?"

"To make sure you two return from this mission."

"Do you think you can do that?"

"I think so, yes."

"What if we should short out a few synapses in your brain, leave you blind and crippled?"

"I don't think you could. I have limited telepathic powers. Kaly inserted a little hypnocommand in my mind this morning. If I feel you inside my thoughts, my brain will project the control command. Do you want to test it out?"

"I don't think so. A stalemate will suffice, I think."

"If you two are through arguing and beating your chests, we have a little hunting to do," Risa said.

She was right. It was well past dark and starting to get a little nippy besides.

We pulled shelter-halves out of our packs. They could be used as individual tents or joined together to make larger ones. We unfolded the shelters and zipped them together, then spread the common floor out on the ground and sat on it. A hemispherical force field sprang up around us. Soon the air was pressurized and warm inside.

"Let's get started," Risa said. She pulled off her camos.

I raised my eyebrows at her.

She smiled. "We're out in the field now. We don't have to be so professional." She pulled off my camos and then Terle's.

I have to admit I was ready. It had been a long day. I lay back and Risa climbed on top of me, inserting my penis into her vagina. Terle knelt behind her. I felt him go into her rectum.

We synapsed into the pathic gestalt.

We floated lazily in the psychic ether, climbing slowly out of the canyon, to soar high above. The ether was disturbed by the battle that day. Traces of thought tendrils lingered, but they were twisted together in a confusing jumble. We were patient. We were in no hurry. We had time to sort things out. We picked up each filament gently and followed it back in time to a mind sleeping the night before. Each led to a sleeping mind of one of the Marindians.

Then one did not. This filament left the camp and meandered through other canyons. We followed it cautiously, careful not to break the thread. The path was convoluted, but we persisted.

It finally led to a sleeping mind. But this mind was living in the present. Geronimo slept in a lodge with a woman a hundred kilometers away. He had ridden his pony hard night and day to get there. She had rewarded him well for his trouble. Now we knew where he slept.

We retreated, careful not to disturb his dreams.

Our orders were to find him, not torment him.

We drifted back to our bodies, letting the gestalt dissolve.

I felt Terle pull out of Risa. I was not yet finished. I rolled us over so I was on top. She put her legs on my shoulders, to more deeply receive my thrusts.

Terle was not through after all: I felt him enter my vagina from behind. The sensations were not at all bad. They were quite good.

Our thrusts synchronized.

I closed my eyes, overcome with delicious friction.

I was about to come. I felt coarse belly hair scraping my back, sharp claws digging into the flesh of my sides.

I came. My orgasm rippled in waves of pleasure through my whole body. But even though overcome with ecstasy, I knew something was wrong. We were not synapsed. I could not be feeling Risa's orgasm, and I could not have a penile orgasm by myself.

I pulled out of her. Nothing spurted from my penis, although delightful spasms throbbed between my legs.

Between my legs!

I knew who was between my legs.

I rolled over, jerking Terle out of me.

He stood over me, in lupine form, long tongue hanging from the side of a muzzle with too many teeth. His eyes burned with yellow fire. His lower body still thrust back and forth. His tail wagged furiously. Semen finally began to dribble from the red tip of his dog-penis.

I remembered the last time I had had my own orgasm, with my skin still on fire from the alphalash.

I had killed that man.

Hypnocommands are only as good as the mind they were in. Terle's mind was distracted by his orgasm.

I struck quickly, rearranging a few synapses that were inclined a certain direction anyway. He would suffer his psychophysio break a little sooner than normal. It would be a long time before he thought a rational thought or could get out of wolf form. I made sure of that.

I felt the command coming. But it was too late to save Terle.

I passed out.

I forgot almost everything.

So did Risa and Terle.

9

Dream-filaments unraveled, winding back into Kaly's mind. She sat up and looked at us.

"Where are we?" she asked.

"In a dream-game in a mind-casino."

"In Chronus?"

"Where else?"

"I suffered a break?"

"Apparently."

"I'm not sure I should thank you for curing me."

"It was unintentional. We wanted to find out what happened on that last mission."

"What made you think I knew?"

"You would not have left us out there alone without a bug. You saw the whole thing. That's why you had a break."

"How did you get away from Terle? How did you overcome the command?"

"He wasn't quick enough. We made him go rogue before he could think the control command. We didn't get away clean. Enough of it made it through to produce amnesia and extinguish the control reflexes. The control commands will never work again."

"Where are you going now?"

"Far away from here."

Her face turned cunning. "Do you still want to know who you were before? Do you still want to break the psicypher?"

"Of course."

"Terle knows the code."

"What! What makes you think so?"

"I know so. Terle was a special project of the Lord Supreme Commander himself. He had access to the psicypher codes. For some reason, he looked up your codes. He can release your memories."

"Why are you telling us this?"

"You could have plucked it from my mind."

"But we didn't. We didn't know you knew. You volunteered the information. Why?"

"I knew you would go after him."

"So."

"I want you to take me with you."

"Why?"

"He knows my psicypher also."

We knew she was telling the truth. We also knew she was not the same Kaly that she had been—the twisted part of her psyche had died when she had the break.

"Will you let me come with you to Mars?" she asked.

"OK," we said.

We rose in the air until the ground disappeared. We tumbled out of the end of a dream-filament. We were tangled in others. We untangled ourselves, and dropped through, finding ourselves again in the amphitheater. Risa got up from my lap.

I had no trouble recognizing Kaly this time. She looked just like the woman in the dream, except for being thin and cachectic. I pulled off the psihelmet. Kaly's persona disappeared from the game. The audience saw her stop breathing and her ECG line go flat. She had died, as far as they knew. Actually Risa picked her up, threw her over her shoulder, and carried her out of amphitheater.

With a little food and water, she should recover.

By the time we got to Mars, she should have back her

fighting strength. Who knows? We might even need her.

Not all the audience was fooled by Nate's illusion. One man had seen everything. One spectator had even monitored the events that had taken place in the dream-crystal.

Dat Lomni smiled as the pedi and the sphinx left, with the sphinx carrying Kaly over her shoulder.

He followed them at a safe distance, careful to keep one set of thoughts innocent. His other set of thoughts laughed with glee.

BOOK FOUR

DREAM-TRADER

1

The wolf lay hidden in an outcropping of rock, watching the lodges of a Marute village. The color of his fur was a perfect match to the rocks—he had a limited chameleon capability—and he was downwind, so he felt safe from detection. The pack that ran with him was foraging and might be a hundred kilometers away at the moment. Wolf packs required large territories, especially on Mars, where prey density was low, and prey was now pretty thin around this village. The annual bison migration would not start for several months. The pack had become hungry. They had probably gone down one of the caravan routes to see if they could pick off a lame horse or forage on some garbage.

Terle could find them when he needed them. Now he had other interests. He was watching the Marindian squaws and maidens as they went about their work. Most of the village men had ridden off on a hunting expedition.

As he watched the Marindian village, strange urgings moved in his body, strange longings rose in his mind. He did not know quite what to make of them.

Terle's perceptions were almost completely lupine. The human circuits in his brain were paralyzed with catatonia. What dim recollections he had of his human past seemed like bizarre dreams to his wolf mind. But even his wolf mind was disturbed by the nightmares of the alphalash and the memories of nights filled with sexual pain. His wolf psyche was not bothered in the least that its existence had begun *de novo* six months ago, as though it had materialized out of thin air, because it knew of no other kind of existence.

And, in a sense, the wolf had appeared out of nothing, waking up alone in a demolished Marindian camp, with his prior memories locked away in a psychotic corner of his hybrid brain. But a wolf did not need his own memories to maintain the continuity of his existence. His own memories had a trivial influence on his behavior. A wolf was directed by his instincts, his DNA dreams, the memories locked in his genes, accumulated over a million years of evolution. Genetic memory was just as valid for the Terra-formed wilderness of Mars as it had been for the wilderness of Earth. He hunted and killed and ate what he killed. He marked his territory with his own urine. He found a pack and if he could establish dominance, they would follow him. He mated when his nose brought the right pheromones into his blood. He howled at the moons of night. Instinct was enough. Thought was not necessary.

But there was something else influencing Terle. His mind still held a command from before. His wolf brain could not understand the reason for the command, but there was no mistaking the command itself. He was to track and follow a certain Marindian.

When he had awakened in a Marindian camp, he was alone. His nose told him there had been two others with him quite recently: one that smelled like a cat and another whose scent was human, but with gender pheromones confused. Fainter scents indicated a great many others had been there not too long ago, including the one he sought.

He followed the scent of the Marindian.

He followed it wherever it led. When he became thirsty, he found water. When he became hungry he killed and ate. During the day he holed up in whatever cover was available and dozed. At night he traveled. He found a pack and fought his way into it and became its leader. The pack followed the scent with him. When they found the Marindian, Terle was content to shadow him. Those were his last orders and they were stronger than instinct.

Terle followed him halfway across Mars, from the Vallis Marineris to the Cebrenian Highlands, stopping when the Marindian stopped, following when he moved on. For the past month, he had stayed in this village, so Terle had stayed nearby. Until now. The Marindian had left the village with the other men. Instead of following, Terle had stayed to watch the village.

Recently, Terle had been bothered by strange, new instincts. His dim wolf consciousness thought there might be something in the air that had triggered a hormone change, or maybe there had been some alteration in his circadian rhythms. His wolf brain did not know what was wrong, why he had become so fascinated by the Marute women. His human brain, had it been functional, would have known that a lycanthrope's hybrid cells began shedding transforming virus and lupine genes after being in wolf form for over six months. Intracellular plasmids destabilized. Those genes in his bloodstream were now producing a peculiar effect on his neuroendocrine axis. His body was shedding excess virons and plasmids in its secretions. The shed virus was infectious, and the DNA it carried was lupine.

Coded instructions in his mind were also unraveling.

But Terle did not know or understand any of it. All he knew was that some compulsion had him lying amid some rocks so he could watch the Marute women work. He could smell them and their musty woman scent made him feel strange, in a way that was both the same and also different from the way bitch wolves affected him when they were in heat. The sight of the women produced an uneasiness within him—like an itch that could not be scratched. Nor did he realize he was psionically broadcasting.

A Marute girl climbed on a horse and rode out of the village. As she rode past him, he examined her closely. Her face was fine-featured, unlike the coarse features of most Marutes; her hair was black and woven into long braids; her skin was as black as her hair and gleamed with monomer; she wore leggings and moccasins, but was naked from the waist up, except for a hishi necklace, hoop earrings and silver bracelets. Her scent excited him, he could still smell the milk-white lochia of a primary menses.

He followed her, keeping out of sight behind brush and rock. Soon they were out of sight of the village. Terle did not understand the urges that overcame his last command; he did not realize his cells were becoming unstable and soon he would become completely wild, in both mind and body.

The trail went by a large red boulder.

Terle ran ahead, keeping low to the ground. He climbed on top of the boulder and flattened down, changing his hair color to red.

The girl and horse approached. His tail stood straight out. As she rode beneath the rock, Terle launched himself into the air, growling loudly. The girl turned a startled face and raised her arms to protect herself. He struck her with his shoulder, instead of slashing her throat with his jaws as he normally would, and she fell from the horse and rolled down a rocky slope. Terle landed on his feet. The horse whinnied, wheeled around, and galloped back toward the village.

The girl lay still, cut and bleeding. She was sprawled on her back over a rock, with her head dangling on one side and legs hanging over the other. Terle sniffed at her mouth, body and crotch. Her smell sent shivers under his fur and spasms into his groin. He licked her cuts: her blood tasted sweet, but did not put him into a killing frenzy. He tugged off her breech clout with his teeth. Her leggings were not full pants and ended at the top of her thighs. He put his nose against her perineum and sniffed in the smell of her maturing genitalia. He licked her vulva, tasting her woman's secretions.

Terle's penis had stiffened, and its red tip protruded from the fur sheath. He climbed on top of the girl, mounted her and thrust his penis into her vault. Vaginal spasms gripped and held him. He spurted into her. As he ejaculated, he howled loud enough to wake the dead. The girl did not wake. Her vagina relaxed and released his penis. Terle leaped off. He heard the sound of more horses coming.

Terle loped away, disappearing into a ravine.

The girl's people discovered her. She was alive. They took her back to the village.

That night, when the moons rose, the wolf howled again.

The girl heard it and woke. When she finally fell back asleep, she too was bothered by strange dreams.

2

The sun, distant and cold anyway, was declining behind the Protonilus Mensa. Carbonic clouds gleamed blue against an already black sky, but would dim quickly. Nightfall came suddenly on Mars.

From the distant highlands, faint in the cold, thin air, came a sound that still sent shivers up the spines of men with any human genes and made their horses snort nervously with instinctive fear: the howling of a wolf pack.

The wagons of a trading caravan wound their way through the huge red boulders of the Utopia Planitia, heading south, toward the Cebrenian Highlands, leaving Marajo country and entering the homeland of the fierce Marutes. Unseen sentries from both tribes made sure the caravan did not stray from the trail. Yellow wolf eyes watched both sentries and caravan.

The caravan consisted of a dozen null-G wagons, each three by fifteen meters and thirty tons gross weight, but easily balanced on their one central wheel, as p-grav gyro-generators provided stabilization while reducing apparent mass to a few kilos. The road they followed was hardly more than a trail, but was typical of the caravan routes that meandered across Mars. Martian tribesmen disdained technology and would not allow improved roads to be built across their grasslands. Nor would they allow civilian modern vehicles—the wagons were pulled by teams of horses instead of semi-tractors. Clouds of red dust hung in the air behind the caravan, marking its passage across the plain.

Between each wagon and horse team, a teamster sat in a saddle seat sprung from the wagon tongue, wearing a psihelmet. A split cable ran from the helmet, each end plugged into a cyborg socket implanted in the horses' skulls. The teamster's and horses' brains were net-worked together into a gestalt: the man provided cogni-tion, while the horses provided locomotion, with no errors between thought and deed. Gone were the shouts and whistles and cracking whips associated with freighters of the previous millennium, replaced by a silent fusion of animal and man.

Armed horsemen rode beside the wagons. Without them, a war party might be tempted to circumvent the rituals of barter. Bands of guerillas ("bandits" to the Terran Colonial Office) roamed freely about the in-terior of Mars. The guards and teamsters were Aster-oidians—a group of sailors and sphinges—which was normal for trading caravans on Mars. They were armed with primitive projectile weapons and stun grenades—hybrids were not permitted to possess more modern armament. Other than their battle harnesses, they rode naked. Sunlight shone from the sphinges' fur and gleamed from the obsidian skin of the sailors. Asteroid-ian merchants controlled commerce in the space lanes; it should be expected they would also monopolize trade on the planet's surface.

The trader chief rode at the head of the caravan. He was a Terran. That was unusual. Terrans did not nor-mally do such mundane tasks as leading a trading caravan. They also were rarely found in the interior of Mars, preferring the amenities of the pleasure domes of Marsport to the primitive conditions found elsewhere on the planet. Terrans did not usually keep the company of hybrids either.

The trader chief raised his right arm, halting the

caravan, and stood up in his stirrups, staring intently
across the plain ahead. A cloud of red dust rose above
the prairie. One of the other riders, a female sphinx,
reined in beside him. She looked typical for her kind:
long and supple extremities, prehensile tail, sleek blue
fur covering her body, a black mane of coarser hair with
tufted ears sticking out, amber eyes with brown pupils
pulled into vertical slits, stubby nose, long whiskers
growing from her upper lip, sharp, pointed teeth.

"What it is?" she asked. Her name was Brit von Yee.
She was second in command. Her cat ears heard distant
gun fire. "Warriors," she whispered.

When the wagons had all stopped, the pounding of
horses' hooves could be heard. Then more rifle shots
sounded. The trader made a circular motion with his
arm, signaling the wagons to assume a defensive formation.

The trader's name was Marc Detrs. To casual inspec-
tion, he appeared to be a Terran of unaltered human
stock: average build, gray eyes, thin lips, skin the red-
bronze of mahogany, short-cropped yellow hair. An oxygen concentrator was clipped to his nose. A closer
look, however, would reveal the tiny scars of cosmetic
surgery and the internal sphincters guarding bodily
orifices, nictitating membranes over his eyes, and the
scalp ridges produced by embedded cyberwires. A
medscan would reveal the anatomy and physiology of a
combat cybernetic hybrid: a triple nervous system,
muscles four times standard strength, skin reinforced
with polymer laminations, bones and joints matrixed
with impact-resistant plastics, subcutaneous brown adipose. He was not human at all, but a most curious
hybrid.

From appearances, he might have been in his late
twenties. But he had been gestated on Earth nearly a
century ago. He was, indeed, an expatriated Terran
Aristocrat, and as such he had received anti-agathic
geneware. He was one of the immortals.

Detrs had always been discreet, shunning publicity.
He had disappeared from public view entirely for eight

years. His appearance as a trader chief on Mars went unnoticed—Martian Tribesmen did not keep up on current events and would not have known about his past. He could not have picked a better place to reappear.

But there was another reason he had come to Mars.

He had come as the Prophet. He let rumors get started that he was the Ghost Warrior, returned to lead the Marindians in war. He was establishing the first new religion to come along in a thousand years. His caravan was trading in theology rather than goods.

The chronotropic crystal had given Detrs the inspiration, or "revelation." He called his new religion Entropism.

Entropism was now well established among the Asteroidians; the monastery on Ceres was training a hundred monks a year, and there were temples on most of the inhabited asteroids. All the members of the caravan were Entropist monks. For several years, other monks had wandered across Mars, preparing the tribesmen for the coming of the Prophet. Detrs was well received in each village he visited. He preached what the tribesmen wanted to hear. He showed them the visions they wanted to see. Among other things, he advocated rebellion against Earth.

That was why the disguise as a trading caravan. The Terran Foreign Ministry's tolerance of theology did not extend to sedition. Detrs would be in big trouble if the Terran garrison on Mars knew what he was doing. He hoped by the time they found out, it would be too late.

At the moment, he was not worried. For the first time in years, he was enjoying himself. When Grychn had left with their baby boys, Detrs had become depressed. Being a tycoon was not a role he had liked. He cherished his memories of when he was a combat cybrid. The few years he was a pirate were particularly well remembered. Now he looked forward to several years as a warrior-prophet who would fight shoulder-to-shoulder with his followers. He would be the great Ghost Warrior. Less pleasant roles would be coming.

Besides, Detrs had always liked Mars. He found the

thin, cold air refreshing. He appreciated the solitude of the vast wastelands. He enjoyed getting away from modern conveniences. He even liked the long, dusty rides between villages, pretending not to notice the warriors who discreetly shadowed them along the way.

And he liked the Martian tribesmen, particularly the Marindians. They were fierce and sometimes brutal, but their word was binding and they would fight to the death for a friend. Such unambiguous loyalty was rare in the modern age. If he could recruit them to his cause and convince them to stop fighting among themselves, it would be a giant step for the rebellion. It was the key step. But each tribe's war chief had to be convinced separately he was the modern manifestation of the Ghost Warrior. That took time. And time was running out. Dinae and Nakai-Tsosie of the Marajos, Yellowfang of the Marcota, and Pimason of the Maraches had been convinced. If Cuthair of the Marutes could be brought into the fold, it would help. With the Marindians in his camp, the other tribesmen would eventually follow. But it was only a matter of time before the Lord Generals found out about his sedition. If he could convince Geronimo, the Marindian tribes would fall like dominoes to his cause. But how can you convince someone you can't find and whose real name you don't even know? Pimason had hinted that Cuthair might know how to find Geronimo, so Detrs had come halfway across Mars to talk to Cuthair. Sometimes he wondered if Geronimo was not as much a myth as the Ghost Warrior.

He wished his precognition would help, but it was totally unreliable. Clairvoyance came when it wanted to, not when he wanted it. The visions he had had of the immediate future were jumbled and confused.

A united Mars would be a formidable enemy, even for Earth. The other hybrid races would join in with a Martian rebellion. Detrs knew they could win this time around.

But a lot depended on convincing Cuthair to join the rebellion. Even more depended on his willingness to put

Detrs into contact with Geronimo. The Marute village was less than half a day's ride away.

But at the moment, there was another matter to consider. Horsemen were approaching at a full gallop. That could mean trouble. The only worse situation was when they were sneaking up on you.

The wagons had formed the classic circle, with each team pulled in behind the rear end of the next wagon. Each driver now crouched behind a turret-mounted light machine gun. The armed escort milled about in front, waiting for the situation to clarify. Detrs and Brit waited side by side.

It was almost dark. A light snow misted down from freezing clouds. The staccato pounding became louder; the rising dust cloud neared.

The traders waited. Horses stamped and fidgeted, while their riders peered into the dusk. Teamsters cocked-back bolts and swung their guns back and forth, making sure the gimbals did not stick.

They saw the wolf first because he was not obscured by the dust kicked up by the horses. He was running five hundred meters ahead of a group of Marindian horse warriors. He had reason to be elusive. A warrior would occasionally rise on his horse and fire a burst from his carbine, sending bullets ricocheting around the wolf. But at that distance and on galloping horseback, he had little hope of hitting the wolf. The warrior's strategy was to keep the wolf on the run and heading out into the Utopia. On the open plain, a wolf could not outrun a horse, as horses had more endurance. In the chaotic terrain of the highlands, a wolf stood a good chance of escaping, as he could maneuver through the tight places easier, and there was more cover. A wolf would not normally have been foolish enough to let the warriors chase him out of the moraine. Now his only hope was if daylight gave out before he became winded. He could elude the Marindians in the dark.

The traders watched as the wolf and his pursuers raced by a thousand meters away. The distance between them slowly narrowed. Daylight faded just as quickly. By the time they disappeared into the dust and gloom, the wolf had a scant hundred-meter lead. His darting back and forth had become more frantic. Soon all that could be seen was red dust settling back to Mars. The sound of gunfire was still faintly heard.

"Do you think he's one of ours?" Brit asked. A wolf pack had been trailing the caravan for several days. This pack had been a little atypical in that it would sometimes range ahead of the caravan, often leaving the bones of its kills scattered in the trail.

"Undoubtedly," Detrs answered. "We haven't heard them for several days. They must have gone ahead to wait for us. This one let himself get flushed."

"Do you think they'll get him?" Brit asked.

"I doubt it now," Detrs answered. "It'll be pitch dark in a few minutes."

"I'm glad." She smiled. Thin lips parted to show prominent canine teeth.

"Loyalty to your xenogenes?"

She laughed. "Maybe. Some of my DNA was derived from creatures as wild as that wolf. So I can empathize with him." Brit had once been a Terran Lady and had undergone hybridization to become an Asteroidian. Most of the Detrs' closest disciples were hybrid Terrans.

"Don't empathize too much. You may have more in common with him than you think."

"What's that mean?"

"I suspect one member of the pack is more than a Martian red wolf." Brit looked closely at Detrs. He continued, "I think one of them is a werewolf. He would just as soon eat a cat as a fat sheep."

"I'm not fat!"

Detrs looked at her. She definitely was not fat. "I might eat you myself," he said.

"Tease. You never keep your promises."

"Maybe tonight I will. We may as well camp here. We're already circled up, and it's too dark to go much further. Post an extra sentry—I don't feel safe with a band of warriors so close. They might be fired up enough to try something brash. I'll be in my wagon."

Detrs rode into the circle, dismounted, and handed his psihelmet to a teamster. The teams were already being unhitched. Feed and water would be placed for them in the center of the circle. Detrs opened the door to his wagon and went inside. In the distance, wolves bayed at the rising moons.

3

Nate, Risa, and Kaly arrived at Marsport.

They had taken a low-G tramp freighter from Chronus, so Kaly's body would have time to recover from the wasting debility of her last dream-game. The sunward trip had taken a month of standard time.

During that month, Nate and Risa nursed Kaly back to health. To the freighter's crew, they appeared to be three out-of-work sphinges going to a construction job on Mars. At first, Nate had to create the illusion both he and Kaly were sphinges, but when she recovered a little of her strength, the chameleon assumed sphinx morphology, so his own illusion was the only one he had to maintain. That was ridiculously easy. None of the crew ever suspected the real identities of the passengers they carried.

During the trip, the three of them got to be close. When Nate had agreed to take Kaly with them, he had never expected he would actually begin to like her. Grudging toleration was all he had expected. But she had really changed from the spook major he had known. And he had changed himself.

Eventually they had made love together, the three of them, and they had actually made *love*. Pleasure took the place of pain. Tenderness replaced nastiness. The neuroses of the past were almost forgotten. Past pain was forgiven. But they still were not completely comfortable in the lovemaking. Dim ghosts from the past still haunted their sex play. Sometimes they woke with the same nightmares. There were demons yet to be exorcised.

When they arrived on Mars, all three were friends.

Clearing customs was their hardest obstacle, and that was a breeze. During the sunward voyage, the freighter's purser had issued crew papers to three new crewmen, although he did not remember doing so, and the ship did not have three new crewmen. A spaceship's crew did not need either passports or visas to visit free ports such as Marsport; their ship's papers sufficed.

Three sphinges disembarked from the freighter; three sailors presented their papers to a bored customs officer, who told them to be sure to return before their ship left in a week. Once past customs, they became a sphinx and two sailors.

They walked to their hotel, anxious to stretch their muscles after the space voyage. The sights and sounds and smells of the bustling city buffeted them like space turbulence.

Marsport was a free port in spirit as well as law. The restrictions that applied to the rest of the planet did not apply to Marsport, so almost every kind of activity thrived there. The Martians hoped Marsport would be a buffer to keep and hold foreigners with their corrupting influences, so the interior of Mars would remain untainted. This xenophobia had its origins in history. The original colonists of Mars had all been derived from ethnic groups that had been uprooted by foreign immigration: Amerinds, Arabs, Abos, Eskimos, Basques, and Massai. They were protective of their new real estate and wanted to make sure squatters stayed away. But they knew the importance of maintaining contact with the rest of the System. So there was Marsport.

Marsport was famous throughout the System. Its Combat Zone was infamous. The Combat Zone separated the spaceport from the city proper. Sailors on leave did not have to walk far for their amusements. And there were many amusements available.

They walked past luxury hotel/casinos that advertized billion credit psino games and glittering floor shows with top name entertainers. In the shadows, mutitutes pleaded pathetically. Along side streets there were peptide parlors, mnemone dens, disease galleries, hybrid shops, death salons, toxic theaters, sliversmiths, and pheromone booths. There was even a brand new Entropic temple. The streets were crowded with humans and every variety of hybrid, including nonoxygen breathers like Elves and Erinyes. Holosigns flashed brightly; display windows flickered with subliminal images. The noise level was deafening—a cacophony of a million voices, footsteps, music, whining gravturbines, screeching tires, slamming doors, subsonic advertising. A thousand scents mingled with each other: mnemone, body sweat, pheromones, food, liquor, even forbidden tobacco smoke.

Vice prospered in the Combat Zone because it was regulated and taxed. The consumer was confident he would get what he paid for, except on Thursdays, which was Bunco Night.

Nate and Risa had once made a fortune there as a path team; Nate was almost sorry they had become reformed. But they ignored the beseeching voices, the entreating images, the imploring subsonics. They walked down Barsoom Boulevard. Soon they came to their hotel.

They checked into the John Carter Hotel and went up to the penthouse. Nate and Risa did not like other minds to be between them and the ether when they were dream-hunting. The deskdroid had sniggered when they registered—his fuddy-duddy synthetic mind thought two sailors had purchased the favors of a sphinx for the evening: Nate could fool any organic brain. But the deskdroid said nothing. Money was money and sometimes the penthouse went vacant.

In the suite, they took off their clothes and took a

shower together. Then they lay on the bed and made love. Three-way sex was a lot of fun with a hermaphrodite and a chameleon—the possibilities were endless. Nate was sandwiched between Risa and Kaly; his penis was in Risa's vagina; Kaly's penis was in his. Each had his own orgasm. Nate was satisfied with one that came from penetration, no longer afraid of female sensations, at least with Risa and Kaly.

"Are you sure you still need to find Terle?" Kaly asked as she lay naked between Nate and Risa.

"No. I'm not sure of anything."

"You don't seem to be so driven anymore. Some of the intensity is gone."

"I am almost contented. I have found peace, except for the lingering nightmares. My mind cured itself. The amnesia was restorative for me, just as dream-gaming was for you."

Kaly snorted. "Don't lie to me. I know you switched around a few functional synapses inside my head. You cured me."

"You cured yourself."

"I don't believe that. You should become a psychsurgeon. You could be the best there ever was."

"No, he can't," Risa said. "We can't do anything like that. We're deserters from the Corps. If we went back, they would demill us. Don't you know how they demill chameleons? It would be the same for us."

Kaly shuddered. "Yes, I do know about demilling. But what's left? Are we to be fugitives for the rest of our lives?"

"There are worse fates," Risa said.

"Maybe if we knew who we had been, we might find out who we are to be," Nate said.

Kaly laughed. "You might be in for a nasty surprise. You might not like what you find."

"That's always a risk with seeking the truth."

"When do we start looking?"

"Tonight."

We soared high in the psychic ether. The hemisphere

below was dark with night. Millions of dream-tendrils
rose from sleeping minds. We plucked them one at a
time, looking for just one. He could run, but he could
not hide his dreams. We would find his dreams, and
they would lead us to him. Eventually, he would dream
again. It was just a matter of time.

Terle flattened himself behind a lone rock, willing his
hair to blend into the same red shade as the soil. It was
pitch dark with cloud cover blocking the starlight, but
Terle's wolf eyes had full night-vision. He hoped the
Marindians' eyes had not dark-adapted yet. They were
galloping toward him. Only the darkness and camofur
would save him from detection. Hiding was his only
hope now. He was winded and could run no longer.

He had been careless letting the Marindians flush
him. He had been watching the village, waiting for
dark. Dim fantasies had risen in his brain, distracting
him from paying attention to sensory input. When he
had finally heard them, they were too close for him to
slink away. He had to bolt from his cover and make a
run for it. Then he had made a wrong turn and had been
forced out on the plain with its scant cover. He had been
very careless.

The Marutes thundered by. Terle held still. They had
not seen him hide; they thought he was still running
ahead of them.

One of the Marutes turned and looked in his direction. Their eyes locked briefly. It was the girl! Terle
remembered her taste and smell. He remembered the
spasm. She must see him. In a second she would shout
and point. Maybe he should bolt again, now that they
are on the other side. Maybe he could make it back to
the highlands and find some decent cover. He knew he
could not. He needed to catch his wind. He remained
frozen, wishing he would have had time to dig a hole.

The girl looked away. She had not seen him. The
Marutes rode past.

Terle followed them at a safe distance. When they

stopped at the traders' camp, he stopped also. When the moons rose, he howled.

The camp heard. Their horses whinnied and stamped their feet. He howled again, wanting to disturb another's dreams.

4

Night had deepened. Stars shone brightly overhead. To the east, two moons were rising.

A cold wind blew in gusts, rattling icy snow against the circled wagons. The temperature had already dropped to minus twenty degrees.

The horses stood tails into the wind, pleasantly chomping hay. They were squat and sturdy, covered with plush fur and padded with thick layers of brown adipose. They were Martian horses—hybrids—with a lot of musk ox and caribou DNA, a little seal and walrus, a smattering of penguin. Minus twenty degrees was a heat wave for them—they had been hybridized to thrive in temperatures of minus two hundred degrees, their breed having been first introduced on Mars over a thousand years ago, before Terra-forming had mellowed the climate much.

Asteroidians were nearly as tolerant of cold as Martian horses. They could survive brief exposure to the vacuum of space at twenty degrees absolute, but did not have sufficiently thick brown adipose to tolerate prolonged cold vacancy. In truth, they preferred to live in a standard Terran climate, though most would not admit it.

The members of the caravan were eating supper inside the cook wagon, in twenty-five-degree warmth and pressurized to a comfortable four hundred torr. At one end were the bins containing ration packs and beverage pouches. Fold-away counters and stools ran along both sides, with similar tables and chairs in the middle. There was more than enough room for the twenty traders. The wagon also doubled as a conference room and lounge at other times.

Detrs and Brit had just sat down together at a table. They each had a standard ration tray. As they peeled the lids off, the microwave generator built into the tray heated or chilled the contents of each compartment to the proper temperature. In thirty seconds, they were ready to eat. Detrs had a seven course neo-French with chilled tossed salad, roquefort dressing, cream of broccoli soup, chateaubriand, truffles, asparagus tips, rice, and a chocolate mousse. Brit favored more basic fare, having shrimp cocktail, steak tartar, cheese soufflé, and ice cream. Both had wine.

Detrs picked at his tray, watching Brit devour hers. He was tired of trail rations. Everything was either cultured or synthetic. He knew that on a molecular basis, one could not tell synfood from organic, but his palate could. Organic food snobbery was the one vestige of his Terran ancestry that he had not shed. He sipped his wine. At least it was real.

The wine began to warm his insides.

He looked at Brit. Light shone from her fur, gleamed amber from her eyes. Detrs had always had a fondness for sphinges. He had met Brit a long time ago on Ganymede in a club called *Critical Mass*. Grychn and he had still been together, but their sexual relationship had been "open" then, as was the current vogue. Brit had just raced in the Ceres' Cup and had nearly been killed when her racer had gotten too close to Jupiter, becoming trapped in its gravity well. Her pilot and lover was seared with radiation during the rescue. She abandoned him to rad sickness and sought a new lover. She found Detrs. She nearly got him killed also.

Brit von Yee was really Lady Brit, and had once been an immortal Terran aristocrat. She had become bored with life as a human and had undergone hybridization into a sphinx, helping build New O'Neil. Construction bonuses only augmented her already considerable fortune. Then she wandered about the System, sampling its vices. She had dream-gamed in Chronus. She visited peptide parlors, mnemone dens, toxic theaters, death salons. She raced in the Ceres' Cup. She became a pirate with Detrs and betrayed him to the Space Guard, resulting in his capture.

Detrs forgave her betrayal. He knew she was driven by feline racial memories, and one could not expect loyalty from a cat. He let her join the Entropist Movement because a premonition told him her next betrayal would not be significant. But he still could not quite trust her. He knew better than to let himself get too close to her. She could hurt him more, if he let her. And he had been hurt by experts.

But she was still fantastic in bed.

A thousand years of practice had honed her technique.

Looking at her still made testosterone spill into his blood. He knew he would want sex with her again tonight.

His reverie was interrupted. Someone seemed to whisper in mid-air next to his ear. *Boss, we've got trouble.* It was Rhondis van Doer, one of the sentries. There had been no sound though.

Detrs wore a gold headband containing standard cybernetic induction coils and a psiwave transceiver. Since he had once been wired as a cyborg, the transceiver could bypass ears and mouth, being connected directly to auditory and vocal cerebral cortex.

What kind of trouble, he asked in his thoughts.

Marjun trouble.

He got up, grateful for an excuse to leave his meal. "You better come with me," he told Brit.

They did not bother with outerwear, not planning to

stay outside too long. There was a faint crackle as they opened the cook wagon's door and walked through the barofield that maintained pressurization within the wagon. Snow stung their eyes briefly before nictitating membranes closed. They walked past dozing stock to the far side of camp.

Rhondis sat behind a turret-gun with an open bolt. The gun barrel was pointed toward a half-dozen Marindian warriors still mounted on their horses. No doubt the same Marutes who had been chasing the wolf. They did not appear particularly fierce at the moment—just cold and hungry. Their rifles were in scabbards.

Detrs walked between two wagons and approached the Marindians, holding his right palm outward. The warrior in front likewise raised his right hand.

"Towaoc," Detrs said.

"Towaoc," came the gutteral reply.

"I am Marc Detrs, chief trader of this caravan."

"I am Sivatuch, first son of Cuthair, leader of the Cebrenian Band of Marutes. We have wandered too far from the village of our people and ask if we might share the campfire of our cousins from the shining asteroids." The Marute looked closely at Detrs, finally realizing he was neither sailor nor sphinx. He did not comment further.

"We would be pleased to share our campfire," Detrs answered. He had no choice—Marindian customs required taking travelers into one's camp. Besides, this was a chance to befriend Cuthair's son.

He led the Marindians past a still nervous Rhondis. Several teamsters helped them feed and water their horses. Then they all trooped into the mess wagon.

The warriors grabbed a ration tray in each hand and sat together at a table. Detrs and Brit sat by themselves at another table. The Marindians must have had trail rations before, because they all seemed to know how to handle the cartons. They apparently did not mind eating synfood, devouring two trays each. It occurred to Detrs they had probably been in the saddle all day without

food or water and could have gone several more days
without complaining.

While the Marutes ate, the rest of the trading party
gradually went to their wagons, leaving Detrs and Brit
alone with the Marindians.

As he watched them eat, Detrs saw that one of the
warriors was a woman—a girl, really, of about six Martian years. She was dressed the same as the men, wearing leather leggings decorated with colorful beadwork,
moccasins in the same design, and nothing else except
jewelry. She wore a little more of that than the men,
with hoop earrings, a hishi necklace, and silver bracelets
on both wrists. Her thick black hair was braided. Her
face was narrow and her features fine for a Marute—her
mother may have been from another tribe. Like the
others, her skin was an ocher-black and gleamed with
monomer sweat. Physically, she was mature, having
completed the changes of puberty; she had a woman's
breasts, though they were still mostly nipple; she was
padded out with brown adipose in pleasing curves; she
was nearly as tall as the men. She would have already
had her primary menses and would be sexually active.
That she was riding with a hunting party meant she had
not started secondary menses—fertile women were married and stayed at home with their mothers-in-law and
babies.

Detrs felt testosterone burn. Brit had started a sex
steroid fire in him, but now Detrs was aroused by the
girl. He felt a little ashamed—she was young enough to
be his great-granddaughter. Then it occurred to him
this girl's mother was young enough to be his grand-
daughter, and she was probably already old and hag-
gard. Marindian women bloomed and withered quickly.

The girl noticed him staring at her. He looked away
quickly, amused that she could make him uncomfortable, and studied the other Marindians.

Except for Sivatuch, the other warriors were typical
Marutes, with squat bodies, round faces, and flat noses.
Sivatuch resembled the girl—brother and sister perhaps.

None of the Marindians spoke while eating. In a

feast/famine culture one did not delay getting calories into one's system with chit-chat. Detrs and Brit sipped wine and did not speak either. It was not long before the trays were scraped clean, lips wiped with fingers, and hands wiped on leggings.

Sivatuch got up from the Marutes' table and sat down with Detrs and Brit. Detrs opened a can of wine and set it in front of the Marindian, who drank half in one pull. He looked at Detrs for a while before he spoke.

"I think you are more than a trader," he said finally. "Who ever heard of a Mitikie trader? I think you are this new Prophet we have heard about."

Detrs said nothing. Sivatuch looked at him. "You don't look much like a prophet."

"What's a prophet supposed to look like?" Detrs asked, careful to use the Marute dialect.

"Well, like a Marindian, for one thing, and preferably a Marute."

"Maybe the Great Spirit is egalitarian in regard to the body in which He places His Prophet."

"Maybe. But I would feel better about it in any other body than a Terran. But that is not for me to decide. The Poagat and my father will determine if you are the true manifestation of the Ghost Warrior. We've waited fifteen hundred years for him to return—I hope you are the one."

The other warriors sat quietly drinking. The girl stared at Detrs—for a moment, their eyes locked together. Detrs looked away. There was no mistaking what he had seen in her eyes. Sweat beaded along his back like it had not for a long time. She got up and stood behind Sivatuch.

"Why were you chasing the wolf?" Detrs asked. "I thought wolves were considered sacred."

"They're sacred until they misbehave."

"How did this one misbehave?"

"He attacked one of our women."

"Was she hurt badly?"

"No. Just cuts and bruises. But once they get the taste of man flesh and the idea they can attack people, there's nothing else to do but hunt them down and kill them. His tail will make a nice ornament for my lance. His hide will make a rug for my lodge."

"How did the wolf get away?" Detrs asked Sivatuch.

The warrior shrugged his shoulders. "He disappeared into the darkness. Maybe he found a hole to crawl into. We will find him again. He will not be so lucky next time."

"Maybe it was not luck."

Sivatuch's eyes narrowed. "What do you mean?"

"Maybe it wasn't an ordinary wolf. Maybe abilities other than cunning and guile allowed it to escape. Could it have been a werewolf?"

"A werewolf? I don't know. I've never chased a werewolf. Ordinary wolves are the only kind we've ever had—they are hard enough to kill."

"When was this pack first noticed?"

"The remains of their kills were found starting about a month ago."

"Then it is probably the same pack that has been following this caravan for the past few days. I suspect one of them is a werewolf."

"I thought werewolf stories were just for old women to tell children to scare them."

"How long has it been since the Marutes warred against the Terran garrison?"

"Too long. Over twenty years. The last warriors to fight Ghost Cavalry are old and fat."

"Then you have not had the WOLVES among you. They were developed only ten years ago."

"What are WOLVES?"

"An elite Terran terrorist unit, consisting of hybrid-ized zooanthropes, mostly lycanthropes—shape-changers, werewolves. They are quite effective against the tribes who herd livestock. The stress of shape-changing sometimes proves too much, and the wolf goes rene-gade, running with and leading a real wolf pack."

"What makes you think this wolf is a werewolf?"

"A member of the WOLVES went renegade six

months ago south-east of here, in Marache land. He has not been killed or captured since. The wolf pack following us has been acting peculiar."

"Wolf or werewolf, it doesn't matter. I can kill either."

"Don't be too sure of that. Werewolves are psionic. They can make you see something not really there. Or not see." Detrs stood up. "You and your warriors are welcome to bunk in here."

Sivatuch laughed. "We are not old women yet. We will sleep with our horses outside." He winked at Detrs. "If a werewolf comes, I want to fight him in the open air." He laughed again.

They all went outside. The girl pushed past Detrs, letting her bare breasts brush his arm.

The Marindians went to the center of camp, where their horses were already bedded down. Each warrior wrapped his saddle blanket around himself and lay down beside his horse. The temperature was minus thirty degress.

Brit followed Detrs to his wagon. "Are you going to keep your promise?" she asked.

"What promise?"

"About eating me." She smiled, showing him sharp canines.

"Not tonight." He looked past her.

She followed his eyes. The girl stood by herself, the only Marindian not yet bedded down. "I see why," she said. "I never thought of you as a pedophile before. A shame we don't have a pedi with us."

"It's not that."

"Then what else."

"Divine Purpose." Detrs smiled.

"More like Divine desire," Brit snorted, as she turned and left.

Detrs went into his wagon and waited.

He did not have long to wait.

She opened the door and entered without knocking.

The only sound was the crackling of the barofield as she passed through it. She stood for a moment in the doorway, looking around warily.

Detrs sat on the couch that unfolded into his bed, sucking on a mnemone tube. He motioned for the girl to sit in a chair. "What is your name?" he asked.

"Musach," she answered, sitting down.

"Can I offer you anything? A drink?" He held out the tube. "Mnemone?"

Musach laughed. "You're funny," she said. "I don't need synthetic feelings. The real ones are still new to me."

"What can I do for you?" Detrs asked with a smile.

Musach laughed again. "You are funny. You know our ways. You know what I want, what I cannot be denied." Her teeth flashed white. Proud cheekbones shone.

"Your father might get angry with me."

"He does not have that right. Not for another six months."

"I thought you might wait for the others to sleep before you came."

"Why? I can do as I please, see whom I want. Besides, Sivatuch has posted a guard; someone will be awake at all times. I don't think he entirely trusts you yet."

"And you? Do you trust me?"

"No. Not yet." She licked her lips.

"Then why are you in my wagon?"

"Trust has nothing to do with what I want from you. Maybe later I'll trust you. I might even believe you in time. The Mitikie have cheated and deceived us for fifteen hundred years. Why should I think you are any different than all the others?"

"Because I am different. And you? Are you the same as the other Marutes?"

"I too am different than the others. They are content to ride about on their horses, chasing wolves, hunting the buffalo and elk. Our women are content to work day and night like dogs, supporting men who think they are too good for anything but war and hunting. In the winter, they sit in their lodges and have babies. I want more than that. Maybe I'll go with you."

"I haven't invited you to come with us."

"You would, if I wanted you to."

"You're confident in your charms anyway."

"I saw the way you looked at me. I know what you want." She laughed. "I want the same thing." She pulled off her leggings and moccasins and stood naked before him.

She was well built, with lithe legs and slender waist. Black braids hung to her buttocks. Monomer shone from her skin and glistened from a scant patch of pubic hair. Her eyes gleamed behind open nictitating membranes with their own fire. She was young and proud of her youth and eager to see what she could do with it.

Detrs admired her youthful beauty. Testosterone throbbed in his brain. "How old are you?" he asked.

Musach laughed. "Old enough. I have been a woman for six months. I'll be free for another six, before my father marries me off, and I must be faithful to one man. But I might not want marriage. I might not want to give up my freedom."

"Those are the ways of your people. You have no choice. You know what they do to a wanton wife. You wouldn't want that to happen to you."

"I can leave the people."

"I thought Marutes withered when they left the homeland."

"Our ancestors left the Earth. Do I look withered?" She pirouetted for him.

Detrs stared at her. He knew lust burned from his eyes.

Musach laughed, enjoying his interest in her body. "Let me see you," she said.

She leaned over him, tugging off his tunic and trousers. She stroked his smooth skin, slick with monomer, and massaged his hard muscles, moving

down his body. Her hands felt his crotch. She jerked
them away when she felt nothing there and stood back,
perturbed.

"Is something wrong?" he asked.

"I thought. . ." she stammered. "From the way you
looked at me. . . I didn't know."

"There's a lot you don't know yet," Detrs said.
"Watch."

He went out of combat mode, relaxing his cremasteric
sphincter, allowing penis and scrotum to descend from
their pelvic pouch. Sex pheromones began exuding from
his pores. "I was once a combrid," he said. Then he
laughed, "But you have never lain with a combrid, have
you?"

The Marindian girl must not have smelled sex pheromones before, because they provoked an immediate
response. She panted and sweat poured from her skin.
Her nipples became erect.

Musach stroked his penis with her fingers, rubbing
stiffness into it. She giggled gleefully as it swelled in her
hand.

"You've been on the trail all day. The wagon has running water. We could take a shower together."

She looked at him like he was crazy. "Water is too
scarce on Mars to waste on baths. What's the matter, do
I stink? Besides, let's not waste any more time. I want
you now."

Detrs pulled her to him and kissed her lips. She
slipped her tongue past his. She smelled of horse sweat
and leather and red Martian dust. She smelled wonderful.

His sex pheromones surrounded them in hazy lust.
Her naive nervous system, with no tolerance, resonated
with his testosterone storm. She quivered.

Musach straddled him on her knees, lifted her
bottom, and reached down to insert him into her. She
placed her hands on his shoulders and bounced up and
down. Detrs was overcome with delicious friction.

Her orgasm took much longer to come than his, but
his penis remained stiff by the tightening of his pelvic

sphincter, until she finally shrieked with delight.

Later they turned down the bed and lay together in it.

"How many women have you lain with?" Musach asked. "You are the sixth man for me, although, in truth, the other five have been boys."

"I couldn't count them all."

"That many?"

"I'm almost a hundred standard years old. Nearly fifty Martian years. That's a long time to remember."

"It's been six months since my first flow. One boy a month. Of course, each one has been more than once. Except Lehi. I didn't like him too much. In another six months, I'll be married to Togwoev. Then he'll be the only man I can sleep with. Maybe I'll have six more lovers before then."

"Maybe."

"I think I may want more lovers than that. What if Togwoev is not good in bed?"

"That's the chance you take when you marry."

"I don't want to take that chance. I like sex too much." She sighed, stroking her thighs. "Are you really the Prophet? The Ghost Warrior?"

"Yes."

"Prove it to me. Make me believe."

"I can't make you believe. You either will or you won't. You want to believe in the Ghost Warrior?"

"Of course."

"Then soon you'll know I am him." Detrs wished she would not have to be the one. But he had no choice in the matter.

"Do you have any children?" she asked.

"I had two sons once. Twins."

"What happened to them?"

"Their mother took them away from me."

"I'm sorry."

"Don't be sorry. You may lose your sons because of me."

"Will I be famous for sleeping with the Ghost Warrior?"

"Yes."

"I'm not sure I want to be famous."

"You have no choice now. How is it you're riding with your brother and the other men? I thought Marute men didn't like women riding in hunting parties."

Musach spat. "I don't care what the men think—I can ride anywhere and do anything until I'm married. Besides, I have a grudge. Revenge is the purest motive for Marutes."

"Revenge?"

"The wolf attacked me and knocked me off my horse."

Detrs was quiet for a moment, thinking. He looked at her naked body and ran his fingers over her smooth, young skin. "You don't seem to be injured."

"A few cuts and bruises. No more than I would have got from falling off a horse. I guess he was scared away before he could eat me. I had been knocked unconscious."

"Don't bet that he didn't eat you."

"What's that mean?"

"Nothing. You were lucky. Let's go to sleep. I'm an old man and I need my rest."

They went to sleep together.

Musach awoke screaming. Detrs held her close. Far away, a wolf howled.

"A nightmare?" he asked.

"I think so. I never had them until a few days ago. It's always the same. A wolf is chasing me. I run away, but I'm running on all fours. When he catches me, instead of slashing my throat with his teeth, he mounts me. And I like it."

Detrs said nothing.

"Does it mean anything?"

"Dreams always mean something."

"I'll ask the shaman. He knows about these things."

"That's a good idea."

"Are there really werewolves? Are the stories true?"

"You talk too much," he said, kissing her.

Detrs made love to Musach again. Her youth made

him more sexually excited than he had been for years. He tried not to think about how quickly her youth would fade.

They slept again and did not wake until morning.

Terle watched the camped caravan from beneath a bush on a hillside a few hundred meters away. He had crept closer and closer to the camp as the night wore on, but now he had approached as close as he dared. If the wind shifted it would blow his scent to the horses and startle them, alerting the sentries. The guards had fallen alseep, even the Marindians. The camp was quiet.

Terle called with his mind. He was not conscious of what he was doing—his wolf mind was not cognizant of much on a sentient level—but he had latent short-range telepathic ability, and he was using it now.

He saw movement in the camp. A dark shape stepped out of a trailer and walked through the camp quietly, slipped through a gap in the circled wagons, and came toward him. It was the girl. She was naked. She dropped to all fours when she reached him.

Her eyes were open but looked blank. Her brain still slept.

Terle licked her lips, and she licked his muzzle, curling her lip in submission. He sniffed her rear end while she smelled his, then he licked her vulva. She began to pant.

He mounted her, hooking his front paws around her waist. Her vagina caught and held his penis. He ejaculated twice before he stopped thrusting. When she released him they curled up together and slept.

Well before dawn, Terle sent the girl back to the camp. He watched as she slipped in without waking the sleeping guards. When he saw she had made it back into the trailer, he waited for a few minutes, then he sneaked close to the camp, howled, and ran away silently.

If his wolf mind had had a sense of humor, he would have laughed at the commotion he created.

5

The whole camp, Asteroidians and Marindians, was awake when Musach left Detrs' wagon. A wolf had stampeded both their stock, and it took hours to catch the frightened horses. There was no doubt she had spent the night with the man calling himself the Ghost Warrior.

Detrs was not quite as sure of the situation, now that his testosterone storm had abated. He knew Marindian mores and realized they had done nothing improper by Marindian standards. But he wondered whether the Ghost Warrior should be sleeping with the chief's daughter. Why not? What Marindian warrior would pass up Musach? None Detrs had ever known.

Brit would be irritated though. He had half promised her the evening. A little annoyance would do her good. She had teased him enough in the past. But she would come around with time—she always did. Besides, it might be good to have her mad at him for the next few days. He knew Musach would want to come back to his bed.

They had a quick breakfast of coffee and rolls. Detrs had to undergo some good-natured ribbing from the others. Sivatuch and the other Marindians did not say much.

They broke camp.

For the Marindians, that was quick and easy: they threw the same blankets they slept in over their horses, hopped on, and were ready to travel. For the traders, it was a little more involved. They secured their wagons, hitched their teams, and were ready to go.

They followed the caravan trail south, slowly climbing into the Cebrenian Highlands. The terrain steadily became more chaotic. A thousand years ago, before Terra-forming, there had just been jumbled rocks and irregular, randomly twisting ravines. Now water erosion was beginning to form canyons. In a few more thousand years, there would be real valleys. They passed deer and elk and bighorn sheep—all successfully hybridized to survive on Mars. Occasionally they would see the scattered bones of an old wolf kill.

Brit rode beside Detrs. Musach rode on his other side. Brit did not say much, but Musach made up for it jabbering away about anything and everything. So much for the silent Marindian stereotype.

At midday they arrived at the village.

The Marindians rode on in to the encampment; the traders circled up their wagons on the outskirts of the village, opened up the sides into counters, and were ready for business.

The arrival of a trading caravan at a Marindian village was a sacred event, precipitating an immediate celebration. Anybody living in remote areas in the vicinity came to the village and set up camp near the wagons. If the tribe had any money, it was dispersed equally to each member of the tribe. A dance ring was quickly constructed and drummers and singers recruited. A cow or two was butchered, and the meat started simmering in big kettles hung over a fire pit. Dogs barked. Boys wrestled each other. Old people spread out blankets and played hand games. Warriors raced their horses and told each other lies.

This caravan was no exception. In a few hours, there were hordes of people at the campsite. The traders were doing a brisk business.

Asteroidian traders brought a variety of goods, mostly manufactured and modern gadgets, foodstuffs, spices, and bulk materials. Although the Marindians professed to disdain modern technology and wanted to preserve their ancient way of life, they accepted some of the conveniences of modern life. Every lodge had a crystalyst power supply, radiant heat, holovision, ultrawave ovens, gammarator, and nearly any other appliance that could be found in Marsport. Detrs suspected their true aversion to technology was that they did not want to live in cities and work in factories. They did not have to do that. Or work at all if they did not want to.

The Marindians brought gold nuggets to trade for Asteroidian goods. They gathered them in the erosion gulleys outside the village.

The treaties that had sent the displaced aboriginal people from Earth to Mars via the hybertanks had specified that they had absolute control over their natural resources. Mars had not had a very good geophysical survey at the time. The situation on Earth had been critical though, and the other Terrans were desperate to get rid of their vestiges of colonialism. So the treaties were signed, specifying there could be no exploitation of Mars at any time. Several decades later, gold, silver, and gemstones were found in scattered pockets in huge quantities. The Marindians never commercially mined them. They were content to gather up a handful of nuggets and trade for goods.

The few non-Martians who had tried their luck were generally not heard from again.

A smart trader acquired his nuggets in trade. That way he would keep his scalp also.

This caravan was indistinguishable from any other, except that the man who called himself the Ghost Warrior was with it. For that reason, the crowds were a little larger than usual and gathered a little sooner than normal. They all wanted to get a look at this self-styled Ghost Warrior. But they would not believe it until Cuthair, their ancestral chief, told them it was so.

Their legends said that a Ghost Warrior would come out of the sky and lead them in battle against the hated Terrans. The legend had started when their ancestors were still on Earth, and the Terrans were white people. The Ghost Warrior had never made it to Earth. But Mars had a sky too. So they had kept waiting. Many hoped the time had come.

At dusk, a warrior arrived and politely invited Detrs to a sweat. He had been expecting such an invitation.

He followed the warrior into the village and out the other side. As they passed through the village, eyes stared at him from doorways and windows. Detrs wore the lavender robes of an Entropic monk and the gold headband of their Prophet. To many, he did not look much like a Ghost Warrior.

The sweat lodge was a low circular structure covered with soil. A few stone steps led down to the doorway. There was an antechamber with hangers for clothes. The warrior disrobed. Detrs followed suit.

They entered the sweat lodge through a barofield doorway. The heat and humidity hit Detrs in the face, taking his breath away. Nictitating membranes snapped over his eyes; other sphincters sealed shut their orifices. Monomer poured over his skin, protecting it from the heat.

It was hot enough that a standard human would have passed out already. They probably thought he was a standard human. Marindians were noted for their wry sense of humor.

In the darkness, Detrs could make out a dozen naked Marindian men sitting on the floor. A crystalyst thermoconverter sat in the middle of the room; its element glowed cherry red. Every once in a while, one of them would pour a pitcher of water on the element and clouds of steam would sizzle off.

An old man stood up. He had gray hair and loose skin hanging from a gaunt frame, but his eyes were as sharp

as his nose, and he had all his own teeth. He took Detrs'
hand; there was nothing wrong with his grip either. "I
am Cuthair," he said, "Chief of the Cebrenian band of
Marutes. You are welcome to sit with us and sweat. We
will share our visions with you." He pointed to another
old man on the floor. "This is Poagat, our shaman. The
others are all elders of the tribe." He did not say there
was no need for you to know their names unless you are
the one, but Detrs knew that was what he meant. "Sit
beside Poagat and me." Cuthair sat down.

Detrs sat beside him.

"My friend, Pimason, of the Maraches, says he
thinks you are truly a manifestation of the Ghost Warrior. But he wants to know my opinion." Cuthair
looked at him with bright eyes. "Are you? Are you the
Ghost Warrior come to lead us in battle again?"

Detrs looked into his eyes. He saw pain there and
glory. He had looked into such eyes before. "Yes," he
said. "I have come to lead you into battle again."

"There is no other way?"

"No. The time has come again for war. I have
modern weapons and hypnotanks to train your warriors
in their use. The Marutes are famous for being fierce
warriors, but you need modern arms to fight the Terran
forces. Let me help you. Let me lead you into battle. Let
me be your war chief."

"I wish I could be sure. War is such a terrible thing.
For a young man, it is wonderful. You come back with
your scars and stories, and the maidens fight each other
to sleep in your lodge. But for an old man, it is different. You know too many of the young won't return.
You are afraid to lose the flesh of your flesh."

A bowl of beaten gold was passed around. It was hot
enough to blister human hands. The bowl was filled
with peeled peyote buttons. Martian peyote was a
hybrid cactus and did not make any other alkaloid except mescaline, so there would be no strychnine to cause
vomiting.

Detrs took a button and chewed its rubbery flesh,
swallowing the pulp. He began an Entropic chant.

The Marindians began singing a chant of their own.

Detrs felt the mescaline begin to affect his sensorium. Colors he had never seen before flashed in front of his eyes. Images formed in the clouds of steam in the center of the sweat house.

The psionic transceiver built into the gold headband Detrs wore interfaced with the induction wires still in his brain, picking up his thoughts and transmitting them. The transmissions were weak, and the best he could hope for was to insert a few visions into someone else's brain. But a brain primed with mescaline was highly receptive to vision insertion.

The images in steam coalesced. There were random faces. Musach appeared, young and lovely and naked. She frolicked outside, dancing amid rocks and bushes. Slowly, she changed. She dropped to all fours. Her face elongated. She grew fur and a tail. She ran away with another wolf. Then they saw Ghost Cavalry descend on the village, dropping out of the air like specters. A terrific battle ensued. Detrs and Cuthair led the warriors in the fight. The Marute warriors fought off the Ghost Cavalry. They had a victory feast. There were more battles—Detrs and Cuthair were leading each. The images changed, but they had a common theme. Different hybrids fought the Terran forces. The hybrids won, battle after bloody battle. The carnage was terrible. But the hybrids won. Eventually, Earth was surrounded by seven great battleships, completely blockaded. The hybrids had won their war.

When Detrs regained his senses, the sweat lodge had cooled, primarily because nobody was pouring water on the heating element anymore.

Cuthair was looking at him.

"Did the visions come from your mind?" he asked.

"I suppose. They were visions I have seen before."

"Then you really are the Ghost Warrior?"

"Yes."

"Why was Musach in your visions? What does that mean?"

"She will become a werewolf."

"I don't believe you."

"You saw the visions."

"They are lies. They are all lies. You are not the Ghost Warrior, false prophet. You are another charlatan."

"As you wish. Believe what you will. But will you except the weapons and training I bring?"

"We will accept that. Even a false prophet may bring us gifts. My warriors will start coming tomorrow for their training."

Detrs got up and left. He walked through the Marindian village. It was quiet. Everyone was asleep.

The caravan camp was dark and still. Sentries were no longer needed. Between villages, a caravan was fair game, but at a village, they were respected guests and would not be bothered. To post guards would be an insult to the host village.

Detrs opened the door to his trailer and went inside. Someone was sleeping in his bed. Musach sat up and looked at him. Detrs had been thinking about her all day. She was as lovely as he remembered her: long black hair, dark eyes, jutting nipples, flat abdomen, lithe legs, with a patch of black hair between them.

"How did you get in here?" he asked, not at all unhappy.

"I walked in. Nobody stopped me."

"No. I guess they would not have stopped you."

"How did the sweat go? Are you the official Ghost Warrior yet?"

"Not yet. But soon."

"Come to bed," she said. "I've been waiting a long time for you. I wish I could go to sweats and see the visions."

He slipped off his robe and climbed into bed with her. She sniffed him.

"You smell like a man, tonight," she said. "I like the way you smell."

"What did you do today?" Detrs asked, much as a parent might have asked his child about school.

"I gathered up a few nuggets and traded for some trinkets."

"I hope you got a good deal."

Musach shrugged. "Who cares? Nuggets are easy to gather." She kissed him. Her mouth tasted different tonight. Detrs knew why.

They made love.

Afterward he asked her, "Have you had any more nightmares?"

"I had another one last night," she answered. "I dreamed I walked out of camp in the middle of the night and met a wolf. I stood on all fours and let him mount me. I loved it. I could not get enough of his red dog penis." She laughed. "All the time, I was sleeping with you. Do you think the dream means something about the way I feel about you?"

"It was just a dream. Go to sleep."

They slept.

A wolf howled.

Musach got up and went outside. Detrs woke up too and followed her. He watched her go to the wolf on all fours. They licked each other's faces, then sniffed behinds. He watched the wolf mount her. He heard them moan and whine in passion. Musach's face contorted into an grimace of lust. He did not interfere. There was nothing he could do. The way to Entropy was often convoluted and seldom pleasant.

He went back to the wagon and lay down. Shortly before dawn, Musach returned. She reeked with the carrion smell of wolf. But her skin still glowed with vitality; her hair shone like spun obsidian. Her breasts were still flushed and sweaty.

Detrs held her close.

He wondered why children were always the first to be hurt in war.

He sometimes wished the will of Entropy did not have to be so cruel.

•   •   •

We found our prey. His dream-tendril was unmistakable, even disguised as it was with wolf dreams. But we remembered. He could not hide from us as easily as he hid from Marutes. His dreams betrayed him.

Now we had to plan how to get closer.

Marsport was easy to get into but nearly impossible to get out of. Martians did not want foreigners to be wandering around the interior of the planet—they wanted to keep out treasure hunters. Trading caravans were the only foreigners with easy access. Then there was the matter of transportation—a trading caravan might take weeks to reach the Cebrenian Highlands. We could not wait that long.

Only the military and the health authorities had access to the interior with skimmers. We would have to hijack a flight. We began plucking dreams near the airport.

A strange anxiety tingled in our nerves. We should have only been excited that our quest was nearly over. Why should we be so apprehensive?

Dim dreams once more tried to rise. Faded ghosts once more tried to haunt our dream-time. We pushed them away. We did not want to hear their warnings.

Our search would soon be over.

6

The next morning warriors arrived for their training, just as Cuthair had promised.

The caravan carried a plentiful supply of small arms, including assault pulsers, anti-aircraft guns and missiles, light artillery, and demolition equipment. Detrs intended to equip the tribes with enough munitions to allow them to defeat the Terran garrison. But his plans went beyond that. He wanted to use the Marindians like cyrines—spaceship based ground assault troops—in the upcoming battle to liberate the asteroids. So he planned to give them complete cyrine software.

He had state of the art hypnotanks, with fifty psihelmets. In ten hours, a warrior could receive complete cyrine basic and advanced training. Detrs had modified the program, making it superior, in his estimation, to the Terran one. Besides, volunteers made better soldiers than conscripts. He had also inserted a little subliminal propaganda to make his trainees more susceptible to Entropic teachings. He did not think there was anything unethical in helping the divine word to be heard.

Before mid-morning, the first fifty warriors were in a trance, receiving their training.

Cuthair summoned him later. Detrs suspected he knew why.

He went to Cuthair's lodge and was taken to a bedroom. Musach lay on a bed with her skin glistening with sweat. Poagat sat in attendance, singing a chant and burning herbs. Cuthair stood at his daughter's bedside.

Detrs felt the girl's forehead—she was burning with fever. Her eyes were bright, but unfocused. She whimpered and moaned but did not speak. Pinching her skin evoked no response.

"When did she become ill?" Detrs asked.

"This morning," Cuthair said. "She said she wasn't feeling well and went to her room. When her mother checked on her an hour later, she could not arouse her."

"Can I have my medic take a look at her?"

Cuthair looked at Poagat. The Shaman nodded.

"Send for the maswetgugat," Cuthair said.

"Go to the camp and ask Firiel to come," Detrs told a warrior.

In a few minutes, Firiel arrived. She had been a chimera in the Ghost Cavalry, had served on Titan with Detrs and had once been his lover. Corpsmen were not demilled when they got out of the Corps—their fleshware was not considered a threat to the military. Cosmetic surgery had brought her back to an approximation of standard human, but she still had the abilities of a combat medic, with a hypodermic needle claw in each finger, each of which injected a different medicine. She had gotten additional hypnotraining and was now a real doctor also. She was an Entropic monk as well, being one of Detrs' first converts.

She clipped an autoanalyzer around the girl's arm and watched its screen for a minute. She took it off, put it back in her bag, and looked up at Detrs. "Viremia," she said, "just as you suspected. Lupine DNA and plasticizing plasmids."

"Can you do anything?" Detrs asked.

"Not out here. She needs some aclovir IV, and I don't have any. We'll need to send for some. I can give her a big loading dose of interferon which will slow down the transformation, but she needs aclovir to abort it."

"How soon does she need it?"

"Within twenty-four hours. Can we get some that fast?

"I think so. I'll radio the Public Health Service people in Marsport. They can get clearance to fly a mercy mission."

"You know what is wrong with Musach?" Cuthair asked.

"The wolf that attacked her was a werewolf. He infected her with the same virus that made him into a wolf. The virus is infecting her tissues right now, transforming them into wolf tissue. If we don't get her some medicine, she will become a werewolf herself."

"You lie. I don't believe you."

"I tell the truth. Ask your own Shaman."

Cuthair looked at Poagat. Poagat nodded. "She will become a wolf," he said. "My magic is not strong enough to stop it. See, already she changes."

Fine fur started to sprout from Musach's previously hairless skin—hair like the underfur of a wolf.

"What do we need to do?" Cuthair asked.

"Make sure she doesn't run away. As soon as it gets dark, the werewolf will start calling. She will want to go to him. Exposure to additional virus will speed up her transformation. Tie her up if you need to, but don't let her leave this lodge. Until the aclovir gets here, we'll just have to wait."

A claw protruded from one of Firiel's fingers. She slipped it into a vein in the girl's arm. A red substance could be seen flowing inside the hollow claw. After several seconds, Firiel withdrew the claw, and it retracted into her finger again.

The effect of the injection was immediately noticeable. The girl stopped thrashing about. Her breathing slowed. She became less feverish.

"Interferon will only buy us a little time," Firiel said. "She needs aclovir soon."

"We'll have it by tomorrow morning," Detrs said. "Make sure she stays inside tonight," he said to Cuthair.

Detrs and Firiel left.

Back in his wagon, Detrs holioed the clinic in Marsport. Genetic engineering had made disease almost nonexistent. The PHS doctors did not normally have much to do. They were supposed to prevent the importation of disease to Mars, but that was monitored by automatic surveillance equipment. They were thrilled at the idea of a case of infectious lupine virus. They said a skimmer with some aclovir would be dispatched as soon as the red tape could be cut—sometime that night, probably—and it would be there by dawn.

There was nothing more Detrs could do.

He went back to supervising the training of warriors. They were doing it in continuous shifts. When a group finished their hypnotraining they were issued weapons and ammo.

That night, Detrs wished someone would have come to his wagon. Musach was sick, and Brit was still angry. He knew it served him right.

Detrs was awakened by a knock on the door.

A warrior stood outside. He asked Detrs to come to Cuthair's lodge. Detrs followed him to the village.

Cuthair and Poagat waited inside the lodge. A Marindian woman wailed on the floor.

"What happened?" Detrs asked.

"This silly woman was supposed to be watching Musach," Cuthair said. "We had tied her up, so she could not escape. She told the woman her bindings hurt and talked her into loosening them. The woman dozed off. While she slept Musach escaped."

"It will soon be dawn. There's no sense looking for her until dawn. Wolf eyes have better night vision than ours."

"Sivatuch has already left to look for his sister."

"That was foolish of him."

"My warriors will follow."

"No."

"Do you tell Cuthair what to do?"

"Yes. If you want your daughter back, you will listen to me. An army of warriors will be spotted a long way off. The wolf will flee with your daughter. You will never see her again. Let me go after her alone. That's your only chance."

"What can you do alone?"

"I'm the Ghost Warrior."

"So you say."

"You wanted proof. Let this be the test."

Cuthair and Poagat looked at each other. "A man's daughter is a precious prize for a test," Cuthair said.

Detrs shrugged his shoulders. "Do you have any choice?" he asked.

"No. You speak the truth. My warriors could not catch a werewolf anyway. I'll put my trust in you. If you can bring her back, I'll accept you as the Ghost Warrior. I'll accept your visions as prophecy."

"I go after her at first light," Detrs said.

Dr. Davis Jefferson was excited.

He was finally going to make it out to the field. He had been on Mars for two years and had spent the entire time in Marsport making sure the automatic disease surveillance machines were operating properly. During that time, the most excitement he had had was a false alarm, when a machine misread a DNA code as the dreaded SANS agent, when in fact, the poor tourist had a simple wart he had become attached to and had not had removed.

There was not much infectious disease anymore. The PHS had done too good a job.

So when the call had come in from the Marindian village in the Cebrenian Highlands requesting aclovir IV for a case of infectious lupine virus, Davis was for once glad he was the OD. Pulling call as officer of the day was normally boring routine. Now he had a chance to see the interior and actually treat a disease.

The PHS was the only entity besides the military that

was authorized for air travel in the interior of Mars. That authorization had to be granted for each mission. It had taken Davis several frustrating hours to run down the right bureaucrats in the Foreign Office and convince them a mission of mercy was a justifiable use for a skimmer. He had to threaten to invoke a planet-wide quarantine before he finally got approval.

But now he had his authorization.

He packed a medical bag with supplies. He made sure he had his holocam. He packed a lunch.

Davis went to the motor pool and checked out a skimmer.

As he climbed into it, he did not see the three others who climbed in with him. He checked the charts, plotted a course and told the skimmer the coordinates. As he streaked through the night sky at Mach two, he did not realize he had three stowaways.

Dat Lomni looked up from a monitor screen in an operations room at the Marsport Headquarters of Corps Intelligence. A cavalry colonel stood behind him.

"They are in a skimmer headed for the Cebrenian Highlands," Dat said. "According to the flight computer, they are going to a Marute village."

"Probably Chief Cuthair's. That's the only one of any size."

"Then Geronimo must be in the vicinity. I want a battalion of ghost troopers ready to go at daylight—as soon as I give the word."

"That will take some doing. We only have a battalion to cover all the Marindian tribes. We'll have to empty every garrison."

"Then empty them. I don't want Geronimo to escape this time.

"As you wish." The colonel turned and left. He hated spooks. They were arrogant and abusive, and this one was no exception. A damn shame a real soldier had to take orders from their kind.

Dat smiled to himself. His plan was working perfectly. Nate had never suspected the ring he stole from

Hitt and now wore contained a beacon crystal. The path team was leading him to Terle. Terle would lead him to Geronimo. The capture of Geronimo would mean a star and a new life—or at least the memories of his old life.

He almost laughed out loud.

7

The wolf lay in wait on the ridge above the Marute village. The night had deepened to dense black, but Terle relied on other senses than sight. He knew where the girl lay bound. He could not go to her to free her. She would have to free herself. His mind spoke to hers, giving her the idea. Then he waited for her.

In two hours, he heard her scrambling up the slope. His nose told him who she was, even though her scent had changed and was now a blending of woman and she-wolf. When she reached him he could see she was a blending herself. Her face was partially elongated; her nose had thickened; her teeth had grown into fine fangs. She walked on all fours, on stubby fingers with nails twisting into claws. A tail was growing from her behind. She was covered with dense fur.

They licked each other's muzzles. She lifted her lip in a submissive grimace.

He loped off, with her following. They had to get away. He led her into the highlands, into a remote canyon where they would not be disturbed. There he mounted her, thrusting his penis into her. They became locked together. Over the next two hours, he ejaculated several times, filling her with his essence.

Before her vagina relaxed enough to free his penis, her transformation was complete; she had become a fine she-wolf. After he pulled out, they lay together, grooming each other with their tongues.

Then they dozed.

Someone else's dreams intruded into the wolf's dream-time. He had seen the images before, but did not know what they had meant; they had disturbed him. The cries of pups would disturb anyone. Pups should not be treated in such a way. Mounting was not done until one's nose told one the female was receptive.

The wolf felt another's pain. He had felt the pain before, but this time it was more intense. He had never known such agony before. He had never been so afraid. Because now he knew the dreams had once been his, the pain had once been felt by him.

The wolf howled, trying to get rid of the coldness inside.

His howls led Sivatuch to them.

During the skimmer ride, we made love.

The pilot could not hear the sounds of our sexplay; he still did not know we were aboard.

I was preoccupied and was not a very good lover, but that did not matter—Risa and Kaly could have gotten along fine without me. I was excited about something other than sex. In a few hours I could extract the psi-cypher codes from Terle. In a few hours, I would know who I had been.

If I also had a slight feeling of dread, I pushed it away.

In a little while, we dozed.

I woke screaming with a nightmare. Kaly and Risa also sat up and also screamed, in synchrony with me.

Our psionic control sprang a momentary leak. The pilot looked around, wondering who had screamed at him. But he did not see anything; we had regained control.

I saw images dance in the eyes of Risa and Kaly. The same images that danced in my eyes: three boys being lashed, being forced to perform sexual acts on themselves, being roughly raped by others. I knew the images in Risa's and Kaly's eyes were not just reflections of mine; they had dreamed the same dreams themselves. Our dream-times were linked by the same grim scenario. I did not want to know what that meant. But I was afraid I would soon find out.

The skimmer streaked toward the truth twice as fast as sound.

Detrs sat in a lotus position in his wagon, chanting an Entropic chant. The chant helped his mind go into a meditative state. He resurrected images he had first seen a long time ago and had studied frequently since.

The images had not changed. The prophecy they told remained the same. When he had first seen them eighty years ago, they were brief fragments. Over the years, more fragments had been added, some by Detrs' doing. He had sent Damiel to Earth, to be sure his own sons did not escape Lady Blue. Lord Surgeon Edbryn had been recruited into Entropism; he had made sure Terle had access to the psicypher codes and would learn them without knowing one was also his—hypnotank commands were not easily ignored.

Now the pattern of the images was nearly complete.

He saw Saraltr and her friends sexually abuse Alix, Craig, and Chris. He saw Grychn struggle with her own incest neurosis. He saw Lady Blue take the boys and watched their transformation in the hybertanks into the creatures they had become. He saw Grychn also become a hybrid. Other images followed, fitting together into a jigsaw pattern. The final image to be fitted was of Musach changing.

Detrs would not have to search for Musach and the Terran WOLF. He knew exactly where to find them and what would happen when he did. He had known that for years, ever since he had first seen that particular augury. He also knew what he must do. But he did not know exactly what would happen after that.

That was the problem with his clairvoyance—it was

incomplete, its images were intermittent and usually fragmentary. He had no control over it; he could not see what he wanted, only what he was shown. He only saw events that would happen to him personally.

The eastern horizon was lightening with day.

Detrs stopped chanting and dressed in his robe and gold headband. He picked up a pack. Inside the pack was a dream-processor unit he had had customized. Lasewires would connect it to his headband. A psifield generator was built into the base of the DPU, which would project a psionic warp ten meters in diameter, trapping any sentient patterns inside it. Talk about a self-fulfilling prophecy. Detrs had the DPU to ensure that the prophecy would become a reality. He wondered what would happen if he left the DPU behind. He laughed. He knew he could not. This augury was too important. He knew what he was going to do, but he did not know what would happen when he did it. Whatever it was, it was going to be spectacular.

He put the pack on his back, picked up a walking stick and started walking east into the highlands. He watched the sun rise, shrouded in fire. The air was crisp and cold. The ground was dusted with both ice and carbon dioxide frost. As the sun rose, the frost sublimated first, then the ice melted.

Detrs saw a skimmer scream in at Mach two, fire its braking jets, and settle down to the ground between the village and his camp. He saw the pilot get out. He did not see the three stowaways disembark, but he knew they were to arrive that day. He smiled, thinking the PHS doctor would be disappointed he no longer had a patient. He briefly wondered why he had summoned him, when he had known Musach would run away that night. What purpose of the prophecy did a PHS doctor serve? He shrugged his shoulders. Then it occurred to him that the skimmer was how the others had arrived.

He continued to walk eastward. He did not look behind, but he knew he was being followed.

When he came to the right canyon he walked up it, winding back and forth for a kilometer. The canyon was

a box ravine with sheer walls of rock. Three sets of fresh
tracks went up it: two wolves and a man.

At the end he found them.

The two wolves had Sivatuch cornered. They were
snarling and snapping at him, lunging in to bite at his
legs with their jaws. He was keeping them at bay with
his empty rifle, using it like a staff. So far there was a
stalemate—eventually the wolves would have won. The
wolves heard Detrs approach. They wheeled around and
growled at him. When they saw Detrs was not armed,
the male leaped at him with his jaws open wide.

Suddenly, the wolf stiffened with paralysis in mid-air.
He fell at Detrs' feet and lay still. His skin quivered with
fasciculations. His fur withdrew and his form remodeled. His tail retracted. His paws elongated into hands.
He became a naked man. At the same time, the she-wolf
became a naked woman.

Lupine genes were once more under neuroendocrine
control.

The man woke up. He shook his head, as though to
clear his thoughts.

Behind Detrs, three figures appeared suddenly out of
thin air: a sphinx, a pedimorph, and a cyrine. Nate had
healed Terle's mind, allowing him to return to human
form, and had also transformed Musach, by telepathically manipulating her neuroendocrine axis.

"Good morning Terle," the pedimorph said. "We've
come to ask you some questions."

Detrs pushed a button through the fabric of his pack,
activating both the dream-processor and the psiwarp
generator. Everyone there was within ten meters of
him—everyone would get to play the dream-game. All
the living minds within the psiwarp were drawn inside
the dream-processor. Detrs had control of the structure
of the game, since his psyche went through a higher
priority gate—his was the only mind hard-wired to the
data bus. Besides, he was a past master at the dream-
game. Jain Maure had tested a lot of players, and Detrs'
mind was the best she had ever found. He probably
would have won without stacking the deck in his favor

by hard-wiring himself to the input port.

Seven naked people sat in a circle, facing each other. There were two Marindians, Musach, and Sivatuch; a telepathic sphinx, Risa; a chameleon-cyrine, Kaly; an empathic pedimorph, Nate; a WOLF in human form, Terle; and the Prophet of Entropism, Detrs. The data bus protocol was multi-echoing—each mind could hear the thoughts of the others. At first, it was a total confusion of uncontrolled thoughts, but Detrs brought things to order.

Everybody just listen.

There was quiet.

Only three of us are who we think we are: me, Musach, and Sivatuch. The other four have all been hybridized from their true selves. I think we should find out who you are. Terle, what are the psicypher codes?

Terle could not withhold the codes from the dream-game. He thought each in turn. As he did, locked memories swirled to the surface. They flashed back two years to Earth; memories of Telluride and Nyssa; simple children's games and also the more complex games of adults; the endless succession of parties and casual sex; of Saraltr in four different ways, none pleasant; of Lady Blue and his anticipation and dread. They all knew the terrible truth. They all found out who the four had been.

Kaly had once been Grychn. Terle had been cousin Alix. Nate and Risa had been the twins. Craig and Chris.

For a long time, they were too numb to think; the truth seemed too terrible to bear. But then they realized it did not matter who they had been, they were someone else entirely different now, and could never go back to past lives.

Then Detrs began showing them all the images the crystal had inserted into his mind more than eighty years ago. He battered their minds with prophetic images. They saw how the hybrid nations would unite behind the Entropic Church and drive the Terran forces out of the Solar System. They saw their own roles and how important they were. They knew it would be futile to deny destiny. Though the karma for each was a little different, though each took a different path, their destinations were the same, and they would arrive there as inexorably as the final heat death. They saw why they had been thrown together now and knew why they had had to suffer so much to get there. They saw that their karma was twisted together; the seven of them were bound together by fate. They saw where their destiny lay and they believed it was so. The Prophet had created six disciples.

The dream-game ended. The seven of them woke up lying on the cold Martian ground.

Detrs stood up first. "Come on," he said. "Let's get moving. We can reminisce and get reacquainted later. There's a battle to be fought now."

They ran back the way they had come, back to the village of Cuthair.

A battalion of Ghost Cavalry was attacking the village. Huvies disgorged ghost troopers in an air assault. Ground troops had the village surrounded. Pulser beams stabbed like linear lightning. The Marute warriors and Detrs' caravan crew were defending the village, using the new weapons Detrs had just brought. The defenders were hopelessly outnumbered; it would only be a matter of time before the Ghost Cavalry prevailed.

But the Ghost Warrior could defeat Ghost Cavalry.

Detrs pressed a switch. A psiwarp surrounded them again. A psychic gestalt of seven formed within the circuits of a dream-chip. Each mind complemented the gestalt in a unique way. The result could not have been predicted by psychengineering theory. The blending of psyches was synergistic—the whole was greater than the sum of the parts.

A giant warrior rose from the ground, astride a giant horse. Bright war paint streaked both warrior and horse; both were adorned with silver and eagle feathers.

The warrior carried a lance in one hand, a tomahawk in the other. He charged across the sky on his steed, smiting ghost troopers with lance and hatchet, bowling them over with the shoulders of the horse.

The seven had formed a macropathic gestalt. Their thoughts struck out, magnified, amplified, resonated, and turned into an awesome force, depolarizing cerebral neurons of ghost troopers, who fell unconscious, one by one in rapid succession. But to any living eyes, a giant Ghost Warrior battled the combrids.

As Colonel Dat Lomni lost consciousness, he knew he would never make general. He was wrong. But it would be in a different army.

Before long, the battle was over. The Ghost Warrior melted back into the dry sands of Mars.

Cuthair was overjoyed to have his son and daughter back. He was also pleased to see a battalion of Ghost Cavalry in catatonic slumber, and his village safe.

Cuthair's warriors had picked up the fallen ghost troopers and lay them in orderly rows. Nate and Risa were going down the rows, rearranging hypnotically embedded commands. When the ghost troopers awoke, they would have different loyalties. They would wake up as soldiers of Entropy.

"What are you going to do with them?" Cuthair asked. "We don't have the facilities to take care of prisoners of war."

"When they awake, they'll all be loyal Entropists," Detrs said. "This battalion will be the first of the Prophet's elite guard. This is the entire garrison for all the Marindian lands," Detrs said. "If the tribes were to rebel now, there would be little opposition. A swift strike and victory would be yours."

"They would pull troops from the other garrisons," Cuthair answered. "There are other battalions on other lands on Mars."

"Not if the other tribesmen were also rebelling."

"Who could arrange such a thing?"

"Geronimo could."

Cuthair looked closely at Detrs. "You know I am Geronimo."

"Who else could you be?"

"And you really are the Ghost Warrior. Of that, there can be no doubt. You brought back both my son and daughter and delivered us from our enemy. The time of war has returned."

"I'm afraid so. We have no other choice. War is our destiny."

"There are worse fates." The old man smiled. He was glad he had lived long enough to see the Ghost Warrior ride.

8

Detrs and Grychn lay together in bed in the John Carter Hotel in Marsport.

Mars had been liberated in two weeks' time. There was no more Terran authority on the planet. Reinforcements could not be sent, because when the word got out about the Martian Rebellion, spontaneous rebellions broke out all over the System. Detrs had made sure the word got out. His monks had made sure "spontaneous" uprisings occurred on schedule.

Detrs and Grychn had just made love. Now they lay in the warmth of ebbing passion.

Grychn looked like the old Grychn—ocher eyes, ermine hair, slender body with full breasts. But she was still a chameleon. She kissed Detrs. "I feel wonderful," she said. "It's good to have you back."

"It's good to have *you* back," Detrs answered.

"I was pretty crazy, wasn't I. I mean, both Grychn and Kaly were pretty crazy. It's amazing how you can mix two flawed halves together and come up with a stable whole."

"Sometimes mistakes cancel out each other."

"And I almost believe your silly Entropism. But you

never showed us what will happen to us in the end. Do you know our final fates?''

"No. There is a limit to my clairvoyance. There seems to be a point beyond which the images stop. It is about fifty years from now. We have established a blockade around Earth, but cannot defeat them. Then they develop some terrible new weapon. But I cannot see just exactly what happens then.''

"Why so much misery? I mean for me and the boys.''

"I don't know. Perhaps the end does justify the means after all. I had to create certain images for the prophecy. Certain images were of my making and I take the blame for them. Sacrifices had to be made. I'm sorry for the suffering. We will need people with unique abilities to win the war. We now have several of those people. We needed a Ghost Warrior, and we have one. There may have been other ways to get here, but this is the way we came. You never would have become a chameleon on your own. But I'm not sure. I don't know for certain what will happen in the end.''

"Do we stay lovers?'' Her voice was vulnerable.

"I have many different lovers, but you have only me.''

"That's not fair.''

"I'm not a chameleon.''

"You mean. . . .''

"Of course. You're my dream-lover. With you I can make love to any woman of my dreams. But I will love only you.''

Grychn laughed, low and sexy. "Shall we put your love to the test?'' Her laugh turned nasty. "I'll give you a dream-lover.'' Grychn changed. Her hair grew out in scraggly locks. Her body ballooned until fat jiggled like gelatin. Pendulous breasts hung flaccid over a huge belly. Her nose turned into a hooked beak. She laughed a crone's cackle. "Prove you love me,'' she hissed. "Make love to me now.''

Detrs smiled woefully.

But he passed the test.

•   •   •

We made love in the penthouse of the John Carter Hotel. Old habits die hard.

Risa lay with me, along with Terle and Musach on a bed of wombskin.

Musach was a little shocked with our morality, or perhaps lack of it, but she would not admit it. We were her ticket off Mars. We were the vehicle that would take her to a life of excitement. After a bit, she became more comfortable, and then she was insatiable. She even practiced her new lycanthropic abilities and changed into a wolf.

I asked her to turn back into a Marindian. Even I draw the line somewhere.

I would always be Nate, just as Risa was still herself and Terle himself. I knew I had once been a little boy named Craig with a twin brother named Chris and a cousin named Alix. Alix's mother had made us do things with her that had hurt because we were too young to understand or want the passions then. But those people did not exist now except in memory. They had died as surely as if their progeria was not interrupted. Each of us was a phoenix risen from the ashes of those little boys.

When I made love to Risa, I was not making love to my brother, because she was a hybrid creature, both mentally and physically, a different creature entirely. Only a little of Chris's DNA and psyche lingered in her, just as only a little of Craig persisted in my mind and body and a little of Alix could be found in Terle.

The recovery of our little-boy memories only made our metamorphosis complete. Just as xeno-DNA stabilized our genes, xenodreams balanced our dream-time; hybrid vigor healed body and soul.

Our morality was that of hybrids, not to be confused with the decadence of Earth. Our mores had an animal innocence. In us, pleasure was not confused with pain. We were not prisoners of jaded passion. We had not lost the capacity to feel the thrill. We still loved.

Our bodies coupled. Which member made union with which orifice was unimportant, because the sensations were shared by all. The origin of an orgasm did not matter, because it was perceived by each. The hippocampal source of a dream was irrelevant, because the dream was dreamed by everyone. Our dream-times coincided. Animal and human dreams became the same.

We run with nose close to the ground, following a scent that sends excitement sparking along our nerves. We howl at a moon.

We stalk the waterholes, lying in wait. When we charge, our roar freezes our prey long enough for us to tear its throat.

We drift high upon the psychic ether, plucking dream-tendrils, following them back to timid minds.

When the terrors try to rise, we let them and laugh at their puny threats. We are not children anymore. We are not afraid of childish fears.

We do not fear death, a mere messenger of Entropy.

When the time comes for us to sing our death chant it will be in a clear, strong voice. Until then. . .

Dreams unwind. . .